Dragon Song

by

Shirley McCoy

Dragon Song

Cover Art by *Kristian Norris*

The Wild Rose Press, Inc.
PO Box 708
Adams Basin, NY 14410-0708
Visit us at www.thewildrosepress.com

Publishing History
First Edition, 2023
Trade Paperback ISBN 978-1-5092-5136-0
Digital ISBN 978-1-5092-5137-7

Published in the United States of America

As they cautiously navigated through the hoard, Morgan detected a slight glow in her peripheral vision. It flared up, then subsided. As they stepped forward, she discerned it again, and this time she whipped around quickly enough to see a small magical symbol etched in the floor behind them light up, then dim.

"Oh no," she murmured.

"What's wrong?" Connor demanded in a sharp tone.

She paced further and showed him. "I think if Meglos doesn't already know we are here, he will soon."

As if on cue, deep within the cave, the sound of an almighty clang of metal meeting metal filled their ears. Then came a roar, the kind which could only be made by a dragon.

Morgan knew her eyes must be wide as saucers, but she couldn't seem to help it or move at all, in fact. Horror rooted her to the spot, unable even to speak, much less move.

Connor was not so afflicted. "Run!"

When she didn't twitch so much as an eyelash, he yelled, "Run, Morgan!"

The volume of his words, his manner, and most of all, the use of her name, snapped her out of her panicked shock at last. She went from utter stillness to moving faster than she ever had in her life.

The dragon, shrieking and breathing fire all the while, flew after them.

Also By Shirley McCoy

If The Shoe Fits
The Crystal Flame

Chapter One

She, Morgan Elizabeth Talbot, was determined to do this. She had come too far and worked too hard to back out now. She took a deep breath, braced herself, and pulled open the door.

From all she could see from her limited vantage point, the Golden Key was as advertised, a tavern and brothel catering to an ordinary clientele, traveling merchants for the most part, wanting a bit of comfort while plying their own trade up and down the north road. The place was clean, if a bit worn, with its tables of dark wood and lanterns positioned at strategic points creating a certain ambience. The whores were, if not precisely discreet, at least unobtrusive.

In addition, the tavern was not so rough that she would appear out of place entirely, nor was it one where she might encounter anyone of her own class she knew. It also boasted excellent food and even better wine. In short, the place was perfect. Morgan hoped finding the right man to suit her purposes would be as easy, but she doubted it. Easy or not, it was time for her to take this step and gain complete control of her life.

She sat near the front window with her back to the door and took her time evaluating the men present. Most, she noted, already appeared to have company. She grimaced and discounted those. Trying to lure a man away from an experienced prostitute was not something she had any desire to attempt. She also discounted those she estimated to be more than ten years older than her twenty-four, as well as those she found unattractive. She couldn't very well go to bed with a man she didn't like the looks of.

She took much care with her attire. She had to appear attractive but not wellborn. This meant showing more skin than she was used to or comfortable with. To that end, she wore a rather daring gown in a bold wine-red color, made from fabric of dubious quality. Her chestnut hair, she left in one messy topknot on her head. Taking such considerations into account would, she hoped, allow her to blend in with more ease.

Her gaze flittered from man to man, assessing, weighing, then rejecting, until her stare fell on a lone gentleman at a table in the far corner of the room. Even in the low light she could see he was stunning. His black hair looked soft and sleek, and she itched to run her hands through it. He was quite tall. His attractive mouth was wide with soft lips, and his jaw was strong and firm. She could not tell the color of his eyes; she was too far away, and his gaze was fixed on the flagon of ale in front of him.

He must have detected her scrutiny. His head suddenly rose, and he stared right into her eyes for an instant before he returned to his previous occupation. Everything inside of her tensed with the effort she expended to not react. The sharp, brief gasp she could not stop was barely audible, but she thought he sensed it anyway, even if he was unable to hear it. Forget the color of his eyes; never had she encountered such an intense gaze. Shivering, she hoped imperceptibly, she broke the connection.

Keeping her own gaze on her goblet of wine, Morgan did some fast thinking. There was no one else more suitable in the whole tavern, and she hadn't much time. Added to that, if she were going to do this, she would not mind having him as her bed partner. The pull of him was strong, and in her present mood she was inclined to go with it and let it take her where it would. Decision reached, she rose and made her way across the crowded room toward him.

He did not look up until her shadow fell across him, but she was certain he was aware of her as soon as she stepped in his direction. He gave her the most fleeting glance then went back to studying his ale. Morgan sank on the bench opposite him.

"I am not looking for companionship tonight. Best try your luck elsewhere," he said.

In spite of the setting and that this was her goal, she was a little shocked that he actually believed she was a prostitute. She did her best to pull herself together. "Even if it costs you nothing?"

"Nothing? Really?" He laughed a little into his ale, and he still wouldn't look at her.

In her estimation, he was not completely soused, but she imagined reality's edges were pleasantly blurred for him.

"Really. I'm no whore, and I have no need of coin. What I do need is companionship, as you termed it."

He raised his head at last and peered at her. His eyes were the blue of a bright summer sky. His gaze, when in such close proximity, was even more intense.

"Why would a beautiful lady of marriageable age and obvious good breeding require companionship?"

"That is my own affair," she said in her most

haughty tone.

He gestured with his half-full tankard. "Forgive me, but it is clear you have little experience of men or the world in general, for that matter. Do you have any idea what this would do to your chances of making an advantageous or even a decent marriage? To your entire life, in fact? That is, assuming I agree."

Impatient now, she spoke in a sharp tone. "I am more than aware of the consequences of what I am doing. I have my reasons. Good ones, I assure you. Ones I have no intention of sharing with you. Now, do you wish to spend a few hours abed with me or not?"

He looked her over, starting from the toes of her serviceable brown boots and going up. His gaze lingered on the curves of her body, then came to rest on her face at last. After a moment, he looked away, turning back to his drink. "You're resolved to bed someone tonight, I gather. You will choose someone else if I decline your offer, I take it?"

It wasn't really a question, but she answered it nonetheless. "Yes," Morgan stated, quick and to the point.

She was as ready as it was possible to be. All of this had been years in the planning. Belmere, her home, was the safest place in the entire kingdom of Esterhaven, perhaps even the world. Although her father managed to make certain it was also beautiful, comfortable, and full of all her heart could desire— from jewels to books, to theatrical performances, to the best tutors—it was as secure as any prison. Yet, she succeeded in leaving without alerting anyone. Because while her father assumed she sat content and protected, even happy, she had been preparing. Preparing for a battle she might well lose.

If Rownar ever discovered the identity or whereabouts of her soon-to-be lover, the results would not be pleasant; the consequences to the poor fellow would, in fact, be disastrous. Not to mention, her father would not be best pleased. There would be the little matter of treason to deal with after all. While she deeply regretted the deception, it was best for everyone. So yes, by all the gods, she was ready.

He downed his last swallow of ale, then got to his feet. "Very well. I already have a room. We can go there."

Morgan blinked. For an instant, she could not take it in. He agreed. He was ready to show her to his room now.

"Wait, I just realized, I don't even know your name."

He swayed a bit but grinned down at her. "Nor I yours. I'm Connor O'Malley. And you are?"

"Morgan," she managed, though she was a little breathless.

He made a valiant attempt to narrow his eyes at her but failed, being perhaps a little drunker than she at first supposed. "No surname, Morgan?"

"No, it's best you not know it."

He raised his eyebrows at this, then shrugged. "Well, Morgan, shall we?" When he offered her his hand, she placed her palm in his.

With every step they took up the stairs, her tension ratcheted up another notch. By the time they reached his door, she could hardly move or speak; her muscles were so constricted.

He paused at the entrance to his room, surprising

her. "Are you sure about this?"

His voice was so gentle that she had a sudden, almost overwhelming desire to cry. Because such a desire shocked her, her tone was sharper than she intended, but she couldn't help it. "I'm sure. Why wouldn't I be?"

"Because your every muscle is locked tight, but even so, you're shaking like you have a terrible fever, and you look as though you might burst into tears at any second," he stated.

When she said nothing more, he sighed. "Why are you doing this? It is obvious this is not typical behavior for you. Even only having just met you, I can see you aren't looking for some illicit thrill. You don't want this."

That absurd urge to weep was stronger this time. She fought it back and did not look at him as she opened the door and stepped inside. "I told you, I have my reasons."

He followed, captured the hand at her side, then repeated, "You don't want this."

"Why should that matter to you or to me? It's what must be done. If you don't wish to share your bed with me, I'll find someone else who will be more than happy to—"

When she attempted to jerk her hand free, he tightened his grip. "I can see your mind is set. Your body might even be willing, but your heart and your soul aren't. So if you want me to do this, I need a bit more. Like why."

"As I have said, that is my own affair, I can't—"

"I'm a bit drunk, and you are very beautiful, but Morgan, I have to understand why."

When she started to protest once more, he held up a hand.

"I understand you cannot give me details, but I must know the motivation behind this action before I can decide what is good and right to do. Because I will tell you plainly, I have never taken a woman against her will, and I don't intend to start tonight."

Now it was her turn to sigh. "You are a kind man, far kinder than I deserve. I won't forget it." She clasped his hand, then released it. "I suppose this makes you worthy enough to be told as much as possible. I am doing this in order to secure the safety of those under my care and for my own protection. That is all I can tell you."

"I see. There's no other way?"

"There isn't."

He searched her face, and she wondered what truths he saw there.

He was silent for so long that she feared he might have changed his mind after all, but then he said, "So all I can do is try to make this as easy as possible for you."

"If you would do what you can there, I'd be most grateful."

He nodded. "If it's any comfort, I'm very good at this."

"Oh, well." She had no idea what else to say to that, so she clamped her mouth shut.

No doubt he was very good, as he said.

"I have no idea if I will be," she admitted. Restless, she moved about the room, unable to remain still. "I've been kissed. I've been touched a bit, but I've gotten nowhere close to—"

On a low table there was a bottle of wine. He poured them each a glass.

"It's all right. Morgan. We will take this one step at a time. First, relax. Have some wine."

She accepted the goblet, sipped, and found the drink superb with a rich note of ripe strawberries. She smiled at him a little. "This vintage is excellent."

"I'm glad you like it. Let's sit." He indicated a small settee, and they sank on it.

"How long do you have?" When she looked over at him, bemused, he added, "Until you'll be missed?"

"Oh, a few hours only. The servants will be up and about before dawn. I must be back before they reach my rooms. So I must leave here by a quarter past five, no later."

"We ought to make a start, then." He set his wine aside on the low table in front of them, then took hers from her and did the same. With the back of his fingers, he gently brushed her cheek, then leaned in and kissed her.

It was a kiss of such unexpected gentleness that she couldn't help but respond. His lips were warm, his touch light as a butterfly's wing, so sweet and oh so enticing. She pressed her lips more firmly to his, and his reaction was immediate. He returned the pressure, shifted his angle, then placed a second kiss, this one hot and open-mouthed, to her lips.

Acting on instinct, she parted her lips for him, and he surged in. And her world narrowed down to him, his mouth on hers, his tongue caressing hers, and his hands framing her face.

When she mimicked his movements and tangled her tongue with his, he drew in a breath, and his hand slid to her breast. He seized it in a strong grip and kneaded. She jerked then arched in pleasure. Loosening her bodice, he pulled it apart then off, leaving her in her linen chemise and skirts.

With a delicate touch, he circled then skimmed over the tips of her breasts. Before she quite knew what was happening, her world tilted, and she ended on her back, sunk into the cushions of the settee.

He made an appreciative sound, then broke the kiss. Those lips of his cruised down her neck and across her upper chest to the edge of her chemise.

"In the normal course of things, this…" One strong hand stroked over her breast, down the length of her body to her hip, and back up. "Would be more than enough for a first encounter. But considering our current situation…." He paused, bent, and took her nipple between his teeth, bit just hard enough. The brief, sharp sound of stunned pleasure she made shocked her to her soul.

"Do you want more?" He whispered the words over her skin, skin already sensitized from his touch.

"Oh yes. May the gods forgive me." Her voice trembled almost as much as her body.

He lifted his head, untied the ribbon of her chemise, and slid it down her shoulders. "So beautiful," he murmured. Lowering his head again, he took her other nipple into his mouth.

Each time he sucked, her body pulsed, most strongly between her legs. He teased and enticed until she thought she might explode; sure, if he would only touch her properly, for long enough, she would. After a while, it dawned on her that he knew exactly what he was doing. He was bringing her ever closer to some sensual brink she could sense just out of reach. All at once, she wanted to go over, and she wanted to take him with her.

"No more preliminaries. I want you."

Was that her voice, so imperious and sensual? One small part of her mind was shaken, but the rest of her accepted the transformation as the most natural thing in the world.

He shook his head. "I want you too. Desperately. But I also want, no, I need, to touch you a bit more first."

He gave her more. Not precisely what she asked for, but she was in no mood to complain, certainly not when his hand slid beneath her skirt and then cruised unerringly to the apex of her thighs.

His hand hovered over her, not quite touching, so she parted her legs in silent invitation. One he accepted a heartbeat later. His warm palm settled where she most wanted it, and an instant later, one long, slim finger glided into her.

He took a deep shuddering breath, rubbed his palm over her, then eased his hand away. "Too many clothes," he muttered, and with a few swift motions, he remedied that little problem.

In a flash, he divested her of her skirts, petticoats, and chemise, leaving her naked as the day she was born. He cast one searing glance over her from top to toe, then rose. He watched her face, perhaps for any sign she might balk, something she did not intend to do at this late stage. He unbuttoned his trousers, then removed them along with his smallclothes. Then, as naked as she, he picked her up and carried her to the bed.

He laid her down then joined her. The feel of skin-to-skin contact over her entire body was decadence itself. She did not have much time to appreciate the effect, however, because Connor parted her legs and settled between them. At last, she felt him poised at her entrance.

"Will it hurt?"

"Just a little if the gods are merciful."

She closed her eyes, but then she sensed him shake his head.

"Look at me. I want to see your eyes when I take you."

Once she fixed her gaze on his, he pressed into her inch by inch. He joined his body to hers infinitesimal degree by infinitesimal degree. When he reached her barrier, he withdrew a fraction, then surged back inside and thrust through to bury himself to the hilt.

The sharp ripple of pain couldn't be helped, but a moment later, the sting was gone, and triumph poured through her. She was no longer a virgin.

"It's done." Tears of sheer relief gathered in her eyes, but she was damned if she would let them fall.

"Not quite." He shook his head a second time. "Not even close."

She shivered at the sound of his voice in her ear, so deep and sensual. Again, he withdrew, but this time almost completely. When he eased back into her, she felt it in every inch of her body. He repeated the motion, and her toes curled with desire.

"Something that feels this incredible can't possibly be right," she whispered when she could find breath enough to speak.

"It is right. Sometimes I think it might be the one

thing in this world that is."

With her legs wrapped around him, he set a rhythm as smooth and a pace as steady as the beat of her heart until they were one, and every fragment of her body was under his sway. She arched up into sensation, into him, and he moaned. Wanting more than anything to hear the evocative sound again, she began to move with him. The friction created was delicious, the touch of his skin enchanting, and she didn't ever want any of it to end.

By mutual accord, they quickened their pace. At the right moment, he changed the angle of their joining so he caressed her inside and out. The pleasure already suffusing her body went white-hot and burst. Her climax shivered through every part of her, claimed every facet of her awareness. It was inevitable and all-consuming. An instant later, when he joined her, it was all she ever wanted.

****

Mere minutes later, Morgan was quite sure she had succeeded in greatly weakening her connection to Rownar. As the remnants of her first climax drained from her body, their connection flared to life. For one instant, it burned strong, stronger than ever before, and all at once she wondered if she had made a serious miscalculation. Then, in that momentary flash of awareness, she felt the depth of his rage, which for once did not frighten her. Soon she became cognizant of a much more gratifying emotion emanating from him. Frustration and a futile anger with no outlet filled the creature. He knew what she had done, and he was livid, but he could do nothing. She almost laughed aloud. Through the now-diminishing link, she sent him her triumph and utter satisfaction.

Our connection is fading. When will you learn, dragon? Whatever I will always comes to pass.

As she blocked what little remained of the link, the last thing she heard was his roar. She had the unexpected urge, the slightly ungallant impulse to consider her lover a spoil of war, one she was more than ready to continue to enjoy. Basking in her victory, she returned her full attention to the man in her bed.

****

Her attention wavered, and Connor felt so connected to her that he recognized it right away. To reclaim her undivided notice, he captured her mouth and kissed her. For a second she remained unresponsive, then her whole being refocused on him. Now that this was the case, he rocked against her, highlighting the fact that, in spite of his earlier climax, he still wanted her and was more than ready to show her how much. She gasped in shocked pleasure, and that was all it took to push him over the edge. His own pleasure crested, and as it peaked again, he cried out her name and emptied himself into her.

Time slowed, spun out, and the moment seemed to go on forever. After a while, the sensations ebbed. His first coherent thought was that he would never forget her or this night. Since she was so brave and so passionate, how could he?

She would never forget it either, he supposed, all things considered. In a sudden rush, he wanted, with an unfamiliar, burning curiosity, to know how she fared and more, what she thought of the experience, especially given the unusual circumstances.

"Are you all right? I didn't hurt you, did I?"

She tossed him a lazy grin. "Not so I'd notice."

"Now it's done, do you have any regrets?"

"It's strange. I assumed I would feel desolate... after. I supposed I would feel as though I'd done something truly awful, even if it was for all the right reasons. I was certain my heart and my soul would feel irrevocably stained, but instead..."

"Instead?"

"I feel strong and vindicated. This was right. It was the right thing to do for my people, and even the right thing for me. As for physically, I've never felt better. There's one final thing I feel: lucky. All my life, I have raged against my various misfortunes, but what a godsend to have met you tonight. What a blessing you agreed to all of this." Her vague gesture encompassed the room, the bed, and the two of them.

"Well, it was no hardship, I promise you. In fact..."

He rolled with her until she was under him. Her pretty eyes went wide once more as she felt him hot and hard again. When he rocked into her, just one tiny inch, she gasped.

"What are you doing?"

With a very wicked grin, he quirked an eyebrow at her. "Are you sure your memory isn't failing? I know this is new to you, but I'm doing the same thing I did a few moments ago. Unless you are too sore." His heart filled with sudden concern, and he stilled.

"I don't think I'm too sore, but... again?" When he nodded against her neck, she struggled to wrench herself away from him. "That isn't necessary. I'm no longer a virgin. You don't have to..."

He shifted back to look at her. The pretty blush

painting her cheek fascinated him. "No, I don't have to, nor do you. I want to. Indulge me and yourself."

When she let out a shivery sigh, Connor smiled.

****

The dragon roared and breathed fire again and again. The link he shared with Morgan was all but severed, and there was no changing the fact now. Nothing could alter what was already done.

He had underestimated her, thinking she was utterly broken after all the years linked with him. For a thousand years, dragons ruled the world long before humanity existed. To dragons, people were nothing more than a source of food and treasure. Sometimes, however, a particular dragon would single out a particular human and would link with him or her. He craved Morgan's purity of spirit and would so enjoy corrupting her bit by bit. And so he forced a magical link with Morgan when she was eight. A link now badly damaged. How dare she!

She was his and no one else's. She would pay for her defiance, and she would suffer mightily when she did. He would make sure of it. Once he had his fill, once he owned her fully, then and only then would he consume her body as well. Still, if he had not been so furious, he would have admired her. Even though his link to her was not what it had been, that did not mean she would escape him.

****

Afterward, Morgan dozed in Connor's arms but woke shortly, afraid she would oversleep. It was still very early to be up, but with her brain so full of all the new experiences of the evening, she didn't mind. She'd accomplished what she set out to do and experienced so much more besides.

She wasn't foolish enough to believe she could fall in love with him in one night. Much of what she was feeling for the man was pure lust coupled with a certain gratitude for his aid; she was well aware. She would be forever grateful to him, beyond a doubt. He'd made what could have been an impossible situation bearable, even, she admitted, a definite pleasure. For that, she would always owe him a great debt. Their mutual and passionate lust was also beyond doubt. Since she was still in his bed, she could hardly dispute the point. That the same lust was perhaps clouding her judgment might be argued.

Yet, there had been a spark of something between them. She was as certain of that as she had ever been of anything in her life. That being the case, she could mourn for what might have developed between them if they had been given time and freedom. That much she would allow herself. So many things had already been taken from her; why not this possibility also?

The little mantel clock in the parlor struck half-past four, signaling it was time for her to dress and be away. Her mind swirled with alarm when she realized she had no idea how to disentangle herself from the man in her bed. Connor's arms were wrapped tightly around her, and she had no notion of how to extricate herself without waking him.

"It's time?"

The sleepy rumble in her ear was a not unpleasant jolt. She nodded and his arms tightened around her, then loosened. He kissed her shoulder and sat up, bringing her with him.

When he rose from the bed, she got one thrilling

glimpse of muscled thighs and a well-shaped backside before he tugged on his smallclothes.

"You didn't need to get up. I am quite capable of finding my own way to my carriage, then home."

"I never do anything I don't want to do. I think I amply demonstrated that fact this evening."

All of the things he'd wanted to do and had, in fact, done to her in the past hours flitted through her mind, and the effect was searing. She drew in a deep breath and put those things aside to remember later.

As if it were the most natural thing in the world, he gathered their discarded attire. Feeling suddenly and unaccountably modest, she wrapped a sheet about her and clambered out of bed.

He saw her swathed in the pure-white linen. "If there were time, I'd teach you the advantages of being less modest." He held out an armful of frothy silk, sighed, then shrugged. "Since there isn't, if you wish to make use of it, a screen sits in that corner."

Feeling a bit silly, Morgan ducked behind the dressing screen. She tugged on her clothing with great haste, and then took up the purse she brought with her and turned toward the door.

They said nothing as they made their way down the stairs, through the now-quiet tavern, and around to the adjoining stables. Standing before her hired coach with him ready to hand her in, she paused.

"Connor, I thank you for your… service."

He grinned.

"Truly you will never know how important your actions this night were."

He acknowledged this, then seemed to come to a decision. "Won't you tell me your surname?"

Regret filled her, but could not change her answer. "No, I can't. I'm sorry. I wish I could."

His jaw set and, obviously quite unwilling to be deterred, he asked again. Passionate and hot, his lips captured then moved over hers, the definition of temptation. Resisting was the most difficult thing she had ever done in her life, and she had done many difficult things. Yet, she had to find the strength, so she said nothing. He groaned and released her.

"Damn it, I have just spent half the night making love to you, and you won't even tell me your name? I am not sure whether to be incredibly fascinated or extremely frustrated. Right now, I'm leaning toward frustrated."

"Not won't, can't. Doing so would endanger you as much as me. Please try to understand."

"How will I ever see you again if I have no idea who you are?"

She took his hand in hers. "We can't ever see each other again. The risk is far too great for us both. It is more than our lives are worth, trust me. Promise me you won't look for me. Swear it."

"To seek you out puts you in mortal danger?"

"Yes. And not only me, but you and many others besides. Connor, please promise me."

"I swear never to seek you out."

His jaw clenched, and a kind of despair flickered in his eyes; then his expression hardened, and she wondered if she had imagined it.

"Know I will be forever grateful, and I'll never forget you, Connor O'Malley."

The utmost reluctance still covered his features, but in the end, he bowed and acquiesced.

"I suppose that will have to be enough." He lifted her hand, pressed it to his lips. "My lady Morgan, if ever I may again serve you by my life or my death, you have but to ask. Send word to me at my home in Swynwick, and I will attend you."

She inclined her head, then stepped up and into the carriage. After a quick signal to the driver, she leaned back against the cushioned seat. She resisted, barely, the urge to poke her head out of the window for one last glimpse of her lover.

As the carriage rocked forward and started for home, the tears she had refused to shed earlier filled her eyes, and this time spilled over.

Chapter Two

After Morgan's departure, Connor trudged back to his room, weary to his bones, but he held out little hope he would be able to rest. In spite of all his expectations, however, he slept deeply. Instead of tossing and turning, he lay down and within minutes, he slumbered.

That night, he dreamed of her. Her chestnut hair, her petite, yet voluptuous figure, and her warm brown eyes filled his sleep.

Hours later, he woke alone with her fresh floral scent still surrounding him. He washed, dressed, and headed to the common room for breakfast. He found he had a hearty appetite for the meal, which was just as well. Important business awaited him, perhaps the most critical business of his life, and he needed to be in possession of all of his faculties to transact it this afternoon.

By the early forenoon, his bill paid, his horse saddled, Connor set out, trying not to think of her. He had little success.

****

Impatient, Morgan hurried to the main audience chamber. Her father's summons arrived as she was dressing and starting her day, late though the hour was. After a night such as the one she'd had, she could hardly be surprised she'd slept until early afternoon. Had the summons not been a formal one, she would have made her excuses in favor of taking a meal alone in her chambers at her leisure. Since it was formal, she made herself presentable and rushed to meet him.

The ground floor of Belmere Castle held a foyer which opened to the audience chamber. Left from the entryway was the library, to the right, the grand ballroom. Each of the three rooms was quite large, and the rooms above were called the north, west, and east wings, respectively.

The audience chamber was one of the most well-appointed rooms in the entire castle. It was an enormous space, bright and airy, with ceilings some thirty feet high, and its area was one hundred feet long by forty feet wide. Massive oak doors opened at one end, and the throne sat at the other.

As the king's subjects proceeded down the room, a fresco was laid out beneath their feet. The oak tree depicted was covered with autumn leaves of red, yellow, and burnished orange and was beautiful to behold. Rich velvet drapes of burgundy hung at the massive windows set down both sides of the rectangular room and were, at the moment, held back with gold tasseled cords to let in the sun. At the far end, her father sat at his ease on his throne carved of mahogany, but he rose when she entered.

"Ah, Morgan, join us, please," her father boomed as she stepped forward. He stood tall and strong, as he had from her earliest memory. Possessed of a rather bulky build, all of it was muscle. He sported a full beard of dark-brown hair beginning to be touched with gray. Still handsome, his green eyes were his most mesmerizing feature. A strong jaw was an indicator of his stubborn nature, a character trait she shared. King

James Talbot was a man of definite views who had no problem expressing them, often in a rather loud tone of voice. Morgan loved him with all of her heart.

Us? The word suddenly registered. She had only just enough time to wonder about that before she saw that her father was not alone. A man was with him. Since the stranger's back was to her, at first all she could see was silky black hair which sent a sudden tremor through her for no apparent reason. It was like *his*, she realized a heartbeat later, like Connor's. Would she see him everywhere now simply because she spent one night with him? The stranger turned, and her world tilted on its axis.

Connor.

Her eyes widened, taking him in while he did the same to her.

"Morgan," was all he said.

The sound of him murmuring her name nearly undid her. His face, blank with shock, told her he was as surprised as she at being in the same room together again.

Her father turned his sharp gaze on Connor. "You two have met? How and when, if you please?"

The question was not really a question at all. It was a demand. How on earth could she answer? She swayed, desperately afraid she would faint for the first time in her life and feeling quite unable to do anything about it.

Connor remained motionless, glued to his spot on the floor. Her father, on the other hand, stepped forward with alacrity to take hold of her.

"Morgan, what's wrong? Are you well? You are as pale as the moon. Kent! Kent, fetch some water! The princess is ill."

Snapping back enough to be sure that the last thing she wanted was the fixed attention and cosseting of her father or any of the servants just now, she tried to pull herself together. She waved Kent away and stood on her own if unsteady, feet. "No, no, I'm well enough, but I just need a moment."

Blinking, Connor came alive at last. He stepped forward, then said her name again. She also caught the word princess.

Panic shot through Morgan. If Connor touched her, or if she even so much as looked at him now, she would be lost. The whole story would tumble out; her father would hear it all, and he would never allow her outside the castle walls again, much less allow her to do what she must do. Before she could organize her thoughts further, James caught her gaze then addressed her in a far sharper tone.

"Daughter, this is the famous dragon slayer, Connor O'Malley. How do you know him?"

"*The* Connor O'Malley? You told me that was your name, but I never thought… You are the man responsible for the downfall of seven dragons?" Laughter bubbled up in her throat at the whims of fate, yet she did not give way to it since it might edge over into hysteria.

Her father gave a curt nod, and Connor, holding her gaze, bowed low. "Your servant, my lady."

Pure desire for him raced down her veins. It was altogether too much. Though she could hardly catch her breath, she forced herself to speak. "No more questions, please. I'm sorry, Father, I feel quite unwell after all. I need to lie down." With no further explanation, she bolted.

****

Her retreating footsteps made no impression, but the bang of the large door as it closed brought Connor fully back to his senses.

Praise the gods for it since the king was looking at him with a face hard as stone.

"How did you become acquainted with my daughter, sir?"

Connor swallowed hard, stood to attention, and faced James. "We met in a tavern on the north road last night, the Golden Key."

"She was alone?"

"Yes. I had no notion of who she was, I swear to you. If I had, I would have returned her to you safe and unharmed."

James inhaled, then exhaled. "My daughter is under my protection and is not to ever leave this castle, not without my express permission. What, by all the gods, was she doing in such a place?"

This last was to himself as much as to Connor, but Connor answered anyhow. "I am sorry, Majesty, but this story is hers to tell."

"Is it indeed?" The king considered him another moment. "But you were part of that story, it seems. Tell me."

"All I can say is that at no point was the welfare of the princess compromised. Nor would I ever behave dishonorably toward any woman, let alone your daughter."

"Do you have any notion of what I could do to you for refusing to answer me? Especially in a matter so very significant and personal as this?"

Connor's every muscle tightened. His expression, he knew, was set and grim. "I know only too well, Sire. Even so, I must, with regret, decline to answer."

The king studied him through narrowed eyes for one long moment. "I see. For now, since she is back under this roof and apparently unharmed, I will let the matter rest. However, be assured I will speak with her about this at the first opportunity."

A little less tense now since it appeared his head would remain intact for the present, Connor turned his full attention back to Morgan and looked in the direction she had gone. "If I might beg Your Majesty's indulgence, I must speak with the princess right away."

The king shook his head, not with heat but exasperation. "No, let her be. I do not know what happened between you, but I know my girl, and she needs some time alone. Until she is ready to rejoin us, why don't we go on as planned and discuss why I summoned you here?"

With little choice, Connor fought back his impatience and followed the king.

King James escorted Connor to his private receiving room and offered him a large brandy. He then urged the younger man to sit in one very comfortable wingback chair while he appropriated the other.

Nerves had Connor looking about him. His darting gaze fell on a thick rug with a pattern of autumn leaves similar to the fresco in the audience chamber, solid furniture made of oak, chairs with seats covered in rich brocade. The drapery covering the windows was of heavy, copper-colored satin. He thought idly that they suited the room and the king very well.

Once supplied with his own drink, James began,

"When humans rose up and subdued the earth, they conquered every species except the dragons. Instead, dragons got stronger, more numerous, and greedier. Humans lived in fear of dragon attack. They paid tribute, but whole villages were slaughtered anyway. Soon enough, their will to resist faded. Their spirits broke, and the entire world lived in the shadow of dragons. With most living as little more than slaves, a mere few continued to fight back. Dragon slayers such as yourself have killed one dragon at a time out of hundreds, hoping for a day when they would be triumphant, and peace would rule again. Rownar is the strongest of these. He laid claim to a vast region and possessed the richest hoard on earth. For time out of mind, Esterhaven, my kingdom, has been his to do with as he pleased. As I told you in my letter, a dragon has targeted my daughter. What I did not tell you is that the dragon is Rownar."

Connor's eyes widened, but he could not help it. He was being contracted to hunt Rownar, the one who murdered his family when he was a mere child of ten. He was being offered the chance to have the one and only thing he had ever wanted: revenge. Perhaps fate was smiling on him at last.

Even if that were so, the task would be far from easy. True, he had killed more dragons than anyone and lived to tell the tale. But just because he survived after battling seven dragons did not mean he could take on Rownar and win. And that's if he could even find this dragon, something he had failed to do in the past ten years of seeking him. Still, if he did manage it, what a feat. Then he thought of Morgan. His very soul trembled, and his belly quaked as he imagined what

Rownar would do if he ever got hold of her.

"It's her he's after? Gods preserve us."

"To be sure," James replied, his expression grave. "This is why I summoned you. You are the very best. I have no intention of playing fast and loose with my only daughter's life. I can, and I will take the best chance on offer, which is, in fact, you. If you kill Rownar, I will give you anything."

A little shocked, Connor met the king's gaze, which stayed steady and true and never flinched from his.

"And I do mean anything, up to and including my entire kingdom. Anything."

"I am honored Your Majesty thinks so highly of me and places such trust in me."

"Yes, well, you have but to name your price. My precious child is worth anything it is in my power to give."

Connor drank a long swallow of his brandy then set his glass aside. "Rownar killed my family. For that, I would do this for nothing. Added to it, I would not see harm come to Her Majesty. I will ask for no recompense." James started to speak, but Connor held up a hand. "But you must understand, Sire, this enterprise is a risk. In spite of my best efforts, I may fail."

James leaned forward, and Connor detected a small glimmer of hope in the king's eyes. "You will have all the aid I can muster. You will have an army at your back, which you and I will train together."

"An army?" A small smile began at the corner of his mouth. "That's… surprising, but has the potential to be very useful. Still…"

"I have watched you for a long time. I have heard of your exploits, each more impressive than the last. I have waited as you have honed your skills. Now, you are second to none when it comes to destroying these creatures. I have been looking for someone like you for years to free the princess and my kingdom from the dragon pestilence. I believe you can do this."

When Connor said nothing more, he added, "I told you I would do anything, not for my daughter alone, but for my people as well. I meant it. So, will you do it?"

Connor studied James for a long moment, then inclined his head. "I cannot promise to succeed, but I do promise to try, Majesty."

"Sometimes that is the best that can be said. I am exceedingly grateful to you."

The king rose, and Connor with him. When he held out a hand, Connor touched his lips lightly to the signet ring his sovereign wore.

"The servants will show you to your chamber. Make yourself comfortable and inform them if there is anything more you require."

"Your Majesty is more than generous."

James waved this away. "It is you who is generous, risking your life for my kingdom. I will see you at supper."

Connor bowed and took his leave.

****

Morgan got herself away as quickly as her shaky legs would carry her. The tapping sound of her footsteps as she crossed the flagstone floor echoed through the passage, but she barely registered the noise. Her head was far too full of her rushing thoughts. First and foremost was the fact that her erstwhile lover was here, and not only that, he could become part of the solution to what she liked to think of as her dragon problem.

Furthermore, he could just as easily make himself part of the trouble if he wished. He could tell her father of their night together, or he could keep silent then do what he had obviously come for—try to kill Rownar. It was within his power to ruin her or save her.

Either way, how on earth was she to deal with him? Gods, when he'd looked at her and said her name, her heart had all but stopped. Then it picked up its beat with a vengeance. It wasn't until she reached the stables that the pounding slowed, and she took her first deep breath. She buried her face in her favorite horse's mane, put her arms about the mare's neck, then waited for her mind to clear. Once her head had, if not stopped spinning, at least slowed, Morgan took refuge and solace as she often did in a wild gallop across the fields.

Once on horseback, she relaxed enough to realize she would have to face Connor again sooner rather than later. Nothing else was certain, least of all her own mind or heart. In fact, she had no idea what she should do next. For a woman who always knew what to do, this fresh indecision was disconcerting to say the least.

In an unfamiliar situation such as this, she finally decided the only thing to do was to take the next logical step forward and see where it would bring her. That next logical step would be to face Connor. There was one other thing she was quite sure of; no one would determine her fate but she herself, not a dragon, not her father, and definitely not Connor O'Malley, dragon slayer.

Determined now and feeling a bit more like herself,

she reined in and headed for home.

****

Belmere Castle sat on the top of a rolling hill that commanded a view of every vantage point for miles around. Constructed of stone, its turrets and four towers, one at each corner, were beautifully designed and crafted by a professional. Morgan made her way to the uppermost one at every opportunity. The walls were three feet thick and contained an outer as well as an inner bailey.

A moat wound about its entire circumference. In addition to these defenses, it was guarded by fifty men, men loyal to her father and more than willing to give up their lives for hers. The entire castle was a fortress doubly protected by a spell cast by a powerful wizard on the very first night of their arrival.

No expense was spared to make her chambers the most luxurious rooms within the castle. Her private apartments consisted of a bedchamber and a sitting room adjacent to a combined dressing room and bathing chamber for her exclusive use. The place was decorated to her taste and designed with her every comfort in mind.

In her sitting room was a window seat she often curled up on to read, and an elegant ladies' writing desk made of maple wood sat in one corner. French doors lead to the terrace beyond. From late spring through summer and into the early fall, those doors remained open during all her waking hours. Fresh air was the one remedy for her feeling of confinement, and she took full advantage of it. The wall opposite the doors was lined with bookcases filled with her own personal volumes. A pair of chairs sat near the windows, along with an occasional table in the middle. Two settees faced each other with the fireplace between them.

An enormous bed took up most of her bedchamber. The four-poster was covered with a counterpane of ivory embroidered with tiny pale-pink flowers with green stems. Linens of matching ivory covered the feather mattress, and pillows of a darker-rose color as well as ones in forest green were piled at the head.

The joint dressing room and bathing chamber consisted of a large steel tub with a water pump concealed in one corner waiting to fill it. A fireplace was centered along one wall. It was situated there not merely for warmth but so kettles of hot water could be heated with ease.

To the left, there was a dressing table cluttered with brushes, crumpled hair ribbons, and chemises. Beside it, a wardrobe stood, containing gowns of the richest fabrics made in the most modern styles, all very becoming. A cheval glass stood in the opposite corner to the right of the dressing table so she might get the full effect of whatever outfit she chose. In all, it was her very own domain, both pretty and fanciful, and it represented the most genteel, refined, and feminine side of her nature.

Connor, the antithesis of everything feminine, had made himself at home in one of the chairs near the window in her sitting room.

In spite of the time alone, now that she was face-to-face with him, she still found it difficult to put her feelings into words. Deciding to do something was one thing; doing it quite another. Determining how best to go about doing that something was also something else entirely. So she stood there without speaking, hoping she would manage to sort through all her thoughts and emotions at some point.

When he saw her, he rose. "Forgive the intrusion. After I finished speaking with your father, I cajoled a maid, got her to show me the location of your chambers, and then let me in."

He couldn't seem to take his gaze off her. In fact, he barely blinked. After some time, he murmured, "I never expected to see you again."

"Nor I you," she managed.

"I did not follow you nor search for you. I swear." After she murmured her confidence in him, he continued, "It was really quite a shock to find you here."

A sudden, inappropriate desire to laugh hit her, but she suppressed it. He possessed a talent for bringing out such reactions in her, and she must take care not to give in to them. Shock was, of course, a bit of an understatement.

"For me also."

"So this explains a lot," Connor commented.

"Yes, well, now you are aware of my reasons for…doing what I did. Breaking the dragon's hold over me was imperative, and the only way to do that was to spend the night in a man's bed, your bed, as it turned out. I hope you don't think less of me for not telling you everything."

"By no means. How could you tell me? It involved the safety of the realm. As for what you did? What you did was very brave. I assume it worked."

"It did. The link is far weaker, and I have not felt this free since I was a child. For that, I owe you my gratitude."

He waved the statement away. "I am glad I was there to keep you safe, and I'm both honored and happy you chose me for that and other reasons." He paused for a moment. "It was no hardship to be the first man in your bed."

"I appreciate the compliment." She could think of nothing more intelligent to say than that but hoped it would suffice.

"As you may or may not have realized, your father brought me here to do what I do best, slay dragons."

"As you may or may not have been told, the dragon is Rownar."

"His Majesty informed me. That does make things interesting."

"Interesting? You think fighting the most terrible dragon in all the world is interesting. I am not sure whether you are mad or astounding. Tell me, should I be appalled or impressed?"

He laughed at that. "Listen, Morgan, in case you are wondering, I am very good at what I do. I'm not saying it won't be a challenge, but I like a challenge."

"A challenge? You'll be lucky to get out alive. I don't care how many other dragons you've killed."

"Look on the bright side; you are no longer a virgin, as I have cause to know. Since Rownar no longer has that hold over you, I might stand a chance."

He rose to take his leave, but her voice stopped him. "Are you as good at slaying dragons as you are at bedding a woman?"

The question was bold, although judging from his countenance he was not at all surprised by it. She, on the other hand, astonished herself.

"I've had less practice killing the foul creatures

33

than I have had bedding women, but yes." His lips twitched, then curved up into a grin. Almost straightaway, however, he sobered and gazed into her eyes. "Even so, we shouldn't indulge again."

Morgan could all but feel every emotion wash from her. "Why?"

He cleared his throat. "Risking your father's very serious displeasure is reason enough. More to the point, it would be far too distracting. I have a job to do, and the relationship between us is already complicated enough. Continuing our previous intimacy would be... inadvisable."

Even though his rejection stung, a distinctive, tingly sensation still ran through her blood, brought on perhaps by the warning look in his eyes. "Do you always do what is advisable?"

"No."

The sensation intensified and tempted her to be daring again. "I beg to remind you, then, that I would never have gotten this far if I always did what was advisable." When he said nothing more, she relented. "All right. I do understand, and I am sure refraining would be the wiser course, especially since I like your head right where it is."

"As do I."

"So, if that is how you recommend we proceed, then that is how we shall proceed."

He inclined his head. "Very good, Majesty. I will do my best for you, and soon Rownar will be dead at your feet."

"I know you will, and I look forward to that happy day. If you want to make a start, you had best speak to my father, then. I'm sure the two of you need to discuss tactics," she advised, surprised and grateful when her tone remained neutral. It required some effort, but she managed it.

"As you command, Majesty." He kissed her offered hand, then strode out.

****

Restless in the late evening, Connor left the guest chambers assigned to him to prowl the halls. Thinking to go out to the stables and saddle his horse for a midnight ride, he halted when he heard footsteps. He caught a glimpse of long, brown hair in a braid down the back of a fresh white linen shirt as Morgan left her chamber. As his gaze travelled downward, he experienced the shock of seeing her shapely backside encased in black breeches instead of skirts. Her tiny feet were enclosed in sturdy leather knee boots, which must have been specially made for her. Utterly intrigued, when she turned the nearest corner, he followed.

She set a brisk pace, and it was soon clear she knew where she was going. As she led him deeper and deeper into the warren of the castle, his curiosity and fascination began to be tinged with alarm. Heading alone, in the dead of night, to an all but uninhabited part of the castle was not without risk.

On the verge of making his presence known, he stopped short. She approached a heavy oak door and entered. Once she disappeared inside, he pushed the door open with caution, and it swung forward on silent hinges.

One look at the room beyond, and his jaw dropped. The place, cave as much as chamber, was large, perhaps forty feet by sixty feet, and well-lit. Candle flame glinted on weapons of all types, which sat on several

35

tables. Every style of sword he had seen or heard of ranged alongside daggers and dirks. Arrows, longbows, crossbows, and even axes were also in evidence.

In addition, one entire wall was covered with book-filled shelves. Nearby, there was one smaller table with a simple, straight-backed, wooden chair. Volumes sat in neat piles atop it, and a large candelabra was perched at the end of the smooth surface.

Yet, by far the most captivating thing in the room was her. In the center, Morgan performed basic practice exercises with a saber. She spun, thrust, and parried, and her form was near perfect. The cool air notwithstanding, a light sheen of sweat already glistened on her golden skin. The same skin he'd caressed mere hours before.

As he continued to goggle, she performed a particularly complicated move, finishing with a vicious upward stroke followed by a sideways swipe meant to chop off a head.

"What the hell are you doing?" The harsh words were out of his mouth before he could stop them.

She gasped as she executed a pivot in his direction and ended with her sword pointed at his heart.

Her eyes widened in surprise at the sight of him, "Nothing which concerns you."

"You've got a bloody sword, and right now it's pointed at me. Try again."

"How did you find this place? Never mind, I don't care. Get out."

"No. Not until I have an explanation, princess," He said the last word with an ironic twist to his mouth. Then he crossed his arms, waited, as if he possessed all the time in the world.

Through clenched teeth, she drew in a deep breath. "Did you think losing my virginity would be it? Dragons crave the blood, flesh, and spirit of a maiden, so I went to The Golden Key last night determined I would be a maiden no longer. But that was only the beginning. That was the easy part, if you'll forgive me. In fact, it was downright enjoyable. You think because I am a woman, I can't or won't fight? Such an assumption is the furthest thing from the truth. Do you think I will allow myself to be taken? No, I've worked too long and too hard. That dragon will not have me."

His entire face slackened with shock for a moment, then his jaw hardened. "So this is what the other night was all about! Not just the bedding. You intend to try to kill that damned dragon." He felt equal parts horror and admiration.

"I *will* kill that dragon!"

He studied her for a moment, dumbfounded until she stepped away.

Abruptly utterly incensed, he gripped her arm firmly and turned her back to face him again. "No, you won't. You'll die."

She jerked her arm away then placed the point of her sword under his chin within seconds. "Are you so sure of that?"

He did not back down but instead held her gaze with his. "I am. You spar well; I'll not deny it. In fact, you spar better than many a man or woman I've seen. That does not mean you have the knowledge or the skill to take out a dragon."

"Not just any dragon. Rownar."

"Ah, gods. Not just any dragon, indeed. The vilest, strongest, most-cunning creature ever to walk the earth, in case you've forgotten. And you want to put yourself up against him?"

"As I made clear last night, it isn't about what I want. There is no other choice, not for me or my kingdom. I told you I will not allow Rownar to have me."

"Tell me, Morgan, do you know where a dragon's single vulnerable point is?"

She opened her mouth to reply, then shut it.

"What about how to track one? Then there's its tail. Did you know that one way to incapacitate a dragon temporarily is to chop off its tail? No? So, you intend to challenge this creature without having the least idea of how to fight him, much less defeat him? By all the gods, I have never heard of anything so reckless. Or so brave. Brave women can and do die every day like the rest of us."

"If it means my death, then so be it."

The thought of her death chilled him to his bones, but with a ruthless effort of will, he quelled it. "There's nothing I can say to dissuade you? Of course there isn't. You're a bloody force of nature; you are. All right."

She narrowed her eyes at him. "All right what?"

"I'll help you."

The look she sent his way was cool and unruffled. "You'll help me. What makes you think I would trust you to train me or teach me or whatever you are suggesting rather than going straight to my father?"

"We *will* go straight to your father, actually."

Her jaw clenched and her face set. "No, we won't." She paused a moment. "I have trained for this for years and I will not be gainsaid. Not by my father and certainly not by you."

"How much does he know about this?"

She shrugged elegant shoulders. "Nothing, and I want to keep it that way. Do you plan to tell him I spent the night with you? If so, I would re-think that. You could end up with your head on the block for treason, and I would have little say in the matter."

"Yes, well, I hope to avoid that outcome, but in this case, I believe complete honesty is best. Besides, even if your father is of a mind to execute me right away, he most likely won't. He needs me. I am the best dragon slayer living, and I might be the one man who can save his daughter." Once again, he studied the room with all its amenities. "He really knows nothing of any of this?"

Morgan shook her head. "If he knew, he would never allow it. He would never let me do what needs to be done. And that I will not abide."

"I think you underestimate him. He loves you, and what's more, he knows you."

"Really, and you know me and my father so well?"

"Perhaps not, but I think given a bit of time, he'll accept. If by some chance he doesn't, I'll back you up, and I can be very persuasive."

He smiled his most charming smile, and she blinked as if the sight dazzled her, then shook her head to clear it.

"I'll just bet," she muttered. "I didn't ask for your help."

"No, but you'll accept my aid because you are many things, Morgan, but you are not a fool. You are smart enough to know you need me even more than your father does. To take on Rownar alone, with little to no proper training and no experience, is suicide. You strike me as anything but suicidal. With me, you might actually stand a chance."

His smile faded, and, giving in to impulse, he stroked her cheek. "As for trust, you've already trusted me with your body. Why not with your life?"

Morgan lurched back as if burned. She lowered her blade, then made a business of sheathing it, managing to avoid meeting his gaze all the while. "Spending last night with you was, in part, a personal decision. It did involve the safety of my kingdom as well, but either way, it does not mean I will allow your judgment to hold sway over mine." She looked straight at him.

"In our short, memorable acquaintance, have I ever betrayed your trust?" His voice was barely above a murmur, yet he knew it carried well enough.

"No," she admitted.

"Then trust me now. Let me help you."

"How can you help me? What exactly would I be agreeing to? Be specific, please."

He hid his grin and the bone-deep relief which rolled through him. She was considering it, a definite positive step forward.

"I agree to keep your secret from everyone except your father. I will train you here or wherever else you choose." He held up a finger. "In exchange, you will agree not to go off on your own or challenge Rownar until I say you are ready."

She shook her head. "I will not go off on my own or challenge Rownar without telling you, but I will decide when I am ready."

It was his turn now to shake his head. "I am the expert, and if I say you are not ready, then you are not."

"I rule here or will someday if I live. Added to that, I am the one Rownar is hell-bent on consuming, body and soul. I will be the one to decide."

For a moment, Connor weighed her viewpoint against his own. "Could we compromise? Make the decision together?"

"We could try, but the safety of my realm is paramount over and above even the safety of my person, so I cannot promise to ignore that in favor of your expert opinion on the matter."

"Fair enough." He held out his hand. "You won't regret this, I swear."

"I'm not so sure about that," Morgan muttered.

Nevertheless, she grasped his palm in hers, then shook.

Chapter Three

"Come."

Her father's voice carried through the door clear as a bell. Morgan shoved it open, then stepped into his study with more than a little trepidation. Her belly roiled, and her nerves jittered, but as she so often did, she ignored both. Instead, she took a deep breath.

She would meet whatever came next.

James sat behind a massive oak desk covered with parchment, quills, and well-used tomes of various sizes and in different stages of disreputability.

"Ah, Morgan, good morning. How are you feeling?" He rose from his chair, and his smile warmed, and his gaze roamed over her as though checking for injury.

She couldn't help but smile at him in spite of her own apprehension. "I am quite well, Father, I assure you. I do need to speak with you on several important matters, however, as does Connor."

Connor stood a step behind, flanking her. When her father sent her a sharp, surprised look, eyebrows raised, she hastened to add, "What I have to say also concerns him."

"I see." James gestured her forward. "Please, by all means, speak."

"To begin with, I will not let Rownar have me. I decided that a long time ago. I won't sit back and allow him to take me."

Her father's expression hardened. "What have you done?"

He knew her better than anyone, aside from Connor, and thus knew she had done something. Her resolve quaked a bit at the stern look on his face. But she gritted her teeth.

"I have been training myself, as best I can, all on my own. I found ancient texts describing battle techniques and strategy. I studied weapons of all types, and I have set myself to become proficient in their use."

When he demanded details, she described her self-training regimen as succinctly and accurately as possible, with Connor adding his experiences and observations.

James looked more and more grim until he finally asked, "But that's not all, is it?"

Although her cheeks heated, Morgan lifted her chin and looked her father straight in the eye. "No, it isn't. I am no longer a virgin. I took Connor to my bed."

For one moment, a charged silence reigned, then James found his voice. "I was aware you left the castle, and I did wonder. But I had no idea you were considering doing something so drastic. I convinced myself you were simply desperate to get out from under this roof, frantic for any sort of independence. I understand the emotion well and was more than willing to let it go, but this? What were you thinking? I cannot believe you would do such a thing. By all the gods, Morgan, why didn't you come to me? There was no need for you to… For that matter, how could you lie to me?"

"I did come to you! Seven years ago."

His face paled as the memory returned, but she went relentlessly on. "Besides, if I told you all I was planning, would you have let me do it?"

James opened his mouth, then closed it and was silent for so long that Morgan wondered whether he would answer at all. "No, of course not."

"There you are, of course not. But despite what you think, it did need to be done, all of it, and besides, it was my decision and mine alone. I was determined I would not be in this prison anymore. All dragons were born to create indiscriminate mayhem and destruction, but you know as well as I do there are times when a dragon will fix on a female and create a bond, form a forced connection. Against my will, this happened to me at eight years old. I resolved at seventeen that I would fight, with your help or without it; that I would defeat Rownar, with your approval or without it! I have trained for seven years on my own, in secret, with no one to aid or support me. When I felt I was ready and the time had come, I sought out a man to relieve me of my virginity, acutely aware this act was vital to weaken the link if I ever hoped to win against Rownar. There was no other way. Fate led me to Connor, a gentle, decent, passionate man. I don't regret it. Not one moment of it. Apart from anything else, at least now I am not so much under Rownar's sway." She shook with a mixture of fury and hurt. "Father, I am sorry I lied to you, but I had no choice. It had to be this way, and if you dare to say any different, I swear—"

He held up a hand. "You are right," James admitted in a heavy voice.

Morgan let out a breath she had not even realized she was holding.

"I suppose I knew from the moment Rownar took your mother when you were a little girl that you would have to confront him. It was only a matter of time. I didn't want to admit it, to face the fact that he had linked with you." He ran his fingers through his hair and sighed. "Do you think I liked holding you here, in what even I could see was a gilded cage?" He shook his head. "Do you think I liked seeing you in pain? No, but it was more important to me that you live. Because I refused to pay tribute to Rownar, it cost your mother her life. I failed to protect her, and I have always blamed myself for that. I vowed I would never let the same thing happen to you, my innocent child, so when I couldn't hunt the creature down myself, couldn't even find him, I built Belmere, this-this bloody prison. All I've ever wanted is to protect you. Everything I have ever done has been toward that end."

Morgan took James's hand. "I do understand, Father. But I cannot let Rownar control my life anymore. I won't, and nor should you."

"I know. All your life, but over these last months in particular, I have sensed your unhappiness mounting day by day. You have grown into a beautiful young woman, and, with your spirit, I also knew that soon I would be unable to hold you any longer. So, in the end, I decided it was worth the risk to contact Connor and see if he would have better luck killing Rownar and ridding the world of him. I wanted this to end. I wanted you to have a life. I should have known you were several large steps ahead of me. I should have realized you are strong like your mother. Stronger than I ever could have imagined." He shot her a bittersweet smile, then took a huge breath. "What would you have me do now?"

When a lump in her throat prevented her from saying anything at all, Connor spoke up. "Let me train her. Your daughter possesses exceptional instincts, Majesty, and has progressed very well, but there is only so far she can go on her own. Allow me to teach her, to guide her."

"And then what?"

Morgan lifted her chin. "Then when I am ready, I go after Rownar."

"With my help and an army at her back," Connor added hastily when James blanched.

"So be it. You are a woman grown and have the right to choose your own path. Do as you will, train, study, do whatever will keep you alive when you face him."

Slowly she inclined her head. Relief filled her as it sank in—first that there would be no more need for lies and, even better, she had gotten what she wanted. "Thank you. You won't regret this, I promise you."

She turned to go, paused, then swung back. "You don't think too badly of me, then?"

"For what happened between you and Connor?" James shook his head. "The opposite. I am proud. I am blessed to have a daughter with the capacity to protect this kingdom and herself, no matter the cost. I do wish you had told me sooner. I wish even more that I had listened seven years ago, and I am deeply sorry I have not been more of a help to you."

He embraced her. For one fleeting instant, she laid her head on his shoulder as if she were a little girl again.

Using gentle, soothing motions, he stroked her

hair. "I swear I will not hinder you, not any longer. In fact, I intend to do all I can to help you. That's why I brought this one here." He flipped a hand at Connor.

Laughing a little, she let go and wiped tears from her eyes. "I love you, Father."

He kissed the top of her head. "And I love you. We will work this out together, but for now, I need to speak to Connor alone."

She glanced at Connor for confirmation. At his all but imperceptible nod, she agreed. But before leaving, she narrowed her eyes at each man in turn. "Do not kill each other. That will do no one any good."

"I make no promises," James muttered.

Morgan gave him a steely-eyed stare, and he subsided. She kissed his cheek, then left them to their own devices.

****

Nerves filled Connor. He had slept with the king's daughter. For the second time in twenty-four hours, he wondered whether he would keep his head.

James fixed Connor with a cool stare. "And what do you have to say for yourself?"

"Little more than before, Majesty. I did not know who she was, and—"

"You make a habit of sharing your bed with strangers then, do you?"

"I–I." For a moment, he could only stammer, then he pulled himself together. "Sometimes, yes." The admission cost him, but his tone was firm and matter-of-fact. He would make no apologies.

"Hmm."

Connor cleared his throat. "I could tell right away she was of good breeding and was reasonably sure she was chaste. When she approached me, I knew it for certain. Added to that, she was so beautiful and bright in every sense. Any man would want her. Soon enough I understood that she meant to bed someone that evening and that she would not be dissuaded. Once that was clear, it was only then that I agreed to do what we both wanted. I have never encountered anyone with such a strong will, so it was easy to believe she would do it no matter what, and at least, I told myself, she would be safe with me."

"And she was lovely, so why not?"

"Yes."

"I see."

"Do you believe in fate, Sire?" When James nodded, Connor continued, "I did not, not until yesterday when she walked into Your Majesty's audience chamber. I never thought to see her again, but there she was. And if that weren't enough, she is the princess you called me here to save. If that isn't fate, I don't know what is. I'm not sure what this means for her or me, but I must find out."

James said nothing for a long time.

Connor kept silent. After all, explaining was one thing, but he'd be damned if he would defend himself, even to his king.

"Perhaps it is fate, perhaps mere chance. Either way, I am inclined to be lenient. Given the situation, you appear to have behaved at least semi-decently. If I accept that you had no idea who she was, and I do, if you had her consent, as she herself states, then how can it be true treason? In addition, Morgan appears to be unharmed by the experience. It might even be beneficial to her in the long run as regards her dealings with Rownar. Time enough to worry over her dismal marriage prospects once her life is no longer in danger. Moreover, apart from anything else, the gods know my daughter is not easy to dissuade."

Connor fought back a sudden grin. "You will get no argument from me on that score, Sire."

"I give you leave to train her without interference. Doing so will be your primary focus. You will also begin working with the rest of my troops, starting with a group of handpicked lieutenants as well as my daughter and myself. You will give her one-on-one instruction. My child is by far the most important person in this kingdom to us, and you will devote your every spare moment to her. She is determined to take on Rownar herself, and no force on earth will stop her, not even me. You will keep her alive, but if you touch her again, I might not be so forgiving, so be very careful. One last thing: if you hurt her in any way, dragon slayer or no, I *will* have your head."

"I am at your command, Majesty."

"Yes." He held Connor's gaze with his own steady one. "You will dine with my daughter and me tonight."

Connor bowed, recognizing dismissal. "Until then."

****

Since this was to be their first training session, Morgan figured it would take time for Connor to accept that he would be tutoring a woman in the physical aspects of dragon slaying. So she would get her daily routine in first, then she and Connor could discuss the more intellectual facets of this venture. Once he was comfortable with the idea, they could move on to the physical.

As usual, she began by stretching her muscles. Trial and error had taught her this was one of the best ways to avoid injury. Done, she started to practice her moves with the sword she favored. It was a point of pride for her that she was becoming skilled with it. In the beginning, even though it was her weapon of choice, she could barely lift the heavy blade. Very good for chopping off a dragon's head or piercing its black heart.

Without warning, in the middle of a thrust, the hairs on the back of her neck prickled. She shivered then looked sharply about her, knowing she was no longer alone. Connor stepped out of the shadows.

"We really must stop meeting like this," she quipped.

He grinned, then bowed. "Forgive me, princess. I did not mean to startle you. I did not want to interrupt."

She shrugged, then sheathed her sword. "That's quite all right." She contemplated a moment. "I can't get used to you calling me by my title. Do call me Morgan, at least when we are in private."

He inclined his head. "I would be honored, Morgan."

"I came down early to get some practice in before you and I began."

His brows rose. "Isn't that what I am here for?"

"Well, I thought perhaps you would like to start with the less active part of the training process."

"Not at all. I would prefer to see what you've got."

The desire to see what sort of moves he had raced down Morgan's veins. Heat filled her as she realized not only did she already know quite a lot about him, but anything she didn't already know she wanted very much to learn.

She stood by as he removed his tunic, leaving him in a loose linen shirt and breeches. He set the garment aside, then turned to the impressive array of weapons. Fascinated, Morgan watched as he examined first one, then another, sometimes testing the sharpness of a cutlass or the balance and weight of a broadsword. At last, he too settled on a saber, less fine than the one she was using but still lethal enough for all that.

He strode to the center of the practice area and took up his stance. "Come join me. It's high time for you to have a real opponent, don't you think?" He gestured her forward. "Don't worry. I know what I'm doing. I won't hurt you."

Remembering the last time Connor said similar words, her cheeks heated even more, but she was determined to meet the challenge.

Morgan set her shoulders and planted her feet in a fighting posture. Observing him through narrowed eyes, she waited as he circled her and wondered when and how he would strike. After orbiting around her several times as if she were the sun and he some distant planet, he gestured her to come ahead. Half-excited, half-anxious, without a word, Morgan did as instructed.

Sword raised, she rushed forward, but he stepped nimbly out of her path. Her inability to halt her forward momentum right away gave him time to circle behind her. She yelped at the smack on her backside from the flat of his sword. Determined not to be made ridiculous, she revolved to face him, thrust hard in the direction of his heart, yet he parried the blow with apparent ease.

Still, feeling her sword connecting with someone else's for the first time was exhilarating, invigorating, in fact, so different from practicing alone. The shocking strength he used to deflect her blows reverberated throughout her entire body as their swords collided, placing her firmly in the reality of the situation.

That first connection of sword to sword was the most startling for her. After that, it was a matter of reacting quickly to defend herself with no time to attack. It was soon clear that he was as expert a swordsman as expected. With no hope of beating him, she focused her attention on not letting him best her too soon. She used every move she had ever taught herself, but he countered each one. Far sooner than she expected, fatigue dragged at her until even lifting her sword was an effort.

In the end, in spite of her best attempts, she finished disarmed on her knees with his sword at her throat. It was some satisfaction to observe that he panted as heavily as she, but not nearly satisfaction enough.

"You put up quite a fight."

She shook her head. "I have a long way to go and a lot to learn."

He shrugged. "Not as long or as much as I anticipated. I've seen professional soldiers with less stamina, and you also have excellent instincts. You do have a lot to learn, I won't disagree, but you also have a natural aptitude for this. That is something that can never be taught."

"So you can help me to hone my skills?"

"Absolutely."

Not quite so discouraged now, she stayed where she was and caught her breath while he sheathed his sword. Then, grasping his offered hand in her own, she let him help her to her feet.

****

They arranged to have another training session the very next day, one hour after the morning meal. This time, Connor arrived earlier than agreed. It was important to him to get a true sense of Morgan's space and of her, something he failed to do the previous day. He also wanted to explore the training room as thoroughly as possible before she appeared.

First he examined the weapons, taking note of each type. They were all well cared for, he observed, though most of them looked to have seen quite a lot of use. Stepping to the bookcase, he perused, reading titles as he went. They ranged from *Flynn: Life and Death of a Dragon Slayer* to *An Encyclopedia of Ancient Weaponry* to *Dragon Defense: The Basics*. He chose a volume at random and read.

He was still engrossed when sometime later, the door opened, and Morgan entered. He heard the sound of her boots on the stone floor, but did not look up. "Your library is quite extensive. I would suggest adding *Dragon Birth, A History,* if possible. It is a very comprehensive, well-written volume, and I believe you would find it quite useful."

"And good morning to you too, Connor." She stepped over to him, and he set down what he had been reading. "There are so many books I have not been able to acquire. Perhaps now with your help as well as my father's, I might be able to get my hands on more."

She made her way over to the shelves and scanned them. "This is how I wanted to start yesterday, with knowledge. With whatever you can tell me that isn't in these books."

"So why didn't you?"

"I meant to, but I got distracted. It was good to have a sparring partner, a trainer."

He accepted this with a nod. "It was interesting to have a trainee." Leaning against the nearest table, he gave her his undivided attention. "So, what is it you want to know?"

"Everything, but most of all, how to fight them."

"First, let me say you are on the right track. Training and gathering whatever information you could have both been very effective tactics."

"But…"

"It takes more than that. If you are going to survive, this is the first thing you must understand— dragons are extremely hard to kill."

She knitted her brow. "I am already well aware of that."

Connor shook his head. "No, you think you are, but until you have actually fought one, you cannot truly know. It isn't just the strength of their physical form or that they fly. Dragons have a very well-developed survival instinct. They can sense a trap more quickly than any other species on Earth. I have never seen one go down without a fight. More often than not, they don't go down at all. Consider this, I cannot count the times I have faced a dragon, yet I have only killed seven."

"So how do you defeat them?"

"With practice and time which leads to skill. But even more important than that, you must understand, these creatures are a malignant magical force."

"Again, I must point out I am more than aware of that, having been connected to Rownar since I was eight."

"Of course. I apologize." He cleared his throat. "By their very nature, they are evil and worse, they are cunning. They are not only good at detecting traps, but laying them."

"So, be careful not to fall into a trap."

He nodded. "Morgan, I can teach you their vulnerabilities; I can train you, and when I am done, you will be able to, if not kill a dragon, at least put up a good fight. I can even teach you to think a little bit like them so that you avoid the pitfalls they will set for you. But there is one thing I cannot teach you, one thing you either understand from the beginning, or you don't."

"And what is that?"

"Above all, never think you are invincible because you are not. Killing one dragon does not mean that the next one won't gobble you up for its next meal. Forget that, and that is what you will become, dragon food."

She scrunched up her nose. "Eww. I definitely want to avoid that. Since I do, I will take your advice. You have been right so far."

"I often am." He grinned at her. "What else have I been right about?"

"Telling my father. He did understand. I never believed he would, but he did. It also helped to have you backing me up. So, thank you."

He bowed with formality and courtesy. "It was my very great pleasure, Majesty."

She nodded and let her lips curve up the slightest bit but then sobered. "So tell me, how do I fight them?"

"There are just two sure ways to kill a dragon, a sword straight through the heart or beheading."

"Yes, from all I have read, that is true."

"But there are things you can do to debilitate them."

"Such as?"

"Cut off the tail—as I already mentioned. This throws them off balance, making it difficult for them to keep on course when flying. It will grow back, but not right away. It takes weeks. Doing this may give you enough time to finish the creature off. If you can damage a wing, that is even better. A dragon's hide is as strong as armor, but his wings, on the other hand? Far more delicate. An arrow is much more likely to penetrate them. On the ground, the dragon is a far easier target because at least it is no longer moving through the air at great speed. This is why you should practice with a crossbow and a sword. One well-placed arrow through the wing, and down the beast goes."

"The sword has been my primary focus thus far, but that can change."

"We'll work on it. Are you any good with a bow?"

She smiled. "Better than I am with a sword, which is why I decided to focus on the sword first."

"Another thing to consider is how to choose your ground. You can opt to pursue the dragon to his lair. In which case, it is much more difficult for him to fly away. On the other hand, this traps you both. Alternatively, you can challenge him when he is away from his lair before, during, or after an attack. Yet, this makes it far easier for the dragon to do serious damage then move out of range."

"Which is best?"

"Neither. It's a matter of taste as well as what fighting techniques you prefer and are best at."

"What if my preference doesn't coincide with my

skill? Can you help me choose between them?"

"I can. I can also help you hone what skills you have as well as shore up your weaknesses. I can do all this, but it won't be easy."

"I am ready for whatever challenges I must face."

Connor studied her for a long time, thinking over all the things she had already done to reach this moment, things done on her own with little to no outside help. He nodded, one brisk tip of the head. "I believe you. All right, let's get started."

Chapter Four

Morgan found herself flat on her back, staring at the ceiling of her training chamber. Again. Bruised in places she had never been bruised before and battered beyond her worst imaginings, she wondered, not for the first time, whether she would ever have what it took to go up against even one man in combat, let alone take on a dragon, especially a formidable one like Rownar.

A strong hand came into her field of vision, and a deep male voice from somewhere above her said, "Come on. We are not done yet."

When she did not move, Connor ordered tonelessly, "Get up."

He was relentless. Even exhausted as she was, a small spark of anger kindled in her. "The hell I will." She started to shake her head, but even that hurt, so she stopped. "No, I am finished for today. Maybe even for good."

"Is that so? I thought you had more grit. I must say I am disappointed. I took you for more than some privileged female. You did commit to this, after all. When you did, I told you it wouldn't be easy."

"That was before. When I believed I had a modicum of training and skill and some sort of a chance, no matter how small. Clearly, I was wrong."

"You did. You do. Morgan, before, you were on your own. Progress is far slower that way. We have only been training together for a month, and already you have learned, improved, and grown so much."

"Have I? Then why is it I still end every day on my back?" She sat up with great difficulty and even more pain.

Connor ran a hand through his hair and sat on the cold flagstones beside her. "Because this sort of skill cannot be gained overnight. I know it's very difficult, believe me, but I am tough on you so that in the end, you will be stronger, more able to defend yourself, and more likely to remain alive when facing Rownar."

She laughed, but was not at all amused. "If I were going up against Rownar, I would be dead."

"Yes, a hundred times over."

She stewed a moment over that unpalatable truth.

"Every day I have to fight harder, think faster, to best you, did you know that? Do not be discouraged."

She stilled. Had he just paid her a compliment? She had to wonder why. Was it to placate her and keep her going? Or was he serious? When she studied his face and saw simple truth there and nothing more, Morgan cursed. She had not let anything stop her, not even when she had been entirely on her own. Now she had him training her. She would be damned if she would quit now, not when she was so close.

Groaning like an old woman, she struggled to her feet. "Again."

The approving look he gave her, one which bordered on admiration, was almost worth the extreme agony.

The renewed strength and determination burgeoning within her definitely was.

****

The days passed with a swiftness Morgan had never experienced before, and Connor's excellent companionship was a welcome change of pace. Mornings were reserved for study—of tactics and strategy and dragons themselves, Rownar in particular.

After sharing a simple meal, she and Connor would train. Having a flesh-and-blood opponent was more than useful. He was a strict taskmaster and an even better teacher, with knowledge of many fields. Perhaps quite as important, he had an exceptional sense of how far to push her and when to let up. Eventually others, a half-dozen handpicked soldiers, joined them.

With so much to learn, at first, she was content. After some weeks, and with every new technique she mastered, however, the more restless she began to feel. As her skill level increased, so did her desire to face Rownar.

"When can we go after Rownar?" Morgan asked as she parried Connor's blow and forced him back a step. The same question she now asked every day, sometimes more than once a day.

"Not yet. Not any time soon."

And there it was, the same answer. She wanted very badly to kick something. Instead, she kept sparring with him, using all he taught her.

"Two months. That's all. That's how long you have been training with me. I realize that may seem like a long time to you, but you aren't anywhere close to ready. Surely you can see that?"

She did a 360-degree turn to avoid his blade, then grimaced. "I suppose so. When will I be ready?"

"I can't say for sure. It could be in three months; it could be in thirty. Each person is different. You are ready when you are ready."

"Fine," she spat through gritted teeth.

Connor swung his sword in a blow meant to take off her head and she ducked, rolled, and stood, ready to land a blow of her own.

****

Sparring with him was exhilarating, she had to admit. In fact, it had become the highlight of her days. The sheer physicality of the action often brought to her mind their night together. Day by day, her desire for him increased, and she reveled in the closeness growing between them. She longed for him to join his body to hers as he had that one memorable evening. Yet, she wanted so much more now. She wanted more than anything to explore her deepening connection to him.

As for him, Morgan had no idea of his wishes on the matter. In all other ways, he was open with her, but not by one sign, not by word or action, did he demonstrate his own feelings or lack thereof for her. Perhaps he had none. Barring that one and only mention when he first arrived at the castle, he gave no indication he even remembered that night at all, so how could she know what was in his mind and heart? It was this which kept her from revealing her own. Taking her cue from him, she kept her emotions locked down tight.

Until the moment everything changed.

One evening, while they practiced alone, as they did every day, she ended gazing at him over their crossed swords. For the first time, she matched him. She hadn't beaten him… Yet. But now she knew that one day, she might. Elation rolled over her. Then she peered up to find him scrutinizing her, his face for once unguarded, and for just an instant, some emotion akin to longing moved in his eyes. The yearning, the passion was unmistakable. She gasped.

She stood still, blade in hand, panting and mesmerized, feeling the tension in his body as well as her own, neither one of them willing to give an inch. His warmth was so close to her, and the long, muscled line of him made her tremble. Then he slammed his shields back into place, and all she could see was the calm she had grown used to. If she had not been watching closely, she might have missed it.

In one smooth motion, he lowered his sword. He turned from her, but Morgan called him back with a hand on his arm. Pretending she hadn't seen what she had wasn't an option.

"Connor—"

What she had been about to say died in her throat because he was kissing her, or maybe she was kissing him. Either way, she was in his arms, and that was all that mattered.

"Damn it, Morgan, I've been trying to keep my hands off of you," he murmured in her ear while he caressed her neck.

"Whatever for?"

"You know why. Because it's complicated. For one thing, I am training you. Your father, for another. He'll have my head if I hurt you. And I...I don't want to hurt you."

For a time, she leaned back against the wall where they had somehow ended up, trying to catch her breath. "Don't worry about my father. You won't hurt me." Never taking her gaze from his, she loosened the lacing of the tunic she wore.

"Wait." He inhaled sharply, even as he pressed his

lips to hers, and his hands fumbled to help her.

"Why? It isn't as if we haven't done this before." She felt giddy, light-headed, like she floated and would never come down.

The look in his eyes said more clearly than any words how much he wanted her. She did her best to tug his shirt free of his pants.

He lowered his lids and looked like a man trying his hardest to resist temptation but recognizing he was about to fail.

"Because I need to be sure you want this. That all you want is this. I need to know you aren't doing this for any other reason this time."

"I'm not. I want you and nothing else."

Connor paused, but it was clear from his expression that his passion-addled brain made thinking difficult. "Good."

A succinct reply rife with finality. It pleased Morgan. Then he kissed her again, and it was all she hoped for. His gaze fell on every surface in the room, then flicked back to hers.

"Not here," he said in a very definite, though guttural tone.

She looked about her and gradually remembered where they were. "Then where?"

"That is for you to decide, Majesty."

"My chambers?"

"Yes, please."

****

How they managed to make it to her bedchamber without being seen was something Morgan could never quite recall. But they arrived there at last, thank the gods. And praise them; he remained as frantic and eager as she.

It seemed like an age since he had shared her bed though a mere three months had passed.

Even though she was reduced to shivery sounds of pleasure, he had little trouble speaking. Still, when he did, his voice was low and urgent.

"When I found out who you were, I thought I would never be allowed to touch you again. I couldn't let myself even think of it. Please tell me I can touch you."

"You can. You are."

Clothes were gone in little more than the blink of an eye. His hands roamed every inch of her body, and she moaned. Caressing her from shoulder to hip, he then trailed his hand inward across her stomach and down. When his fingers eased into her and then his palm pressed and stroked her center, she flew over a jagged peak, swift and unexpected.

When he knelt, then replaced his hand with his mouth, she tumbled over again. She couldn't have stopped it even if she'd wanted to. Yet even as the sharp edges of reality blurred into smooth pleasure, one thought remained crystal clear.

She wanted him with her.

****

He could not stop touching her. Everywhere. In every way he could think of. It was clear she felt the same, as she was doing the same to him, touching him everywhere with no inhibitions whatsoever.

During their first night together, at least at the very start, she had been nervous, a bit skittish, but not so now. This made it very hard for him to maintain his own control. She was still so new at this, and he did not want to frighten her. Yet, nor did he have any wish to discourage her. He had to walk a very fine line, but he could do it for her, for as long as she needed him to.

So he set a pace as slow as it was excruciating. He watched her every move, her every expression, not at all inclined to rush. He wanted to be sure she was with him every step of the way, but even more than that, he wanted to savor.

"Connor, please." The words were barely audible but insistent.

"Soon," he promised.

Unsatisfied with his answer, she shook her head. "I've thought of nothing but you and this since the one night we spent together. I don't want to wait any longer. Stop holding back. You didn't hold back that night."

"No, but I didn't—" He clamped his mouth shut. *But I didn't know I loved you then.*

"You didn't what?" She caught his gaze for a moment, but he looked away.

"Nothing. You are right. I won't hold back anymore."

He hoped this reply would suffice because he wasn't ready to say the words. He wasn't ready to speak of the love he was only just realizing and admitting to himself was there. There was nothing he could do now but show her. She all but demanded it, and he was, as always, at her command. So, clasping her hand in his, he did as she decreed. He gave her every iota of himself—body, heart, and mind—and felt her do the same.

****

Once her mind cleared sufficiently, she found herself sprawled atop him. More than content to be there, Morgan let her hand drift lazily over his chest. "Let's not wait so long to do this the next time."

"Hmm, we won't. Not if I have anything to say about it, Your Grace." He stroked her hair. "Morgan?"

"Hmmm?"

"There is something I need to say to you."

She sent him a dreamy smile. "You can say anything to me now. Go ahead."

He tilted her chin so he could see her eyes. What he needed to say was very serious. "I don't share. You are royal, but I don't give a damn. You are mine and mine alone. For as long as you and I are together like this, no other man will touch you."

"I am yours," she said. "And you are mine."

"I am." With no more words, he took her again.

When she came back to earth once more, she lay on her back, and he was beside her. There was nothing but the sound of their labored breathing.

"Can I confess something to you?"

"You can say anything to me too; I hope you know that."

She faced him. "I am an absolute wanton. I suspected it before, but now I am sure of it." He said nothing, so, a little nervous now, she rattled on. "I have wanted to be with you like this again since the moment I saw you in the audience chamber. Tonight, when I was a match for you at last, I must say I was ecstatic, practically euphoric. Then I looked at you. For an instant, it was as if you wanted me. Then you shut down and pulled away, and I couldn't let you go. Not this time. So, I suppose what I am trying to say is that I hope you don't mind my enthusiasm. Or my directness."

Several moments passed and yet he did not respond. The slight tension she felt from making her declaration ratcheted up a notch. "Connor? Could you say something, please?"

He refocused his attention on her. "Of course, I'm sorry. I am just trying to imagine how I could get any luckier." His hand ran through her hair; then he kissed her shoulder. Instead of ticking points off on his fingers, he kissed his way down her arm. "You are beautiful. You are intelligent. You are kind. You are of royal blood. You are becoming a formidable warrior. And now you are telling me you greatly enjoy sharing my bed. So, do I mind your enthusiasm or your directness? No, not at all."

Morgan's lips twitched. "Oh, that's good, then." Lips still curved, she kissed him.

"As for tonight? I did want you. I have since the moment we met. Tonight, I couldn't hide it anymore. Maybe I didn't wish to."

"That's even lovelier."

She supposed her smile must be bordering on besotted, but she didn't care. This time he kissed her, then settled her head on his shoulder. He stretched out one long arm to douse the candle on the nightstand, then smoothed the covers around them.

"So, what do we do now?"

"Now? We sleep. When we wake, I'll have you again."

A thrill of anticipation rushed through her, and she relished it. "That wasn't exactly what I meant. What about after?"

"Come the morning, we continue training as we have been, only with the subtle difference of being lovers who are intimately familiar with each other's bodies."

"And what about my father?"

He sighed. "The gods alone can say."

She considered. "At this point, does he need to know? I think perhaps not. This is my own private life, after all, no one else's."

He snorted, and she glanced over at him in surprise. "What?"

"You are the crown princess of Esterhaven. You don't have a private life. Nor do I, now I am your lover. You belong first and foremost to your subjects, and even though I hope to be chief among them, I must still share you. We might manage to keep our relationship private for a short time, but eventually people will find out. That being the case, we ought to tell those who matter most to us first."

She pulled a face but acquiesced. "But what do we tell them?"

Connor yawned. "No idea. That we are lovers? That I will be by your side for the foreseeable future, at least until you are safe from Rownar? We can worry about all of that tomorrow. For now, sleep."

He kissed the top of her head and she did.

****

James decided it was long past time he saw his daughter's training firsthand, not to mention begin his own. Never one to waste time having made a decision, he went down to the training area the very next day. Without making his presence known, he watched Morgan and Connor spar together without even glancing at the other perhaps dozen men doing the same.

Connor shouted directions, threw out mildly mocking comments when she missed, and was equally generous with his encouragement when she hit the mark. She followed his directions, worked all the harder on the rare occasions when she made a false step, and soaked in the encouragement.

His daughter was fast becoming an accomplished fighter. While the realization disquieted him, it also filled him with pride. Her movements were fluid, and her strength was clear. In addition, she possessed a head for strategy it seemed, judging from the bits of conversation in between blows and the moves and countermoves she used.

All at once, his instincts prickled as the couple stayed close for a beat too long over their crossed swords. Heat flared in Connor's eyes and drew a similar, unmistakable response from Morgan. *Well, well, we'll just see about this.*

As soon as there was a pause, he called out, "Well done!"

Morgan looked over and smiled. "Father, I'd hoped you would come! What do you think?" Her gesture encompassed the whole of the room.

"I think I am very impressed with my beautiful daughter. Or should I say, my warrior."

She beamed. "Let me get some water, then show you around."

When she was out of earshot, James murmured, "What do you think you are doing?"

Connor, who had been focused on Morgan as if unable to take his eyes off her, whipped his head around. "I beg your pardon, Sire? I don't know what you mean."

James scoffed. "You don't know what I mean? Let me speak plainly then. You are bedding my daughter again and on a regular basis. If I'm wrong, I'll melt my crown and sell off the remnants."

Connor's jaw tightened. "You aren't wrong. She offered. I accepted. It's what we both wanted. It's as simple as that."

"Simple! Nothing about this is simple. I wanted her to make a very advantageous match, perhaps with the young prince from Prith. Now, well, that isn't going to happen."

"Why not? Charge me with treason and execute me. Then you could marry her off, if not to the highest bidder, then to someone less fastidious." Connor's voice was as cold as the king's was hot.

"Why not? You know damned well why not. Because she is falling in love with you if she isn't already there. Furthermore, how dare you talk about my daughter as though she is some commodity to be sold. She isn't. She has never been that to me."

"Nor is she a mere bed partner to me."

"Oh? Then what is she to you exactly? It is clear you are willing to risk a traitor's death for her, so I suppose she must mean something to you."

Connor fixed his gaze on her. "She is what I need to live, and I won't let her go, not even for you, Sire. Not, at any rate, until she is safe. Certainly not for some…potential husband who might never become a reality."

James assessed Connor for a long moment. Then glanced over at Morgan, who was headed back toward them, smile undimmed. "I suppose that answer will do. For now. But once this threat is neutralized, you will have to determine what your intentions are. You will have to decide what you want. In short, choices will have to be made and acted upon."

"I am quite aware of that and am considering it, Your Majesty."

His daughter stopped to organize some of the weapons on the table. James doubted she was aware of it, but she hummed to herself. "She's happier than I have ever seen her. Since this is clear, I am trusting you for the present. Her life is in your hands in every possible way, it seems. There also seems little I can or should do about that at this point. As you know, she is dearer to me than anything on this Earth. Do not disappoint me, much less her. When I said if you hurt her, I would have your head, I meant it."

"I think I am falling for her, and I know I would guard her heart, her soul, and her body with my life. I would protect her even from myself, if need be. Please believe that."

James nodded to Connor, then held out both hands to his daughter as she joined them.

****

That evening after supper, Morgan announced she could not resist the bright stars and the balmy air and suggested a walk on the terrace. Connor responded with eager agreement, and they stepped out into the night.

Once they were alone, he said, "I take it you have not spoken to your father yet about us."

Morgan grimaced then shook her head. "No, I keep putting it off."

"There's no need to tell him now."

Morgan stopped dead. "What? What do you mean?"

"I mean he knows. I didn't volunteer the information. When he came to see us train this morning, he took one look and he knew."

"What did he say? How did he react?"

"He asked me what my intentions were."

"Gods protect us," Morgan muttered.

"Then he told me not to disappoint him or you. He also reminded me that if I ever hurt you, he would have my head."

"Oh, for pity's sake!"

Connor held up a hand to stop the impending diatribe. "No, it's all right. He is your father, and like any loving parent, he is looking after you, trying to protect you."

"But he never should have threatened you so. To treat you as if you have not done more than anyone apart from himself to safeguard me is inexcusable." She paused, "You do understand that no matter what my father says, no matter that we share a bed, you are not obligated to... A betrothal is not..." Cheeks aflame with utter embarrassment, her voice faded.

He reached for her hand, squeezed. A moment later, he tipped up her lowered chin and met her gaze. "I know. It's all right. Besides, your father and I understand each other now."

Her eyes narrowed. "Oh, do you? What does that mean exactly?"

"It means he sees I make you happy. In the end, that is all that matters to him, just as you said. So long as I continue to do so, all will be well." No need to go into the particulars of his feelings, which were growing and deepening every day.

Although her eyes remained wary, her expression

softened a trifle. "In most circumstances he is a kind and generous father. Since these are not most circumstances, however, I assumed he would put up at least some resistance. It has always been his dearest wish that I make a good match, one comprising love, respect, fulfillment of duty, and a strengthening of political position. In short, he has always wanted me to marry well in every respect. So I admit to being surprised he has given that dream up."

"So being my lover, much less my wife, was something he never had in mind for you?"

She shook her head and blushed, then after an awkward pause, said, "Not that you wouldn't make a marvelous spouse if you were to ask me but… a strong political position, at least one backed by experience, is something you have not got, it must be said."

He shrugged. "Political machinations are nothing I ever aspired to become an expert at."

All of a sudden, she would not meet his gaze. Instead, she spoke softly to her hands which she held clasped in front of her. "I know. You are an honorable man in every respect."

"You said an advantageous match was your father's dream. Was it yours?"

Her gaze stayed fixed in the middle distance as she considered the question. Then she made a small sound. "I don't rightly know. There has been precious little time to contemplate such things with Rownar ever and always a threat. I know I wish to please my father, and I know I would not shirk my duty. However, I know also that, first and foremost I want a loving husband, one who sees me as an equal. When reflecting on the matter, that is what I dreamed of. I am not sure such a thing is possible. With a powerful man, one who, as a king, is used to giving orders, it is, to say the least, implausible. One who, in addition, would be a stranger to me. Of course, I never truly expected to marry. I never believed I would live long enough."

He framed her face in his hands and murmured, "If I have my way, you will not die anytime soon. Years from now, when you are an old woman, safe and warm in your bed, only then will you take your last breath."

"May the gods will it so." After a moment she asked, "And you? Have you given any thought to marriage at all?"

He shook his head. "Very little. Let's say the life I lead would not fuse well with matrimony. For another thing, I, like you, doubted I would live long enough to enjoy it. So no, I've never considered it, at least not until recent times. Even now, I am not sure marrying me would be advisable. I am not a very good bet."

He took her hand. "In spite of all that, I care for you more than I have ever cared for anyone."

"But?"

"The reasons I haven't considered marriage up until now still apply. Just because I have met a woman who makes me question everything I've ever believed to be true, doesn't mean I should change my stance. No matter how much I want to. Added to it, I'm surely tempting fate by even considering something so monumental right now."

"I see," Her tone was carefully neutral, then she turned away, but not before he glimpsed the hurt on her face she tried to hide.

"Morgan, wait." He tugged her into his arms. "When I think about you, sometimes I can hardly breathe. I have never felt this way before, and I have no idea what to do with it. It's so much and so strong, and it hit me so fast. I need time to figure it out, that is all. In the meanwhile, can't we enjoy whatever time we have together?"

Her expression softened a trifle, and after a moment, she murmured, "All right." Then her countenance went mock-stern and imperious as she offered him her hand to kiss. "But don't take too long."

Lips twitching, he kissed her knuckles. "Yes, Your Majesty."

They strolled in the moonlight for an hour or more. Then he kissed her one final time and led her back inside.

Chapter Five

Weeks passed and, as Connor predicted, Morgan grew stronger. Each day she evolved, and her moves became sharper, her reactions quicker. In addition, Connor proved to be as excellent a lover as he was an instructor. With days spent training and nights in his bed, Morgan had never been happier. She was at the top of her game in every way. Then one morning, the inevitable happened.

The point of her sword hovered a bare inch above his throat, and her booted foot was on his chest. He was quite unable to move. At last, she had bested him. Absolute triumph rushed through her.

"Am I ready now?" This time the words were not a question so much as a demand.

He assessed her, then shook his head. "Not to go after Rownar, no. But to go after other prey, yes."

As she continued to stare down at him, intrigued curiosity rose. "Other prey? I take it you have a particular dragon in mind?" She wanted Rownar, but for now she would take what she could get.

"As it happens, I do."

"It is Rownar I want, but I could use the experience. When do we leave?"

"When can you be ready?" he countered.

Morgan offered him a fierce smile. "Oh, my bags are packed and waiting."

****

As promised, all was arranged with great speed, and Morgan was soon prepared for her journey. There was only one final thing required. Her father must be told and his permission granted. She could not leave without informing him.

After the evening meal, Morgan joined her father in his private sitting room as she often did, to broach the subject. The place was very much her father's and reflected his taste. Decorated with well-crafted, heavy oak furniture, the settee and the chairs were large and comfortable. There was always at least one book lying about, often more than one as both her parents had enjoyed reading and passed the love of it on to her. Drapes of midnight blue hung at the windows, which looked out onto the grounds. She and her father often spent time there together, deep in discussion of their favorite authors, and she took strength from the familiar surroundings.

"Connor says I am ready to go out and test my skills. We will hunt a young dragon called Meglos."

James sighed. "I knew it could not be much longer. Who shall I send with you?"

"No one, Majesty. We need to do this alone. Morgan must have this practice and experience."

"You want me to send my daughter out to kill a dragon with you alone to safeguard her? Out of the question."

"With all due respect, Sire, Morgan, and only Morgan, is Rownar's target, and she may well have to face him alone and unaided at some point. I will do all I can to prevent it, but it may still happen. Added to that, I have taken down seven dragons alone. It can be done.

Moreover, she won't be quite all on her own. I will be with her. Do you doubt my expertise? Or perhaps it is your daughter you lack confidence in?"

James opened his mouth, but before he could speak, Morgan did.

"Father, please."

Stepping to him, she took his hands in hers and put every ounce of pleading she could into her voice. "I need to do this. You promised me you would do all you could to help."

"So I did, but how can I allow you to go into such danger all but alone? You were supposed to have an army at your back. An army I have barely been able to gather, much less train as yet." He shook his head, and the look in his eyes turned to steel. "I will come with you myself."

"No, Father. You have a kingdom to rule. Connor and I must go alone. For now, this is how it must be done."

James studied her for a long moment. "So be it." Then he directed his attention to Connor. "If any harm comes to her and you are still alive, I will find you and kill you myself."

Connor and James, both their jaws set, both pairs of eyes narrowed, exchanged a look, then Connor inclined his head. "Understood, Sire."

"In the meantime, I will continue gathering and training the army. When you are ready to face Rownar, you will not be alone."

"Thank you, Father." Morgan rushed forward into her father's embrace.

"Promise me one thing, both of you. Promise me that even if you find him, you will not attack Rownar by yourselves."

"But, Father, if we have the chance to take him, we have to try."

"No, not at the cost of your life. Promise me."

"If it means certain death, then I promise you, I will not engage with Rownar."

Connor repeated the vow, which appeased the king.

"Be careful, be victorious, and be well, my dearest child." He murmured the words into her hair, then kissed the top of her head.

"And you." Tears spilled over, but she did not try to hide them.

Instead, she let them fall.

With a handkerchief, she wiped away her tears and dabbed at her face. Letting go was wrenching, but for the first time, Morgan felt ready to face whatever fate might have in store for her.

When Connor offered her his arm, she accepted it without hesitation and marched to meet her destiny.

****

"So where is this dragon, precisely?" Morgan asked once they were on their way, traveling on horseback down the north road.

"Precisely? I am not sure. I received a missive from an acquaintance who lives in the village of Camston, informing me that the place was attacked the night before." He skirted a low-hanging bush. "Now, when most dragons destroy a village, there are no survivors. But this one, Meglos, is young and foolish and has not developed the skill, or perhaps the ruthlessness, necessary for that."

"That is all very well, but I don't see how any of this helps us find him."

Connor scratched his chin. "It so happens I have been a step or two behind this one before and am familiar with his habits. In fact, I was tracking him before your father summoned me. He will have gone to ground very nearby. Somewhere concealed and a bit away from the village so he can pick off any strays. Once that is done, he will return to his lair. When he shows himself, we will take him."

"You make it sound so simple."

"It is." When she widened her pretty brown eyes at him, he shrugged. "At a certain point, it becomes that way. After you have trained and done the best you can to prepare, then all you can do is place your fate in the hands of the gods. Entrust yourself to them and do what you are meant to do. I—" He stilled. "Quiet," he snapped.

At first, she heard nothing then a rushing wind reached her ears. An instant later, a gorgeous sapphire dragon bulleted out of the mouth of a remote cave. In the distance, the dragon banked and wheeled in the darkening sky. He circled above the mountains a few times, then descended back into his dark lair.

In all her life, Morgan had seen only two dragons, Rownar and one other. She could not help her fascination with this one, particularly since they were about to kill him. Or at least try to.

Abruptly, she couldn't quite manage to move. "Connor, either this dragon is a lot bigger than I remember dragons to be, or it is larger than you said. Are we really going to try to kill that?"

He tossed her a roguish grin. "Yes, we are." He glanced over. "You all right, Morgan? You've gone pale. Don't tell me you're nervous?"

Gaze fixed on the spot where Meglos had disappeared, she watched for his return. "I would be a fool not to be, now wouldn't I?"

He ran a hand through his hair. "Well, yes, but I guess I didn't expect it. Not from the same woman who was bold enough to take me, a stranger, to her bed."

Morgan's gaze, which had been glued to the sky, shot to his. "That was entirely different."

His grin widened and she blushed in response, but then he sobered. "Indeed. This will be very different."

As suddenly as nerves had come over her, they were gone. "You're right; it will be. It's time." She started to urge her horse forward, but he caught the reins.

"Wait a moment. Remember your training. Look out for the tail; it can be deadly. The fire, of course, don't forget that. And…"

Now it was he who sounded nervous. To comfort and reassure him, she patted his hand.

"I won't forget. You've trained me well. I admit I clutched for a minute, but I am all right now. Let's do this."

Without warning, he pulled her into a swift, fierce kiss then just as quickly let her go. "Come on."

****

The cavern was dank, dark, and downright eerie except for the jewels, shining even in the dim light of the torch he carried. Those, Connor admitted in a whisper, were magnificent. As for Morgan, her eyes were unblinking as she did her best to take in everything.

"Connor, this is amazing. I have never seen anything like this before. Is this a typical dragon hoard?"

"No, I have never seen one so rich, but let's focus. The dragon we want to kill is somewhere in here. He may be a young, reckless one, but he is still dangerous. He is responsible for the destruction of two villages, and, make no mistake, he will kill us the first chance he gets. We can't let anything fracture our concentration."

"Right."

"So we keep moving. Quietly."

Morgan nodded, and they pressed on into the next cavern, which contained an even denser portion of the treasure.

As they cautiously navigated through the hoard, Morgan detected a slight glow in her peripheral vision. It flared up, then subsided. As they stepped forward, she discerned it again, and this time she whipped around quickly enough to see a small magical symbol etched in the floor behind them light up, then dim.

"Oh no," she murmured.

"What's wrong?" Connor demanded in a sharp tone.

She paced further and showed him. "I think if Meglos doesn't already know we are here, he will soon."

As if on cue, deep within the cave, the sound of an almighty clang of metal meeting metal filled their ears. Then came a roar, the kind which could only be made by a dragon.

Morgan knew her eyes must be wide as saucers, but she couldn't seem to help it or move at all, in fact. Horror rooted her to the spot, unable even to speak, much less move.

Connor was not so afflicted. "Run!"

When she didn't twitch so much as an eyelash, he yelled, "Run, Morgan!"

The volume of his words, his manner, and most of all, the use of her name, snapped her out of her panicked shock at last. She went from utter stillness to moving faster than she ever had in her life.

The dragon, shrieking and breathing fire all the while, flew after them.

They sprinted back the way they had come, heedless of the noise they made. No need for stealth now, just speed.

In the end, they had to run for their lives. There was no other choice.

"We failed."

It was all Morgan could do not to hang her head. Out of the cave and back to the relative safety of the road, they took a moment to collect themselves.

Connor shook his head. "No, this is a temporary setback, nothing more. This one is careful about guarding his lair, that is all. We will have to fight him out in the open."

"But how do we draw him out? For all we know, he might stay there for a century or more. Some dragons do."

"Some do. Most can't resist fresh prey or finishing what they started."

"So we go to Camston village and wait, then?"

Connor nodded, and when he indicated the proper direction, Morgan followed.

****

Camston had once been cozy and had even bordered on prosperous until Meglos decimated the small village. The place consisted of a church with a tall spire, what must have been several shops, an inn, and perhaps a dozen houses spread over a quarter-mile area. Many of the buildings were burned to ash, with not even a foundation left to show where they once stood.

As they rode through the grassy square of the village, several men approached and hailed them.

"Are you the dragon slayer Connor O'Malley?" the first man asked. He was thin and about forty.

Connor inclined his head. "I am."

"And who is with you, sir?"

"This is my new partner, Morgan."

Morgan bobbed her head and tried not to appear too regal. Earlier they agreed that if she were not recognized on sight, they would not reveal her identity.

"I thought you worked alone. That's what I was told, leastwise," a second, younger man said, giving Morgan a suspicious look from under his dark, heavy eyebrows. "Instead, you bring a young woman with no chaperone."

"Until recently I did work alone. I have trained this young woman. Taking out a dragon is not quite so difficult with a well-trained companion at your side."

The first man gave the second a quelling look. "You are the expert, of course." He bowed low to Connor and Morgan. "You have arrived in good time. Each night for the past four nights, the creature has attacked one hour after sunset."

"So you said in your letter. There is more than time enough to find the best strategic position from which to hunt the beast."

The third man spoke for the first time. "We hope you might even have a moment to spare for a meal."

Connor glanced at Morgan, who gave him an almost imperceptible nod. "We would be honored."

****

By sunset, they positioned themselves in the bell tower of the local church, ready and waiting. This was a situation Morgan found difficult to cope with, even in spite of all of her recent training. Keeping still right then was impossible for her, so she paced the small room.

After a time, Connor glanced at her. "Morgan, relax."

"I can't."

"Sure, you can. Clear your mind the way you taught yourself to do years ago."

"I am trying, but a dragon and a fiery death for both of us keeps popping in there."

His lips twitched, but he put a hand to her shoulder to comfort her. "Well, I've been there a time or two myself, and it's not a bit fun, is it? When he does come to mind, remember this: you are the bravest woman I know. You were prepared to take on this task single-handedly. You aren't alone. I am here with you, and together we will triumph."

She lost herself in his eyes, in him, for an instant, and let his confidence infuse and strengthen her. If he said it, she believed it. She trusted him beyond question. Buoyed by the realization and, if not soothed, then at least somewhat calmed, she focused and kept watch.

As the last of the light died, she heard it. The unmistakable sound, which would haunt her worst nightmares for the rest of her life, filled the air. Connor heard the dragon screech as well as she did. He rose with great alacrity to peer out of the narrow window but kept out of the view of anyone or anything outside. Seconds later, Morgan joined him and caught sight of Meglos.

The creature appeared on the horizon, a dark blur against the orange sky, then raced toward the village. Toward *them*. For some time, they were both silent, mesmerized by his beauty and majesty, yet sickened by the atrocities he was responsible for.

At last, Connor murmured, "We aren't running this time, so it is vital you listen to me. It could mean the difference between life and death, both yours and mine. Follow my orders without hesitation. Do you understand?"

"I do. You've trained me well. I won't fail you."

"Excellent. He'll come around for another pass, and after he flies by, I want you to take a shot at him. Aim for the back of his right leg. This will wound and enrage him. He will turn toward us again. Then I will aim for his heart. If I miss, we both go for a wing."

"Got it."

The creature swooped down toward them. Once he passed their window, Morgan sent an arrow flying right into his leg.

The dragon roared with pain then spun his head around to determine what caused it. Seeing Connor, he rotated his massive body effortlessly in mid-air to face in their direction.

Connor waited until the angle was perfect. Even when Meglos spotted them and shot flame through the small window, he did not flinch or rush to action. In fact, he took so much time; Morgan grew more and more concerned about the rather large dragon bearing down on them, and the possibility of that fiery death replayed again in her mind.

"Connor."

"Wait," he muttered.

She did so, heart pounding, throat raw. "Connor, shoot him."

"Wait."

Meglos was closing in, mere feet from them.

"Connor!"

His focus never wavered. Finally, at the very last possible second, he murmured, "Now." He loosed his arrow, and it went straight through Meglos's tough, scaled hide right to his heart. Hot blood spurted from his chest into the frigid air.

The creature plunged toward the ground, roaring and tossing his head in pain. It helped that she put another arrow through his wing, but he was still very much alive even as he hit the ground with a thunderous crash.

"Damn it! I pierced the heart, but not deeply enough. He will die, but not before he does a lot of damage on his way out. Come on, we must finish him."

Barely able to tear her mind away from Connor, she raced with him down the stairs and out.

Meglos lay on the ground, writhing like the snake that was the ancestor to all dragons. He was still breathing fire but with no sense of accuracy, control, or even malice, causing a great deal of chaos and destruction.

The noise was deafening, but Connor shouted to her over it. "Would you like to do the honors?"

"What? Me?"

"Yes, you helped take him down. Don't you want

to finish him?"

"Yes, I do." Morgan realized it was the absolute truth. She was ready and willing to kill her first dragon.

"Stay out of his line of sight, if you can, and out of range of his flame for sure. Do it now."

She positioned herself. "Now what?"

"What do you think? Pierce its heart!" When she hesitated, he added, "Now, Morgan!"

Acting on instinct, she struck at the beast's heart when he reared up. Her blow found its mark. The dragon roared and shrieked in pain. She ducked to avoid his writhing head and snapping jaws.

With a mighty swing of her sword, Morgan struck once more. It took three blows, but eventually she relieved Meglos of his head.

As he died, Morgan was unable to look away. When it was over, Connor grasped her gently by the shoulders.

"It's done. Come."

Suddenly her arms were weak as water, and she lowered her sword. Her head swam, and her lungs were full of smoke. She had never felt so triumphant in her life. This particular dragon would never harm anyone ever again, and it was thanks to her.

To her and Connor.

As she took Meglos's head, the villagers rushed out of their homes. A bucket brigade formed, and others were building a makeshift firebreak to contain the flames and put out the numerous fires the dragon started.

Connor by her side as always, and so she gradually began to feel a bit more like herself.

After a time, she croaked, "He really is quite dead.

What do we do now?"

"Burn the body, preferably using his own flame, and salt the ground. Then I suggest we adjourn to that rather fine inn at the far corner of the square."

Still a little shaky, Morgan was more than ready to fall in with this plan. She nodded and helped the villagers put out the flames

That done, she gathered as much wood as she could carry and began to build a pyre.

Chapter Six

Some hours later, with Meglos burned to ashes, Morgan and Connor traveled to the inn. The place was small, and she speculated idly on how comfortable their accommodations would prove to be.

It was only then that it occurred to her to wonder how they would handle the issue of their lodgings. Separate rooms for the sake of propriety, she supposed. What a pity. As it turned out, when Connor requested two rooms, the innkeeper's wife explained that, while several single rooms were available, she could also offer their best suite containing two bedchambers and a private parlor they might find more comfortable.

He used his brilliant smile on the woman, and her answering one was almost as bright. "That would be most satisfactory. And if it isn't too much trouble, could you prepare two tubs of hot water? We would both like to rid ourselves of the dragon filth covering us."

"Of course, Lord O'Malley, sir. Right away."

When he reached into his purse to hand over payment, the inn wife waved it aside. "Oh no, put your coin away. You have rid us of that revolting dragon, and our whole village can't thank you enough. The least we can do is allow you to spend a night here at no charge."

"No, I wouldn't hear of it. I insist."

The inn wife hesitated but finally bobbed her head and accepted with a murmur of thanks.

She handed him the key. "The room is at the top of the stairs, first door on the left. I will send Lily, our maid, up with the water in a moment. If there is anything else you need, anything at all, please ask."

"I think that will be quite sufficient for the present. You have our gratitude."

Then he took Morgan's arm and led the way up the stairs.

The room was simple but quite comfortable and more than adequate for her needs, Morgan decided, once they stepped inside, and she spared a moment to look about her.

A short time later, there was a brisk rap on the door, and when Morgan opened it, a young girl of perhaps sixteen stood on the other side holding two kettles of steaming water, along with two other servants, each carrying a large wooden tub. The girl also brought two cakes of lavender-scented soap, several bits of toweling, and two linen sheets. She lined the tubs with the sheets, then set one tub by each bedroom fire. She and the other servants, after many trips, filled the tubs with the water, then she curtseyed, the men bowed, and they went out.

Morgan undressed with alacrity, anxious to lower herself into the blissful warmth. As soon as she did, her sore muscles eased, and all of her tension drained away. She rinsed off the soot and dirt clinging to her, then let her mind drift.

As so often happened, she found herself thinking of Connor. Witnessing him in action had been a revelation. Never had she seen anyone so cool under pressure. The scenes of the last hours replayed themselves in her head, and she would never forget the look on his face right before he took down Meglos. Such concentration. The only other time she had observed such laser-sharp focus in him was when they made love. Until the final instant when his focus blurred.

Thinking of that would do her no good, at least not right at the moment, so she shook her head to clear it. Instead, she directed her attention to the rest of the battle. She believed she had acquitted herself well and hoped Connor felt the same. At any rate, it was done, and she was still alive, which was more than many could say. The rush of it all was still coursing through her veins even now. Never had she come so close to death, and so she found it odd that she had never felt more alive. Perhaps she could discuss it with Connor? He ought to be familiar with the sensation.

Morgan noticed the water had gone cold and decided she had indulged herself long enough. She rose, stepped out of the bath, and grasped the towel in easy reach on a nearby stool. Then, washed and dressed, she rejoined Connor in the parlor.

He nodded a greeting then gestured to the food covering the small dining table. "I took the liberty of ordering a late supper. Even though we had a meal beforehand, I thought you might be hungry enough for a light repast."

"I am starving. Thank you." With no further prompting, Morgan sat and filled a plate with a savory mutton chop, brown bread, and peas.

They ate in a companionable silence for a while, then Connor said, "You did well."

The welcome, unsolicited praise heated Morgan's cheeks, but she hoped he would not see her blush in the soft candlelight. "You truly think so?" When he nodded, she beamed. "I thought the same. I mean, I did manage to stay alive. Quite a feat, especially for my first encounter with a dragon."

"Indeed." He raised his glass in toast. "To beautiful warrior women and the dragons they conquer."

She acknowledged the compliment with a regal inclination of her head; they both lifted their glasses and drank.

The meal was simple but delicious, and Morgan ate a far larger portion than usual. Replete, she sat back and did her best to enjoy the wine, but her thoughts kept racing. Images of the battle, of Connor, of the dragon in the air, then minus its head, and particularly of the final thrust into the creature's heart hovered just inside her consciousness.

As she set her empty glass down on the table, she gave voice to the predominant feeling inside her. "I can hardly believe it! We did it! We killed a dragon!"

****

Connor found it difficult to hide his grin but did his best to remain stern. "We killed a very young, very reckless dragon. But yes, we did, and what's more, we worked well together."

She beamed. "We did." She rose and paced about the room, unable to keep still. "I am as keyed up as I was when we defeated him. I have never felt quite like this. Does it ever go away?"

"It's the high of battle; you aren't used to it. It usually dissipates after a few hours. Don't worry."

She threw herself back into her chair. "Well, that's

93

a relief. I don't think I could cope with this all the time. What should I do in the meanwhile?"

He could think of so many things, but… "We've got an early start home tomorrow. You should at least try to get some sleep."

"Sleep? I couldn't possibly sleep. Not for hours."

His control snapped. "Come to bed, then."

She shot him a quizzical look. "To bed? But I told you I—"

He grasped her flittering hand, trapped her gaze with his, dropped his shields, and let his desire show. "Come to bed."

Her pretty eyes widened once she realized he wasn't asking her to sleep. Rising, he held out a hand to her.

After taking one deep breath, she rose in her turn and placed her palm in his.

****

The next morning, they breakfasted in private in their rooms. In Connor's estimation, Morgan looked rested, well-fed, and downright energized.

"As soon as we have eaten and are done here, we will head out. I got word this morning that there's another dragon terrorizing Hamstead," Connor said.

Morgan offered him a questioning look. "How on earth do you always find these things out so quickly?"

He shrugged. "Many people know me by sight and will volunteer any information they have. If it happens I am not recognized, I spend an hour or two in the taproom of wherever I am staying. If I ask a few of the right questions, I can often find out the latest news. Since people love a good tragedy, any recent dragon attacks are surely the talk of whatever town I happen to be in."

"Interesting. So we aren't going after Rownar now?"

"Not yet."

"Why not? We've beaten a dragon. I still can't quite believe it, but we have. But not the one I want. I want Rownar. I want to pierce his black heart with my sword."

"Not yet." He reached across the table for her hand, and was gratified when she allowed him to take hold of it. "Morgan, right now you are riding high on last night's victory."

Her expression softened yet intensified infinitesimally. "I am. Yesterday was wonderful. For the first time, I did what I have been training for years to do. The dragon we hunted together is dead, and I am… We are still very much alive. And that's not even mentioning after."

Unable to stop last night's heated memories from flashing through his mind, he admitted, "Yes, it's exciting in the beginning. You feel invincible. I confess that feeling came back to me last night when we fought together. Having you with me instead of having to fight alone as I have always done was invigorating. Then coming back here and spending the night in your bed… Now that was truly amazing, incredible in fact. But I promise you, it won't stay that way. Well, at least the fighting won't. As for bedding you, I doubt that could ever be anything less than brilliant."

"Hmm," was all she said. From her expression, he could tell she was replaying the memories of last night's encounter over in her head also.

He shook his head to clear the sensual fog from his

brain. All at once it was vital to him that he get through to her on this important point. "You think it will be easy to exact your vengeance. You are sure it is the one thing you need to make you whole. It isn't. You believe that you will have your revenge, and it won't take its toll. I assure you it will."

Her expression shuttered, and her gaze turned cold. "Perhaps. Whether it does or not matters little. I said as much the night we met. Rownar must be wiped from the face of the earth. No matter the cost."

He tried another tact. "Did you know I have been trying to find his lair for years? He killed my parents when I was ten, and as soon as I was old enough, or what I, at the time, considered old enough, I began searching. I have been searching ever since, for more than half my life. He attacks and then leaves, never spotted again until his next onslaught. Until we find him, why not fight others of his kind?"

"So we wait until he comes after me? No, that is exactly what I have sworn not to do. I might as well be back safe in my tower room doing nothing!" Her strong, yet still feminine, hand slammed on the table. Then she rose to pace, agitation in every movement.

"I am not asking you to do nothing. We will search for him. If we can't find him, then we will wait until the next time he shows his face. Once he does, we will track him and do our level best to end him."

"Again with the waiting? No, if you cannot find him, I will make him come to us."

"No, you cannot go after him on your own. Haven't you learned that yet? I realize you were alone in this for a long time, but the only way we will succeed is if we do this together. We will find him, and when we do, I will bathe in his blood if that is what you want. I swear it. And believe me, I will enjoy it for your sake as well as my own. But what good will any of that do if you are dead!" His words ended with a shout, so he took a deep breath and tried to regain some semblance of composure. In a somewhat calmer tone, but one invested with steel and all the personal power he possessed, he finished, "Not. Yet."

She studied him, unblinking, measured him for a long moment, then inclined her head. "Very well. Not yet, but soon. Or I will have no choice but to go after him myself. That I swear."

Everything about her, her posture, her tone, her air of confidence, made her a queen. As so often happened these days, he assented with a bow of his head. He had little choice but to accept this compromise as the best he was likely to get and be grateful for it.

****

As they traveled and then tracked another of the beasts, this time to the south, Connor gave her what she suspected would become the usual rundown on their prey.

"This one, Bres, is older, larger, and meaner. She is a very strong female. It won't be so easy to take her out. If she is breeding, it might not be possible at all."

Morgan wondered if the second time would be any less challenging than the first. She doubted it since, according to Connor, this dragon was far more daunting.

Soon enough they spotted her. Right away, and even at that great distance, she sensed a much stronger air of menace about the creature. It was almost enough to rival what she detected from Rownar.

As the dragon circled overhead, Connor took stock. "Everything I've ever told you, remember it. It could save your life."

She bit her lip, stiffened her spine, and nodded.

A bare instant later, the dragon's head tilted in their direction, then she shrieked in triumph. Fast as the wind of a hurricane, she flew toward them.

"She's seen us. Take cover."

Morgan did not need telling twice. The forest was thick beside the road, and Connor led the way straight into it. Morgan flattened herself over her horse's neck as she galloped into the trees. Once in the relative safety of the wood, she leapt from her saddle and landed in a crouch beside her mare.

As fast as possible, she concealed herself in the lower branches of a large beech tree. Well-hidden at last, she moved not a muscle and tried to control her ragged breathing with little success. For what seemed like an eternity, she heard nothing. The air stirred as a cool breeze wafted past her flushed cheeks.

Then there was more than the breeze. A swishing, whooshing sound, which could only be the beat of wings, reached her a split second before the roar and the heat of flame. The sky lit up for miles around. Through the small gap among the trees, the massive dragon circled high above, her bright-green scales flashing in the fading sunlight.

Without warning, the beast dove straight toward her. As it did, flame erupted from its jaws to scorch the ground mere feet from where she stood. She dove out from cover, her crossbow at the ready. She got off one shot, which glanced off the armor-like skin instead of the wing she was aiming at, before the dragon engulfed the area in flame. The fire singed the arm she threw up to protect her face.

Before she could react any other way, a strong hand grasped the arm still at her side and jerked her back. Connor propelled them both along a nearby path at breakneck speed toward a dense copse.

"Damn it; I told you to take cover!"

"I'm sorry. I had the shot. I took it. Or at least I tried to. I missed."

He gave her one fulminating look which promised the discussion was not over and marched her deeper into the trees.

All but deafened by Bres's incessant roars, she struggled to keep pace with her now very angry lover. With a rough jerk, he positioned her where he wanted her. Her back scraped against the rough bark of a large oak tree while she caught her breath.

"What now?"

"Now? Since she knows our approximate position, which you gave away, I might add, I will draw her out and kill her. You stay here." He gripped her upper arms roughly. "I mean it, Morgan."

He had released her and was striding through the trees before Morgan managed to find her voice.

"No."

He spun on his heel to face her. "*No*? Morgan, I do not have time to argue with you. Stay here."

"No," she repeated. "What am I here for, if not to fight, if not to guard your back? Yes, I made a mistake going after her just now, but I don't want you to take on this creature alone. I swear I won't make another move without your say-so. Let me help you. Let me do what you have been training me for. Please."

Without warning, dragon wings beat quite close by, and seconds later, trees mere yards away burst into flame.

When he still hesitated, she sighed. "You are right. We don't have time to argue. I speak now as your future queen. Please do not force me to make this an order."

Connor's jaw tightened as she knew it did when he was intent on being stubborn about something, then his gaze shifted to the burning trees. "All right, come on."

He led her to a clearing with the dragon on their heels. She had dealt Bres a minor wound after all, if the small river of blood running down her underbelly was any indication.

"You stay undercover here while I draw its attention. When I give you the signal, send an arrow through its wing. Then you come and help me finish her off. Yes?"

Morgan nodded and headed in the direction he indicated.

With a gesture, Connor ordered her to stay where she was, some steps behind and to his left within the trees. A moment later, he sprinted out of the woods and to her right. Bres saw and with an almighty roar dove straight for him.

He stood rock solid as the creature hurtled toward him. Then he evaded her flames. This enraged Bres and she roared again as she circled around for another pass, this time coming in even closer and faster.

"Now!" Connor bellowed.

Morgan let fly her arrow.

This time her arrow found its mark. It pierced Bres's wing and she plummeted. Unfortunately, the battle was far from over, and she was not yet dead. She lay semi-stunned for a second or two after she hit the ground, then shook her massive head as if to clear it.

Connor strode forward until he was all but nose-to-nose with the beast. Far sooner than Morgan expected, however, full sense returned to the creature, and she fixed Connor with a murderous glare. If the shocked look on his face was anything to go by, Connor was more than a little surprised at her speedy recovery as well. With a groan, Bres rose to her feet. The flame she breathed next was strong enough to knock Connor onto his back. He scrambled away, holding his shield up for the meager protection it offered.

Morgan had been paralyzed with fear, but now fury galvanized her into action. By all the gods, she would not stand by and watch as a dragon stole yet another person she loved from her. She rushed to his aid, sword at the ready.

Connor was weakening. His shield arm trembled. Now on her hind legs, Bres rained fire down on him. This put Bres in the perfect position for what she, Morgan, needed to do. With as much force as she could manage, she launched her sword straight at Bres's exposed heart.

Gods be praised, she hit her target! Bres let out an epic roar full of rage and pain, then her flame guttered out. She collapsed. Then after a resounding, thunderous crash, she stilled, never to rise again.

As the creature spluttered, choked, and finally died, relief filled Morgan. *What an incredibly narrow escape.*

For a long time, Connor said nothing, merely stayed on his back while he caught his breath. Then he rose, straightened to his full height, and faced her.

"Don't ever question, much less disobey, my orders again, not while we are in the field. I am well aware you are a princess, and even with the training I have provided, you aren't used to taking commands, but you almost got us both killed."

"I know. I am sorry. I will never make that mistake again. I promise."

"Good." He sheathed his sword and turned on his heel.

"Connor?"

He halted but did not turn back to face her.

"I need you to promise me something also."

"Oh?" The look he shot her was just short of intimidating.

She stuck out her chin and stood her ground. "Stop treating me like I am made of glass. We both know I am stronger than that. Nothing went well, and it was my fault, but you have to stop trying to protect me. That, too nearly got us both killed. I want to be your partner even if I am not yet your equal when it comes to dragon hunting."

His jaw clenched. But then he sucked in a breath, let it out again. "You have a point. That was a tactical error. So, I'll try if you will."

Relieved, Morgan nodded. "I also promise to try if you will." When he nodded, she inclined her head in approval. "That will do then."

****

Injured and bloody, they said little as they acquired rooms at the inn in the small town of Hampstead. Morgan strongly suspected shock was beginning to set in, at least for her.

Silence still reigned between them as they headed

up. Servants brought in hot water to the one room they shared. Morgan started to get out of her torn shirt and scorched pants, then sat beside Connor on the edge of the bed.

"How do you do it? It was exciting at first but now... You almost died. We both almost died, in part because of my recklessness, in part because of the job at hand. I cannot imagine doing what we just did on a regular basis. How do you cope? How do you do this every day? How in the name of all the gods do you face all of that evil?" How could he give her an answer he did not have? He didn't try; instead he simply stayed beside her.

"When you stare too long into the abyss, the abyss stares back at you. Or so they say. I've become used to it I suppose, but it doesn't get any easier. For so long a time, nothing helped, not really anyway. I drank. I—"

"You what? It's all right. You can tell me."

"There were women," he admitted. "Not often, but when things got bad, I sought out female companionship. I went to whores, to be blunt."

"That's what you were thinking of doing the night I met you."

"Yes. I would bury myself in their bodies and try to forget. But now, I have hope. Hope that if we can kill Rownar there might actually be an end. And then there's this."

He grasped the back of her neck, drew her to him, into a kiss, and down, down into oblivion.

****

As Connor touched her, he left a streak of soot down her neck, and suddenly he wanted every trace of the dirt and grime gone from them both. Dragon filth

103

had no place here.

As if in some dream, he drifted toward the warm bath and brought her with him. He undressed her first, then removed his own clothes and left them all in a messy pile on the floor. Taking the kettle, he poured water over Morgan then himself, drenching the floor and not much caring.

When the worst of the dirt and muck was rinsed away, he led her over to the tub. He lowered himself into the warm water then drew her in with him. With her settled in front of him, her back against his front, he extended a hand and grasped the small cake of soap and bit of clean cloth provided, worked up a lather, ran it over her, then himself. Once they were both well scrubbed, he cupped water, then sluiced it over them, rinsing the last of the grime away.

That done, Connor turned her, and they sat face-to-face, washed clean. He drew her in then down until he was inside of her. As he did, she moaned and arched back, allowing him to sink in even more deeply. With gentle fingers, he brushed a wet strand of hair out of her eyes; then he closed his own. Steam billowed as he rocked against her in tandem with the gentle motion of the water. Both it and she enveloped him.

Clinging to her, the only good thing in his life, he let all the pain go. The weariness of his heart and soul lightened. Feeling better on every level than he had in a very long time, he let his body take over. Their joining was slow and easy until the last, and their simultaneous climax broke over them, surging and cresting in an endless warm wave.

They drifted on a dreamy, infinite sea of pleasure for an indefinite amount of time until the water grew cool. Utterly relaxed, sated to his toes, and loose in every limb, he somehow got them both to their feet. Once dry, they fell into bed and, wrapped in each other's arms, they slept.

****

Much later, morning sun brightened the room. While Morgan changed into a comfortable day gown in the tiny adjoining space which served as a dressing room, Connor exchanged the ruined leather tunic and smoke-filled trousers he had been wearing the previous day for a fresh linen shirt and sensible grey broadcloth breeches. As he finished, there was a light tap on the door. Since Morgan was not yet fully dressed, he went to see who it was.

The young maid curtseyed. "A letter came for you by courier, sir."

She held it out. When he took it, she curtseyed again and hurried off.

Chapter Seven

When Morgan returned dressed and ready for the day, she found Connor sitting on the edge of the bed. While this in and of itself was hardly unusual, his posture and stillness were. In fact, his whole demeanor was uncommon strange. Something was very wrong.

"What's happened? What is going on?"

Connor said nothing. Instead, he poured himself a drink, gulped it down in one, and ran a hand through his hair. He was stalling and frustrated. When she kept her gaze level with his, he grimaced.

"I have news of Rownar. Information on where to find him and even more important, where his lair is. An acquaintance sent me a letter, which arrived while you were dressing. With this knowledge, we might find him. " He produced a crumpled bit of parchment.

She did her best to hold on to what was left of her composure. What she wanted to do was shout, "At last!" but she refrained. All but snatching the missive out of his hand, she then read it. "What in the name of all the gods are we waiting for?"

Connor said nothing, merely poured himself another drink. This time Morgan took his glass and held it out of reach.

After setting it on the table beside her, she searched for parchment, quill, and ink. "I must get a message to my father straightaway."

He placed his strong hand over hers and held it still. "So you should. Remember, however, your father has begun building an army, but it is rudimentary at best. Also, it is untrained and, most importantly, it is five days' march away. They would never make it here soon enough, and even then, we might not find Rownar at all. I have been this close before, only to have it all slip through my fingers. It could be another dead end. If we go after him—"

"If!"

"If we go after him without your father's army, we are on our own."

"As we have been so far. I think it's worth the risk." She considered a moment, then murmured to herself, "If…no, *when*, we do this, even if we make it out alive, my father may kill us himself when he finds out."

"It is more than a risk. It is tantamount to suicide."

"That's debatable."

When she continued to fix him with her stare, patently uncaring of any real or imagined danger, he groaned.

"Come now, you are the greatest dragon slayer in the world, and you trained me. Don't you think I am up to the challenge?"

He refused to meet her gaze. "It isn't that. I'm not sure I am."

Genuine shock filled her, but she managed to splutter, "What? Why?"

"Morgan, I have never taken on a dragon as powerful as Rownar. No one has. Yes, I am the most experienced slayer out there, but even I have never done that. Yes, I have wanted to destroy him all my adult life. He killed my family, and the memory I have of him is of an irresistible evil force. I have done my best to train you and instill you with confidence, but the truth is, I am not sure whether we will survive this."

He reached for the glass again and, with a sigh, she let him have it.

"Forgive my hesitation. It is taking time for me to adjust. We will get him, and soon, I believe that. But my life has been all about the hunt for so long, to know it might soon be over is disconcerting. To come so close and to fail again is unthinkable, yet I can't help but imagine it. Not to mention, it would all be so much worse since I have so much more to lose. Risking my own life is one thing. I am not afraid to die. Risking yours is something else. Added to all of that, while I am willing enough to risk my life, that's a different thing than being ready, willing, and eager to die. Which I am not, not yet, not unless I can win, and I'm not sure I can."

"So my life is at risk as it has been since I was eight years old. So what? If you think I am going to give up now, then you are crazy. I have not come this far, done all I have done, to not even try. Nor, by all the gods, have you."

Connor leaned his head against the back of his chair, closed his eyes, then sighed. "I know." Then his beautiful eyes opened. "I know."

"Well, then what are we waiting for?" The smile she sent his way was fierce and determined.

His grin was slow in coming but, in the end, every bit as fierce as her own. "Indeed."

Silence reigned for a time.

Then Connor murmured, "Given that we will be on

our own and that this is Rownar we are talking about, I must consider our strategy. We cannot rush in without a plan. That's a good way to get ourselves killed."

"True." A bowl of fresh fruit on the table caught her attention. With a delicate hand, she chose a grape, then popped it into her mouth. "Do you have something in mind?"

He shrugged. "At long last we know where he is, or at least where he is purported to be. We also have a good idea of what he intends to do: attack the most convenient village whenever it suits him. Since we have the approximate location of his lair, we travel there. If he is gone hunting, we set a trap for him and we wait."

Fascinated by the idea, Morgan demanded, "What sort of a trap? Do we engineer a cave-in or what?"

Connor shook his head. "Too dangerous and probably not enough to kill him. A cave-in would be plenty enough to kill a man, though, and many dragon slayers have died attempting such things. Trying to be too clever never pays. If it doesn't kill him, you have an extremely angry dragon to deal with."

"Well, what then?"

"I'm not quite sure. I won't be certain of anything until we arrive at Rownar's lair and I can assess our options."

"So there are options then? Different ways we might hunt him?

The idea touched a cold, dark place in her heart.

Connor rumbled his assent, then rose. "We will find him and his lair. Gather your things. We'll leave within the hour."

****

At mid-morning they set out. After close to a full

day in the saddle, they arrived in the general area where Rownar's lair was meant to be, according to all reports. Connor's own theories and calculations jibed with what little new information he had, making him cautiously optimistic. Upon their arrival, they had, in his estimation, perhaps an hour of daylight left to search the immediate vicinity.

"Should we split up? We could explore more ground that way."

Connor shook his head. "We cover each other every step of the way. We'll search, but a dragon's lair is secret. This naturally makes it difficult to find. Rownar's in particular is almost impossible to locate."

"You don't say."

Connor gave her a quelling look, but his lips twitched, and he had to hold back a laugh. "We have no time for sarcasm. Let's get started."

The last of the light was dying when he found the place. The cave's entrance held an air of magical foreboding, which discouraged any from coming near it. However, since he wasn't most people, he fought the urge to flee. He walked closer, and in good time, he was rewarded. The entrance was well-concealed by the normal, everyday sort of camouflage as well as being masked by magic, but in spite of the bushes and small boulders obscuring the opening, Connor recognized it for what it was.

He tapped Morgan on the shoulder then pointed. "We've found him."

He kept his expression solemn, and his tone almost reverent.

****

Doubtfully, Morgan studied a very ancient cave

opening in the side of an even older mountain. "You're certain?"

"Oh, I'm certain. Every dragon carries a unique magical signature, and his leads right here. This is his lair, no question. But if you doubt it, you still have some slight link with him. You tell me."

Not at all willing to open herself up to Rownar again, she nevertheless cleared her mind and focused on the small part of her still linked to the dragon. Certainty that this was indeed Rownar's lair filled her within seconds. As soon as possible, before the dragon could become aware of her, she severed the link.

"You are right; this is his lair."

Connor inclined his head in response. "I've hunted Rownar for a very long time, but I've never gotten this close before."

"This could all be over soon."

The thought was both appealing and unsettling. How odd. After all, she had lived under the threat of possible attack by Rownar for most of her life. What would it be like when the threat was gone? What would her world look like? Aside from feeling free and knowing that she wanted Connor to be a part of it, the brave new world she envisioned did seem a bit vague. She would have to work on refining that nebulous outlook and clarifying that mental picture.

"Connor, why now? After all these years, how is it we have been able to track Rownar now?" Morgan hesitated. "You don't think it could be a trap, do you?"

"Of course it could be a trap."

"Oh, my. Well, that's not very reassuring."

"Come on, Morgan, cheer up. For the first time, he is letting us close, and that is worth the risk. No matter what trap he sets, all I need is ten minutes with him. That will be enough to finish him."

"So you hope."

"If it isn't enough, if I die, then at least I have given my life for a worthy cause."

The mere idea of his death made Morgan go cold.

He looked toward the horizon, then Rownar's lair. "Let's go."

Morgan remembered Meglos's lair as eerie, but Rownar's was a thousand times more so. The malignant magic he was imbued with permeated every inch of the cavern.

As they went deeper, the link she had with the dragon began to regain its strength. Before her first night with Connor, it had been a substantial weight, like a large bundle of wood on her back. Since then, though, it had been barely noticeable, like a necklace worn a long time rubbing slightly against her neck every so often.

The closer they got to what her instincts identified as the center of the cave and the heart of the hoard, the stronger the link became.

"At last, you've come to me as I knew you would."

Rownar's voice in her head was almost a purr.

"I've come to kill you."

But her voice did not sound as assured as she hoped it would. In spite of the sword in her hand and all of her training, having the monster back in her head after so long disconcerted and alarmed her. Deeply disturbed, she stepped forward with caution.

Connor stopped her with a hand on her arm. "Are you all right?" When she didn't respond, he turned his shrewd gaze on her for a long moment. "It's Rownar, isn't it?"

She managed a nod.

"Stay close to me."

He took her free hand in his. She was grateful for the contact, and her racing heartbeat steadied right away.

The atmosphere of the cave grew ever more oppressive, hotter, and danker the further they got from the surface. Or perhaps it was the closer they got to Rownar.

Without warning, the narrow passageway opened up. Before them was an enormous chamber partially illuminated by Connor's torch. The light caught on something shiny, and Morgan gasped. First, a sapphire as big as her thumb lit up, then diamonds even larger, and gold in great piles covering every inch of the floor. The hoard was massive. Full of untold wealth, it stretched for what Morgan estimated to be miles, bigger by far even than Meglos's. It had to be the richest dragon hoard on the face of the earth. She could barely take it all in.

As she and Connor stood there gaping, a gentle clinking noise reached Morgan's ears. Then it got louder and closer, and Morgan's heart picked up its beat again.

It was Rownar. His black-and-gold scales blended so well with the shadowy environment that she only discerned he was there because he moved. At first, he seemed to be part of the dark, and then he slowly materialized out of it. Once her eyes adjusted, she got her first look at him in almost two decades. His movements were economical and sinuous, yet lethal. There was a certain eerie beauty to them that riveted

Morgan.

She could not look away. Connor's voice filled her ears, but his strident tones could not reach the distant recesses of her mind. Not while the dragon came closer.

"You are mine." Rownar spoke aloud to her for the first time.

Morgan's ears vibrated to the resonance of his voice, and the sound echoed through every part of her. In spite of everything, even with every precaution she took, she had still been half-bewitched until that moment.

Her will to fight surged back. The man she loved was begging her to return and remember her training. With his next breath, he cursed Rownar and pleaded with the gods. It was his voice she wanted in her mind and heart, no one else's. She lifted her blade, tensed arms gone slack, and faced the creature.

"No! I am not yours. I will never belong to you."

He roared, and her ears rang, all but deafening her. Rownar's fury was unprecedented. He flew at her, fierce and brutal, and the chamber lit up bright as day with his flame. His great jaws snapped inches from her, but she dodged this way and that, then dashed into a small recess at the last instant. Rounded and just deep enough that he could not get to her, it offered some small, temporary protection, at least against his teeth. He could, of course, burn her to a crisp, but she banked that he still wanted her alive, at least for now. As the seconds ticked past and she remained breathing and unburnt, she accepted that her instincts were spot-on.

Her small feeling of triumph at being right on this point was short–lived. Rownar positioned his gleaming, golden eye close enough to peer at her. Morgan did not move a muscle; she did not even breathe. Then the ground reverberated with the creature's steps. A heartbeat later, Connor's shouts echoed in her ears.

Morgan left the corner she cowered in and ran straight for Rownar. The foul thing went after what she loved since he couldn't capture her. They would see about that.

The dragon now faced the mouth of the cave, and Connor was in front of him. Her lover put up a tremendous fight, but the creature was strong, even injured. The dragon limped and blood poured from a wound above his right foot. It seemed Connor had tried for the dragon's heart and missed. In addition, his tail had been hacked off. Her own heart dropped into her stomach when Connor turned. He was also hurt. Every instinct she possessed urged her to go to him and get them both somewhere safe.

Every instinct save one, her desire to remove Rownar from the face of the earth.

Rownar breathed fire, and it filled most of the cavern. Over and above the terrible sound rang Connor's shouts, then his agonized screams. Rownar then used what was left of his tail to knock Connor down the passageway and through the entrance of the cave. Then all that filled her ears was the dragon's roar. Like some heated, fierce storm, it matched the noise reverberating in her own head.

When the creature followed him, obviously anxious to finish him, Morgan regained his attention. "Come for me, dragon! I am the one you wish to claim! Leave him and take me if you can."

Rownar jerked his head back to her

"Both of you are mine. I will devour him, then

you."

"You will have to kill me first!"

He took her at her word. Her world became a nightmare of flame and falling rock. She dodged razor-sharp claws and teeth as large as her hand. She lost her sword and shield within moments from a nasty swipe of his talons. That was when she knew for certain he was playing with her. He wanted to make her suffer before he killed her. Not if she could help it.

When the stub of his tail slammed her against the rock wall, she wondered if this terrible dragon would be the last thing she would ever see, just like her mother had. And she determined she wasn't dead yet. She would never give up, not until her last breath.

She gathered her strength and her wits and ran for the cave entrance.

****

Battered, burned, and bloody, Connor regained consciousness lying on the ground a short distance from the mouth of the cave. His temples pounded. The pain beat against his skull with every thrum of his pulse. He opened his eyes and lifted his head, but this was a mistake. The pain became blinding, and he was forced to roll over and retch. He could not stop himself. Afterward he felt somewhat better, at least fit enough for his brain to start working again.

Morgan.

He dragged himself upward. But dragon fire bursting from the cave knocked him down again. For an instant, his heart almost stopped. "No!"

She couldn't be dead. He wouldn't let her be.

Forgetting pain, nausea, and the blood pouring from the wound in his thigh, he hurtled toward the gaping maw in the rock. Another surge of fire came close to burning him alive, but he scarcely felt the heat. He shouted her name as he ran.

Amidst yet another torrent of flame, he glimpsed her racing toward him. He took one fleeting moment to thank the gods for her survival and to stand in awe of her. Though flames engulfed her, she was not burned. It was as if she were shielded from them somehow. No matter the whys of it, his princess and the love of his life looked like a goddess rising out of the inferno, and that was all he needed to know.

When at last they got within arm's length of each other, they embraced and clung. Her body trembled, as did his. Soon however, he shook his head to clear it.

"Let's get out of here."

As if to emphasize the point, fire burst from the cave entrance, the dragon roared loud enough to shake the ground under their feet, and rocks fell, trapping him. Rownar had damaged the cavern, and now it collapsed.

Morgan held tight to his hand as they sprinted away.

Chapter Eight

They ran for what seemed like hours to Morgan. At last, Connor signaled that they could stop a moment, and she was grateful to have the chance to catch her breath.

Looking about her, she recognized the place they had left the horses. While the animals stamped and snorted, they were unharmed, for which she was thankful.

"Your wounds need tending."

She looked over at him. His expression was unreadable. "So do yours."

He shook his head. "Minor burns, superficial cuts, and scratches. I'll do. Yours are much more serious."

Saying nothing more, Connor rummaged in his saddlebag and drew out bandages and salve. He freed the skin fixed to the pommel of his saddle, pulled its cork, then poured a bit of water onto a strip of fresh linen. He wiped at the shallow slash running down her upper arm, and she winced. Then he dabbed salve on the cut. Finally, he bandaged it tightly. When she examined his handiwork, she was relieved to note the bleeding had slowed to a trickle.

As he tended to his own minor wounds, she asked, "How long will it take for him to get out and come after us do you think?"

"A day, perhaps two, if he was uninjured by the

cave-in. By that time, we need to be far from here. On the other hand, if he was hurt, who can say? It could be weeks, even months before he is fully recovered. Either way, we should leave."

"I agree. Still, I don't fancy running around unfamiliar territory in the dead of night and wounded, to boot."

He grunted. "We haven't much choice."

Not very pleased with the idea, she nevertheless confined herself to asking, "Where are we headed?"

"For now, back to your father unless I can think of a better plan."

"That sounds reasonable, I suppose. I don't relish returning home with my tail between my legs, though. I also am not looking forward to explaining to my father why we went after Rownar by ourselves when we promised him we wouldn't."

"Nor am I, but we must."

"Somehow I think my definition of certain death and his will be quite different, in this instance in particular."

"At least your neck is safe, unlike mine."

"At this point, the one reason my father would ever do you harm is if I ended up dead. Not just because I would never allow it, but because he has grown quite fond of you."

Connor snorted. "One can only hope that will be enough. Still, I put you in danger. He might find that unforgiveable. I would." After tying a last bit of bandage around his muscular thigh, he rose, then offered her a hand up. "Come on, we have to keep moving."

Although every muscle in her body protested and

her wounds burned, Morgan obeyed.

****

They rode all night and into the next day. It was not until then that Connor judged them far enough away to stop at yet another inn. Once they obtained a room, they headed for it with alacrity. As soon as they entered, they dropped onto the thin, but to them blissfully comfortable, mattress without even undressing and were asleep in moments. Neither woke until evening fell.

The sun had long since set, and after eating a simple repast of cold pheasant and baked bread in their room, they opted to remain for another night and ride out with the dawn. He ensconced himself on the settee with a book while she sat at a table made of rough wood. Several letters needed to be written, and she volunteered for the task, but her mind refused to settle.

"I'm a coward." She could scarcely believe she had said the words aloud, but there was no going back.

He looked up from the volume on dragons and their history he was reading. "What? No, you are not. Don't be ridiculous." He shook his head at her, then turned back to the text in front of him.

"I am."

He closed the book with a snap, rose, then joined her at the table. He took her hand, then waited until her gaze met his. "The last thing you are, Morgan Talbot, is a coward. You are the bravest person I have ever known."

"No, there's something I've been too afraid to tell you for ages." She touched the center of her chest. "It's been here inside of me since the night I met you, and I've been hiding from it for almost as long. It's taken us both almost dying at Rownar's hands for me to get up the courage to say it out loud."

"You've come this far and whatever it is can't be worse than the things I've done in my life. So no matter what it is or what you might have done, I'm here with you and always will be. Be brave now and tell me."

Morgan took a deep breath and leapt off that emotional cliff. "I love you."

He stared at her, then laughed. Her heart leapt with hope. At least he was not running away, screaming.

"Well, it's a right mess we're in then, darling, because I love you too."

Now her heart soared. "Why would we be in a mess if I love you and you love me?" Her wheeling heart tripped a little at the words.

Now the joy faded from his eyes. They filled with yearning and sadness. "Because what we do is dangerous. Either or both of us could be killed at any time. Not only that, this work eats away at the soul until there is almost nothing left. That's where I was when I met you, and I don't want that to ever happen to you. Since you walked into the Golden Key, I have felt more alive than I have in years. And so I know I can't go on like this. I want a life, a real life, with you, but I also will not stop; I cannot stop until this world is safe, until you are safe. That's why I didn't say anything, not even when I believed we were both going to die."

Connor rose from his chair. With slow, deliberate steps, he closed the distance between them and drew her to her feet. "Do you have any idea how I felt as Rownar shot fire at you? If you were dead, I would break. You were running toward me, and I was racing toward you, but I thought for sure I wouldn't make it to you in time. Then you walked out of the flames, unharmed, like some goddess. I wanted to kneel at your feet. I wanted to take you right then and there, but I did nothing. So who's the coward?"

Dazed, Morgan lowered herself to the firm, cool mattress. She was mesmerized by him.

"I don't intend to be a coward anymore." He framed her face with his strong hands. "I love you, Morgan Talbot."

From that moment, passion ruled them both. No, not passion alone, she realized, but love. She loved him. Even more astounding, she was now aware he felt the same way about her, that his feelings were that deep. To know he loved her, to hear the words from him, and then to feel it in her soul and her body was astonishing. With every beat of her heart, the remarkable knowledge sank in until it permeated the very marrow of her being. And it rocked her to her very core.

Words were not enough to express all the emotions welling up inside her. So she let her actions speak for her and then relished his enthusiastic replies. When she caressed every inch of him she could reach, he responded by burying his tongue in her mouth and his hands in her hair. His touch sparked fire beneath her skin, and she jerked his shirt from the waistband of his trousers and ran her palms over his flat belly.

He lifted his arms and whipped the garment off. The rest of their clothes soon followed. In a blur of movement, he reached for her and tumbled her onto the bed. Then, in one smooth powerful motion, he entered her. They both moaned at the contact. Shaking, she held on to him as they found a rhythm which was not his or hers but theirs.

When she was a heartbeat from going over the edge into climax, he whispered, "I love you. Always."

****

"When did you first know you were in love with me?"

Connor smiled, a gentle curve of his lips. "I think a part of me suspected it the moment I saw you, but I didn't truly comprehend it, not fully, until we spent our second night together. Then I knew with every fiber of my being that you were the love of my life, that there would never be another. Not for me."

"When I saw you the next morning in the audience chamber, I thought, that's it, I'm done for. He is the only one for me. He is my fate. I'm in love with him and will be for the rest of my life."

"I almost told you that night, our second night together," he admitted.

"Why didn't you?"

"Too damn scared, I guess. Now the one thing I am scared of is losing you."

She placed a gentle kiss over his heart to comfort them both. "I feel the same way. Let's make a pact."

"A pact?"

"That we will both do our best to survive this."

"I can agree to that, of course. But what if we don't? What if one of us dies?"

She shivered, even the thought chilled her. "Then we pledge to go on. We vow to at least try to find a new life."

"Being without you wouldn't really be living, but very well, I accept. How do we seal it?"

"Like this, of course," she said as she stretched to kiss him.

****

"I've had a chance to think, and I have come to certain conclusions," Connor told her the next morning over breakfast in the inn's common room.

"What sort of conclusions?"

"At first, I was very angry. This was our one shot at Rownar, and we blew it. Yet, after one immediate burst of fury, what I felt most was surprise. Surprise that I did not feel worse about the outcome. Then I realized, we both made it out alive so, it's not all bad."

"You are right about that." She squeezed his hand. "You know, I've also been thinking."

"Have you now? May the gods preserve us."

Morgan smacked his shoulder. "I think we need an entirely new strategy. We lure them; we capture them; but we don't kill them."

"What?"

"Hear me out. When we got close to killing Rownar, I felt something. It was like a tremor through the earth, but it echoed in my soul."

"It's just your connection to Rownar. It isn't—"

"No, this was something separate and apart from my sick connection to that dragon. This was an altogether different force; I know it in my bones. Whatever holds this world together trembled as if it might break. I think if we had killed Rownar, then the world itself might have shattered. I think if we kill all the dragons, it would forever change the balance of good and evil, and something far viler would rise up."

"Are you trying to tell me we cannot kill that creature?"

His voice was so low and dangerous she almost did not recognize it. "No, not at all. We can kill Rownar.

What I am saying is that killing them all is not possible. Not only that, it shouldn't be done."

Connor stared at her, eyebrows raised.

"Trying to dispatch dragons one by one is a miserable, almost impossible, battle. One you will eventually lose. I have only been doing this a few weeks, and I can see that. You said it yourself; it is a dangerous business which leaves the soul damaged. So, why not end it? Why wait until the day some dragon is too much for you and kills you?"

"So instead, you want to capture them." He sounded more baffled than angry now.

"Yes. All but Rownar. Him I would see dead, no matter what."

"How?'

"This is something you and I must figure out together."

"It is strange and a lot to take in. I've fought dragons for fifteen years, close to half my life. Yet what you say resonates with me, and I believe it to be true. There is no light without dark and no darkness without light."

"I'm not sure whether we can succeed or what any of this will mean for us or the world, but to continue with this work, until one day I die, never to complete it? That I cannot and will not abide. So, I suppose what I am saying is: I am willing to try."

Morgan savored her relief, then beamed at him. "Wonderful!" Her smile faded. "Now all we have to do is figure out how to do it. It won't be easy."

"No, it won't, but I have a few ideas on that. There might be someone who can help us. We will need all the aid we can muster. I know dragons, how to fight them and how to kill them. What I do not know much about is how to capture them without killing them. But there is a sorcerer I am acquainted with who may be willing and able to assist us."

Her smile returned. "Fight dark magic with light magic? Excellent idea. Makes perfect sense. I'm so glad you thought of it."

"So it does, and I wish I had thought of it long before now." He kissed her.

In between bites of savory toast and eggs, she asked, "So where do we find this sorcerer?"

"His name is Sebastian Hanson, and the last I heard he was living as a hermit in the Sagebrush forest."

"How did you become acquainted with him?"

"About five years ago I had a problem with a particular dragon. Sebastian lived in the village nearby and was there to help. He concocted a potion that temporarily incapacitated the dragon I was hunting, an old creature as powerful as he was sly. Once we defeated the beast, I told him I could use a man of his skill and asked him to come with me, but he said he had other matters demanding his attention. I hope to convince him to help again in some similar fashion."

"Do you think he will?"

"It can't hurt to ask," Connor said.

"So, when do we start?"

He smiled. "It is several days' ride from here. We will leave as soon as we have finished our meal."

Chapter Nine

Three days' slow trek through dense forest brought them at last to the magician's cottage nestled in a clearing. The structure was smaller than Morgan expected. The building itself was a simple wattle-and-daub construction with timber framing. A rather charming thatched roof kept out wind and rain, and two unshuttered windows opened to the air on each side of the oak door.

Yet, even as they headed nearer, a distinctive pressure oppressed her, mind, heart, and soul, the polar opposite of what one would expect from the appealing look of the place. Dread filled her. It seemed vital she come no closer. Knowing this for the defensive spell it was, she fought against it.

"There is magic here,"

For once, magic did not panic her. Perhaps because she knew deep down to her soul these spells were different. White magic versus the dark magic of the dragon she was all too familiar with.

Connor squeezed her hand. "Don't worry, it is a protective enchantment. So long as we mean no harm, no harm will come to us."

"Sure about that then, are you?" When he said nothing to reassure her, she shook her head. "Never mind; for once, I'm not worried."

The closer they got, the more her trepidation

increased, but at last, it eased. At the entrance, they dismounted, leaving their horses to graze on nearby vegetation.

Connor led the way to the door and knocked. The door opened a crack to reveal a young man with old eyes of crystal-clear blue. Thick blond hair worn a little past his shoulders was the next feature of his appearance to capture her attention. His build bordered on slender, but he carried himself in a way that whispered of power.

Connor broke the silence. "Sebastian Hanson?"

"Who is asking?"

"The dragon slayer Connor O'Malley and Princess Morgan Talbot. I am not sure if you remember me, but you helped me defeat a dragon once. We've come to ask for your help again."

"Many do. Others have a far darker purpose. I am honored to have a visit from a princess of the blood but understand well: no one can do harm within my walls, royal blood or no. In fact, most wishing to do damage cannot even find this place."

Without warning, a weight pressed against the barrier of her mind. She held fast. Morgan sensed that if that weight broke through the barrier, there would be a test she would not want to fail. An instant later, Sebastian's mind pierced hers. Since his will was strong, bright, and above all, powerful, she could do little to resist. When she realized he was not trying to harm her but was instead attempting to discover any malicious intentions, she ceased struggling. She let him do all he needed to.

"We wish harm to none. All we want is your aid."

An instant later, his mind departed from hers. From

Connor's strangely blank expression, he was receiving the same treatment. Before she could become uneasy, the magician released him.

He gestured them through the still-open door. "You should come in."

****

The tiny cottage was as charming inside as it was outside, Morgan decided. It contained a common room and kitchen, one private bedchamber to her left, and a loft over the kitchen.

The inside was warm from the cheery fire in the hearth situated on the back wall. When she glanced to her right, she gasped, and excitement filled her. The wall before her was lined with bookshelves filled to bursting. The place smelled of herbs, as well as the leather bindings and the paper of the books. Reading was her first great love and would always be a joy to her.

To the right of the hearth stood a table with wooden chairs, to the left was a pair of armchairs perfect for snuggling in with a favorite story. Morgan hoped she might be allowed the privilege and the time to do just that. For now, there were plans to make.

"So, what sort of help have you come for?" Sebastian inquired as they settled themselves at his table.

"Don't you know?" Morgan quipped.

Sebastian laughed and shook his head. "I don't have the gift of second sight, at least not without much preparation. You'll have to be specific with me."

Morgan and Connor exchanged a glance, then Morgan began. Between the two of them, they told Sebastian everything about their situation up to the present point.

"Don't tell me it can't be done. I've spent the last ten years of my life believing it can be," Morgan said.

"I would never contradict you, Your Majesty. However, I will need some time to think about this. I have to consider whether it should be done, then if so, how? Ways and means must be contemplated."

Connor leaned forward. "We understand, but we haven't much time."

"I am aware of that, but I must have the night at least."

Morgan and Connor exchanged another glance, then nodded.

"You are more than welcome to stay until morning. The cottage is small, but there is room enough. Take my bedchamber. I can sleep in the loft. I will have an answer for you on the morrow."

As she rose from the table, Morgan hesitated. "We won't wake in the morning to find two hundred years have passed will we?"

Sebastian laughed aloud. "I could make that happen if I wished it, but I won't."

Morgan let out a slightly nervous giggle. "That's good to know."

"Come, I'll fetch all you will need for your comfort."

****

Late in the evening, in the silvery light of the full moon, Sebastian ventured out alone and struggled to see. Once settled on the bank of the river, he did what he could to clear his mind.

"Bright moon, silver river, sweep the dark from my vision.

Let the future be as clear to me as a reflection on the water.

May the power in my blood strengthen my sight and my every pure intention.

What will be, will be, this I do not seek to alter.

Yet, I pray to see.

As I will, so mote it be."

At first, a variety of images played before his eyes in the clear reflection of the river, little more than a kaleidoscope of color. Then the images slowed and sharpened enough to make out fire, blood, and dragons, as well as he himself conjuring a spell.

Then the prism revolved, the scene shifted, and he could see himself bedding a beautiful woman and gasping her name: Trista. Knowing it for a previous encounter, he murmured, "Not the past. It is the future I seek and will not go until I see it at last."

He focused his mind and his power, and the scene changed yet again. In the water before him, a vision of himself and Trista completing a powerful spell arose. The vision ended with the tormented shrieks of dragons in his ears.

Returning to the present, he remained where he was, motionless. He was reminded why he so disliked the art of divination. It was so open to interpretation, and those who practiced it so prone to error. Yet, as luck would have it, this vision was remarkably clear. He would have to see her again, Trista Norris, the woman who nearly destroyed him. That realization troubled him far more than the idea of going into danger or facing dragons uncounted. Yet, if the vision was any guide, and his whole life was predicated on a belief in such things, he would need her help to accomplish the task before him.

Was he strong enough? Could he be in her presence again and not be ruled by her? Foolish, needless questions.

He would have to be.

****

Dawn was breaking when Sebastian returned to the cottage. Connor and Morgan were sitting down to breakfast. He joined them.

"Have you decided, then?"

He nodded to Morgan. "I attempted to see, but I perceived very little. All I know is that this is meant for me to do. The answer is yes. I accept this task."

Morgan's smile was as bright as the sun. "Wonderful!" As if unable to help herself, she rose from her chair, raised him from his, and embraced him.

When she let him go, he sat and filled a plate for himself. "Yes, well, how to do it is another matter. I do have a few ideas on that."

"As do I—we go back to the castle and set a trap." Morgan all but clapped her hands.

Sebastian smiled over at her, indulgent. "An excellent notion, but first, there is someone I must call on and enlist to help."

Connor glanced from Morgan to Sebastian. "Who might that be?"

"If this is going to work, I cannot do it alone. Casting spells as powerful as the ones we will need would kill me. There is a sorceress. I trained her. Together, I am certain we would be strong enough. If I can convince her to join us, she will make a powerful ally."

"I'm sure once we tell her what we are trying to

achieve, she will have no objections. We won you over, didn't we? I am certain we will persuade her as well." Morgan said.

"We will see. I must warn you; she will be far more difficult to sway. Even so, I believe she is our best chance."

"Well then, let's not waste any more time. Pack your things, gentlemen. We move out in an hour." Head high, confidence in every step, she went to follow her own advice.

****

In the darkest hour of the night, Rownar freed himself from the ruin of his lair at last. With a roar that shook the earth, he burst out into the open sky. His first thought was to find and kill that girl at last. He would consume her immediately this time. No more games. Morgan's body and soul were his.

He was two miles away before he realized his revenge would have to wait. Blood poured from reopened wounds, and he tired. His wings grew heavier and heavier until he could no longer lift them, and he had to lower himself to the ground. His landing was awkward, not his usual graceful touchdown at all. His strength was not what it had been, and he needed time to heal from his wounds.

Of far greater concern, his link with her grew weaker with every passing day. He could no longer pinpoint her location, and he could not invade her mind unless he were physically close to her.

Though impatience burned, Rownar resigned himself to waiting to go after her. He needed to regain his strength before attempting anything. In the meanwhile, he would make plans.

Perhaps he would refuse to give her a quick death after all.

****

Several days of travel brought them to a small village attached to a medium-sized estate. The large stone building had been impressive once, but now showed clear signs of neglect. Yet, as they drew near, small hints of reversal were apparent. Indications of recent repairs were there if one cared to look. A fence mended here. A field cleared there. A vegetable garden revived. Sebastian took these as positive signs. That Trista was returned home and treating it as such, caring for it as such, could only be a good thing.

"You're certain this place is hers?" Connor demanded.

"Very sure. I have been here more than once. This is where she grew up. Besides, can't you feel the magic? She has protected this place well. Just as I taught her."

Morgan nodded, though Connor still looked far from convinced.

Unperturbed, he strode to the door and knocked. Silence reigned as they waited. Then he rapped on the door again. Still nothing. Another few minutes, then this time, he pounded on the thick oak panels.

At last came the sound of latches clinking and hinges squeaking, then the door creaked as it swung open. A servant girl stood on the opposite side.

"Tell your mistress Sebastian Hanson needs to see her right away."

The girl's eyes widened then her lips thinned. "I am sorry, but the mistress is not receiving today. She is not at home to anyone. In particular, she is not at home to *you*."

With a sigh, Sebastian turned to Connor and Morgan. Connor's eyebrows rose, and his lips twitched while color flooded Morgan's face.

"You might have warned us we wouldn't be welcome," she muttered.

An irritated shrug was his response. "Give us a moment, if you would please."

Connor and Morgan stepped back while he paced forward. "Tell Lady Trista I know she is here. Explain to her that I am not leaving until she listens to what I have to say. I will break down this door and through her protections if I must, but she and I both know that that won't be pretty, and I'd rather not. Such a ridiculous waste of energy. Therefore, she should make it easy on all of us and see me. Go."

The girl's mouth gaped open, but after a moment, she managed to sputter, "But I can't do that, sir."

He gave her a steely-eyed stare. "You can and you will."

Still obviously reluctant, the girl slowly opened the door with her gaze lowered. She bobbed a shaky curtsey, then ushered him into a very comfortable drawing room. Morgan and Connor were left to stand out in the hall for the time being as he needed to meet with Trista alone first.

Sebastian settled into a damask-covered chair to wait. He studied the room. Much remained the same, but again he noted some minor improvements just as with the larger environs. The chair he sat in had been re-covered, and, at the large bay window, the garish purple drapes he remembered had been replaced with ones in a cheerful sunny yellow. There was also a crackling fire in the hearth, unusual in this house at this time of year despite the early spring chill. Two settees sat perpendicular to the fire, one on the right, the other on the left, as always, and an occasional table sat between them. A new painting graced the wall above the fireplace. It was a landscape of the view from the terrace overlooking the back gardens. In his humble opinion, the scene was not only peaceful but also beautiful and had surely been done by Trista. The whole piece gave off a sense of rebirth.

For the first time, Sebastian allowed himself to hope that perhaps they had not ruined each other utterly, nor had black magic.

The young woman who joined him some five minutes later was quite as beautiful as Sebastian remembered, perhaps even more so. The last time he saw her, her face had been ravaged by tears and the injuries done by dark magic. Trista tried to cover up the damage using every sort of artifice with little success. The harm done seemed to have healed except for the pain in the depths of her emerald-green eyes. Her glorious red hair fell in a long braid down her back, and her fair cheeks glowed with natural health instead of the rouge he had so hated. All in all, she looked very well indeed, although he had to admit he was biased when it came to her.

As he studied her, she studied him, then met his gaze.

"Go to hell." She followed this up with a turn on her heel in the direction of the doorway.

Sebastian stretched out a hand and, using his power, kept the door closed. He had always been stronger than her, physically and magically. "Trista, I–

we need your help. I would never have come otherwise."

"You want *my* help? After everything? You have a lot of nerve. As I already said, I'd prefer it if you went to hell, but to be honest, I don't care where you go so long as it's out of my sight."

Trista turned her back on him and faced the still closed door. With a burst of her power, she attempted to open it, and when he let her, she sailed through. Not waiting for any further response, he followed Trista down the corridor.

****

Trista still could not believe it. He was here in her home, bold as you please. And he was surprised she would refuse to see him and throw him out. Surprised!

When he followed her, she said the first thing that came into her head. "You want my help? You should count yourself lucky I do not turn you to ash. Go away, Sebastian."

He shook his head. "Not until you hear me out."

She did not dignify that statement with a response. The truth of the matter was no one could make him leave, perhaps not even her. He would have to choose to go. Suppressing the strangled sound of frustration rising up in her throat with great difficulty, she stalked back into the receiving room she had come from. She'd be damned if she would entertain him in her private parlor or out in the hall for all in sundry to see.

With an ill-tempered jerk, she tweaked her skirts out of her way and sat. "Fine. Speak. Say whatever you need to say. Anything to get you out of my sight."

"I abandoned you before, and I am sorry, so sorry, I hurt you. But I had to do it. I was drowning in dark magic and in you. I had to do everything I could to break free. For that, I will not apologize."

"Do you have any idea what it was like for me? I was drowning, too, even though I would have died rather than admit it. Then you left, and that nearly killed me in truth."

"I know." The words were a gentle whisper.

Her eyes stung with tears she would never shed in front of him. "How dare you come back here." Much as the fact humiliated her, she couldn't quite keep her voice from shaking.

"I'm sorry, Trista, truly, but I had to."

It took one heartbeat for her to be completely furious again. "You had to, no matter the cost to me! Well, isn't that just perfect? Your answer for everything! I wouldn't throw water on you if your head were on fire! So don't you dare anticipate any help from me."

"Now that is childish. I expected better from you." Crossing his arms, he leaned back to study her.

"Childish!" For a moment, she could not speak. Instead, a loud, feral sound originated deep in her throat, and she let it out.

When she noted him trying and failing to hide a smile, she clutched his arm and did her best to haul him bodily out of the room.

"Trista, stop!" He planted his feet, then grabbed hold of her and whirled her about to face him. "Stop this! This is far more serious than anything that ever happened between us. Even as much as I…cared for you and knew how much seeing me again would hurt you, I could not let that weigh. Please, this is a matter of life and death, and not only yours or mine."

Her shoulders slumped in utter defeat, and she let him have his way. "All right. Tell me."

****

Once Morgan and Connor joined them in the receiving room, Sebastian paced for a moment, then ran a hand through his hair. To Trista, it was a familiar sign that he was gathering his thoughts. Then he stopped and sat beside her on the settee while Morgan and Connor took the one directly opposite.

"Lady Trista Norris, may I present Princess Morgan Talbot and Connor O'Malley, dragon slayer."

Once the formal introductions were made and Trista had a chance to marvel a princess was in her home asking for help, Sebastian began the tale. "The dragon Rownar has targeted Her Majesty. He wants her for his own. Morgan disagrees. She'd rather remain alive."

With a twist to his mouth which assured her he recognized the irony, he gestured to Morgan to continue.

"To that end, I have been training. I have also lost my virginity. It was essential I break Rownar's hold over me. I met Connor at a tavern, where I convinced him to relieve me of my maidenhead. What I was not aware of at the time was that my father had hired him to deal with Rownar."

Trista's eyebrows rose at this, but she remained silent.

"She is determined to kill Rownar herself, and I intend to help her," Connor said.

Interested in spite of herself, Trista asked, "What does any of this have to do with Sebastian and me?"

"Morgan and Connor have decided that they don't

just want to kill Rownar; they want to rid the world, or at least this kingdom, of dragons," Sebastian said.

Trista let out a derisive snort. "Impossible. There are far too many of them. Even if there weren't, killing them all would tip the balance of good and evil."

"Not if we capture instead of killing them. That is where we come in."

Intrigued now, Trista demanded more details. Sebastian leaned forward as he expounded. "The way I see it, we need two spells, one to draw the dragons to us and one to entrap them."

"So you truly mean to imprison all of them?"

"Every last one except Rownar. Him, we will see dead," Connor said, tone firm.

Trista sat back, impressed. "Such a thing has never been attempted, much less done, not on such a massive scale." She glanced over at Sebastian. "Doing it alone would kill you."

Sebastian met her level stare, then shrugged. "That's why I came to you. Together we might manage it."

"Will you do it?" Morgan asked.

A spark of excitement kindled in Trista's soul, and she felt alive for the first time in more than a year. "A grand piece or two of magic, danger at every turn, and the chance to rid the kingdom of all dragon spawn? Of course, I'll do it."

"Just like that?"

"Yes, just like that. I live for danger. You, of all people, know that, Sebastian."

He gave her a searing look but said nothing more.

Morgan grasped Trista's hand. "From the bottom of my heart, I thank you."

"Thank me once it's done," Trista said, but she couldn't help but smile.

****

As evening fell, the two men tended their horses. Connor always tended to his own mount no matter where he was, and Sebastian led him to the simple but functional stable nearby.

Connor cleared his throat and at last, asked the question Sebastian was sure had been on his mind for the last several hours and more. "Will you be all right working with her? Trista I mean?" When Sebastian said nothing and continued to groom his horse, Connor went on. "I gather the two of you have a complicated, not altogether pleasant, history."

"That's an understatement. We were lovers, and it ended very badly." He set down the currycomb and faced Connor. "I don't relish the notion, I admit, but it's the only way. Besides, apart from anything else, it was my idea. I'll be fine."

"I realize we barely know each other. In fact, we're practically strangers, but if ever you're not fine, if you ever need to talk, I will be here."

"I appreciate that."

"What we are proposing to do will be very difficult. We have to help each other. If one of us has a problem which might affect the whole, the rest of us need to know about it. The support works both ways or so I would like to think."

"It does indeed." Sebastian held out a hand.

With no hesitation, Connor put out his own palm and the two men shook.

****

Late that night, when she and Sebastian were alone

in the receiving room, Trista demanded, "Can we really do this?"

Sebastian contemplated the flickering light of the dying fire and shrugged. "You said it yourself: something on this scale? Attempting it unaided would be suicide. Even together, it might kill us. Human magic alone is not strong enough to physically harm, much less destroy a dragon, not directly anyway." He paused to let that unpalatable fact sink in. "On the other hand, you are looking at the best sorcerer and sorceress who ever lived. If we can't do it, no one can."

Trista's lips quirked up. The words sounded arrogant, but none were ever truer. She had forgotten what it was like to hear such talk, how it felt to be around someone like Sebastian, a man so full of strength and confidence, and possessed of a single-minded focus that was very compelling. She decided she might not mind falling under his sway again so much after all, at least within certain limits.

Returning to the task at hand, she rose. "What sort of spell were you thinking would draw them?" How would she need to organize her workspace to include Sebastian?

"I was thinking an illusion of all the things a dragon might desire, such as gold and other treasure, dark magical objects, young maidens."

Trista shook her head. "An illusion like that would have to be strong and carry over a vast distance. More importantly, it would be far too easily shattered."

"You're right, I know it. But what if it didn't have to carry over a vast distance? What if we use another spell to draw them and then this one once they are within sight?"

"Perhaps we could manage that, but then what do we use to lure them?"

He beamed at her, then murmured, "A song."

"A song? You mean something like a siren song? But only sirens have this power, and their song is fatal."

"If we write an enchanted song to be sung by the princess and any virgins we can enlist, though, it might work."

"But we don't want to kill the dragons."

"And we won't. We could not, in any case. As you said, sirens alone have that power. We can captivate and enthrall, however. We can create our own dragon song, one the creatures will be powerless to resist. Together we have skill enough for that, I think."

Trista blinked and considered the possibilities. "You are right. It might work."

"Good, it's settled then," Sebastian said. "You know, I've always wanted to compose something especially for you. Something to showcase the beauty of your voice."

Trista peered at him for one shocked instant then avoided his gaze. "You wanted to compose a song for me?"

"Yes, not just one, any number of them," he said, with an absentminded gesture of the hand.

She recognized that faraway look. He got it on his face when creating a new spell or composing a piece of music, and it signaled his mind was focused on his self-appointed task rather than the conversation. She, on the other hand, was quite riveted.

"One for your every mood."

Trista smiled. "Oh? Do I have so very many?"

"So many. I have never been able to count them

all."

After a moment, he looked at her. "So, an enchanted song and an illusion to lure them. Then when they arrive, we conjure a magical net to hold them. So far, so good, that is if we can manage all that. There is yet another problem, however."

"If they are trapped together, they will tear each other to bits."

"You thought of that too."

"Of course."

He waited, but she said nothing more. "You have an idea. Out with it."

"What if the song also tamed them? What if, once they are trapped within the magical net, they will not be able to struggle? They won't like it, and at first, they will try to fight the effects of the song—like they will try to escape the net—but eventually, they will realize they have no choice and surrender. This one simple fact will seep through their thick skulls and into their tiny dragon brains: while they are strong, nothing is stronger than the magic we can do."

He contemplated her suggestion, then glanced her way. "Doing what you propose shouldn't be too difficult. All we need do is make the taming spell part of the song itself."

After a pause, he said, "You've given me a lot to think about, but my mind is weary with travel. Best to start fresh in the morning. This will require a song of unparalleled beauty, not to mention spells of tremendous power. I want to give all of this my best effort."

He rose. She did as well.

"I am confident if anyone can write such a song

and cast such spells, it's you."

"May your faith in me never be misplaced," he murmured. In a normal tone of voice, he said, "I will see you on the morrow." Then he bowed and left.

****

Morning dawned, and after breakfast they gathered once more in the drawing room. Between them, the two sorcerers did their best to communicate the rudiments of their plan, but questions still spun about in Morgan's head.

"A song? A siren song?"

Morgan was nonplussed by the idea. Siren songs killed, didn't they? Mystified, she looked to Sebastian and Trista once more for clarification.

Sebastian shook his head. "Not a siren song per se, but rather an enchanted song. One which will draw every dragon in the realm to us, then subdue them."

"It won't kill them?" Connor asked.

"No," Trista said. "Mix this method with some far-darker magic; then we could kill one dragon, perhaps. That is all we would have power to do, even with dark magic. But as I understand it, that is not our goal here. Our goal is to kill Rownar and trap the rest." She faced Morgan. "If this is what you want done, then this is the way, Majesty."

Morgan tapped a finger to her lower lip as she considered. Intrigued, she stated, "I like it. Connor?"

"I like it as well, but all the dragons in the realm? What if some of them resist? Hell, if even one resists, it would be a massacre."

Sebastian shrugged. "That's where the army you trained comes in. Some will resist, you can be sure, but Trista and I will do our best to prevent that. Leave the spells to us. Let us lure them. Let the army fight them if need be while you and the princess worry about Rownar."

Connor glanced at Sebastian and Trista, then Morgan, and nodded. "It sounds like the beginnings of a very good plan to me. I've faced worse odds and come out alive anyway."

"Let it be done, then," Morgan said.

****

The tower room where Trista worked possessed a high ceiling and was brightly lit, with windows overlooking the fields of the estate. Her space was organized much as the one they used to share in his cottage, Sebastian noted, although this room was far larger. Facing the door was a table of oak with a mortar and pestle as well as a decent-sized cauldron at one end.

At the other end was a softly rounded object set on a wooden pedestal and covered with a blue velvet cloth. Beneath the velvet rested her crystal ball unless he missed his guess. Shelving along each wall held books and bottles filled with various potions, all organized according to her efficient system. The one break in shelving was made by the small hearth to his left, in front of which sat two wingback chairs covered in green-and-gold silk brocade.

Judging by the fine dust covering many of the jars and vials of potion and that a fire was not in evidence, the room appeared to have been unoccupied for quite a while. He also observed the dark objects she had been wont to use were nowhere to be seen. An iron chest, chained and padlocked, which sat on the floor in a dark corner, was where the items ended up. He would bet his life. Even shielded as it was, the evil emanated from it and chilled his soul.

He stopped and tilted his head toward the large container. "The dark objects are in the chest, aren't they? Why keep them? Why not destroy them?"

"Some of them are very difficult to do away with once made and used. I was unsure whether I could get rid of some of them completely. I did not want to risk any of these objects falling into the wrong hands. In addition, the stronger the object, the more likely it would be to infect me. That was the last thing I wanted, not when I went to so much trouble to rid myself of all dark magic. Second, I keep them to help me resist temptation. Also to remind me of all I lost and all I still stand to lose if I ever practice the black arts again."

He studied both her and the chest for a long moment. "I understand."

She gave him a curt nod then moved about, clearing a space for him to work. The gesture was so homey and familiar that nostalgia shot through him, sweeping away the last of his melancholy.

"You haven't practiced in some time, I see."

She tilted her head. "No, not for ten months or more. I thought it best, particularly at first. It is only in the last week or so that I cast a few harmless spells. I put a protective enchantment over my flower garden to shield the blooms from a late frost. It might sound silly, but when I did, I found the pure joy of doing magic again."

"That doesn't sound silly at all."

Now that she had cleared an area, she turned to him, her eyes wide and eager. "So, where do we start?"

"With these books. I see you have acquired a few new ones. I'd like to take a look at them. Also, there are several spells I recall from some of the older volumes which might be useful. My memory is vague on those, and I'd like to refresh it. Why don't you do the same, and we will see what we come up with, yes?"

She chose a volume titled *Creating Lasting Enchantments* and began to read.

A mere hour, according to the chime of the carriage clock on the mantel, had passed when Trista announced, "Sebastian, I think I may have found something."

At her call, he rose and joined her. "Already?"

She pointed to a spell about halfway through the book she was perusing. "This potion, once concocted, is poured onto the ground. An incantation is said, and an enchantment is then done. After that, any dragon that passes will see the deepest, most desperate desire of his heart, whatever that might be. This is exactly what we are looking for, isn't it?"

He read the list of potion ingredients and the spell. His mood rose, then plummeted. "This is a very difficult spell. As for the potion, look at the ingredients, bat wing is not so hard to find, but a phoenix feather? It may not be possible."

"Oh, come now, Sebastian, I admit some of these things may be hard to find, but we can do it. Between your stores and mine, we already have most of this. I even have a phoenix feather."

"You have a phoenix feather? Where did you come across that?"

"I bought it off a man in a pub a year and a half ago. He wasn't at all respectable, but he did have a few disreputable things I wanted, and he included it. He had no clue what he had, and nor did I until our business was concluded. I kept it, of course."

"Of course." He sighed. "You are right, I suppose. If you have a phoenix feather, then we have everything we need."

"What about the song? Is it ready yet?"

"Nearly."

"Will you let me hear it then?"

He was far from sure that he was ready to do that, but he cleared his throat and sang. His rich baritone suited the song well enough though it was written for a woman. Even so, the seductive nature of the song rang in every note. It gave desire and temptation a voice.

When the last note died away, Trista remained still and silent for a long while. She cleared her throat before speaking. "That was amazing. It was beautiful. It was raw, and powerful, and feminine. If we sing this and it doesn't call them to us, I do not know what will."

"I want to tweak it here and there, but yes, I think, on the whole, it will do." His cheeks heated, and even he could hear the pride in his voice. With great care, he put away the precious sheets of parchment the composition was written on. "Add this to the spell you found, and they won't be able to resist."

Trista grimaced. "Yes, I wanted to talk to you about that. Perfecting this potion is proving difficult. I would welcome your input."

"Of course."

They soon fell into their former rhythm and slipped back into their old habits. Working together was so natural, easy, and right that it was all but unconscious, from Sebastian's point of view, at any rate. So much so that after just one day, it was as if they had never been apart, at least on a professional level.

With a soft tap, Sebastian closed the book he was thumbing through when the clock chimed five. "Let's put this away. It's time to dress for dinner. I'm sure the princess will expect us, and you shouldn't neglect such an important guest after all."

Trista looked up from her reading material and glanced out of the window.

Studying her face and yet unable to read her expression, Sebastian asked in an abrupt tone, "What are you thinking?"

She shook her head. "I was thinking today was far more enjoyable than I expected it to be. It passed quickly and pleasantly. Wonder of wonders."

"We did work well together once upon a time. I am glad we haven't lost that ability."

"So am I. I expected things to be tense, if not downright explosive, between us. At the very least, I prepared myself for a certain amount of awkwardness. Instead—"

"Instead, it's almost as though I never left." He pushed back his chair and stood before her. "I can't promise it will always be this easy. Explosive is an accurate term for us, more often than not. Can you handle that?"

"Absolutely. Can you?"

"Definitely."

Challenge delivered and accepted. He held out a hand. She took it, then even permitted him to help her to rise. Saying nothing more, he offered her his arm and with perfect decorum, escorted her to her chambers so she could change for the evening meal.

Chapter Ten

A few nights later, the dream began. Trista laughed as she and Sebastian did magic together. The scene shifted, and she was in his arms, then in his bed. Steeped in pleasure, she moaned and gave herself up to it and him. Then, night fell, and the dream turned dark.

In an instant, she was cold and alone in a desolate landscape, with Sebastian nowhere to be seen. Then Rownar's voice invaded her consciousness. The dragon assaulted her mind. Insidious, tempting darkness surrounded her, and with no warning, she stood on the edge of the abyss.

"Embrace the dark," he crooned. *"Accept your true nature, pitiful human creature, and draw on the black magic in your blood. That power is the one worthwhile thing in this world, and it is the only thing that will save you. Give yourself over to it and me or die along with your lover and your new friends."*

"No!"

She did her best to shout the word, but it came out as little more than a choked gasp.

"Surrender yourself."

"Never again!" Her throat closed, leaving her mouth hot and dry and her lungs unable to take in air.

Finally, the trapped scream erupted from her throat. The next thing she knew, someone was shaking her violently, and she awoke with a jolt.

Sebastian gripped her arms firmly. His eyes, the ones she could never resist falling into, were fixed on hers. He kept repeating something. Her name, she realized, along with curses and pleas.

"Come back, darling. Breathe. Trista, wake up! Wake up, damn it!"

She gulped in air and started to weep without a sound.

The tension went out of his muscles, and his grasp on her relaxed slightly.

"What in the name of all the gods was that?" Connor sounded a little angry and very frightened.

Sebastian was not the only person with her. Morgan and Connor, also awakened by the noise, were there to see what all the fuss was about.

Sebastian released her, his hands fell limp at his sides, and he sat back a little. "I'd like to know that myself. A glass of water, please," he said to a hovering servant.

"Of course," the girl murmured and left to fetch it.

"Catch your breath," he said.

Then Sebastian handed her a cup of cool spring water, and she gulped down half of it in one satisfying swig. She shook so hard she had to hold the glass with both hands, but the beverage cooled her parched throat.

After she drank down the rest a bit more slowly, Sebastian asked, "Can you tell us?"

Once she filled her chest with one more deep lungful of air, she nodded. "It was Rownar."

Exclamations and imprecations erupted from them all.

At last, Sebastian held up a hand for silence. "How?"

"I'm not sure. I was dreaming; then he was just…there. He was in my mind, part of my dream, making it a nightmare."

Haltingly, voice trembling, she told them the rest. "He tempted me. I could see the dark beckoning. It was more beautiful and terrible than ever, and for an instant, I wanted it. I wanted all of the power I used to have back again. Even knowing what I would be giving up, even knowing it would destroy me and all of you, I wanted it. Even after everything. What does that say about me?" Her words ended with a sob.

Sebastian gripped her hand tightly. "Did you say yes?" His tone was fierce, and he asked her the question as if he already knew the answer.

She blinked. Of all the things she had expected him to say, that was not one. She shook her head and then wished she hadn't been so vigorous as it began pounding. "No. I fought as hard as I could. I fought him and, even more, myself."

He smiled. "That says you are brave, you are determined, and you not only want to change, you have changed."

Trista shook her head.

"You have. Think back. Two years ago, if you had been offered the same, you would not have been able to resist. But right now, tonight, you did. Take comfort and strength from that."

She hesitated, searched his face then murmured, "All right, I will."

Eyes grave and shoulders tense, Morgan said little but instead urged another glass of water on Trista. Then insisted she step behind the dressing screen to change into a fresh nightgown. Far more comfortable physically but only slightly calmer emotionally, Trista got back into bed.

"You should try to sleep now." Sebastian urged as he fussed with the sheet and pulled the twisted counterpane straight.

"I couldn't possibly. Not after such an upheaval."

"Tomorrow, I will create a protection charm for you. Making one for each of us would be even better. Until then, I'll stay with you."

Abruptly, tears threatened again. To take advantage of his strength was tempting. To lean on him, the one rock-solid person in her life, was an alluring prospect. In fact, it was far too appealing a notion to resist, all in all. "Very well. I would be most grateful."

He nodded, and as the others said their good nights, he pulled a chair beside her bed and settled in for what was left of the evening.

****

The morning was far advanced when she woke alone. When she looked about for Sebastian, he was nowhere to be seen, but there was a folded bit of parchment on the bedside table with her name on it written in his hand.

Trista,

I did not wish for you to wake alone, but I am not far away. I am in your tower room working on the protections we discussed. Join me there if you wish or send for me if you have need of me.

Sebastian

Smiling slightly to herself, she refolded the note and placed it in the small drawer of the table.

It was almost midday before she dressed and headed to the library seeking peace, solitude, and the comfort of a good book.

For an hour, she found what she was seeking. So she was in a somewhat steadier frame of mind when Morgan entered. For a time, the princess remained silent and perused the shelves, ostensibly in search of a book.

"I understand what it is like, you know. To have Rownar invade your mind."

Trista looked up sharply from the book. "You do?"

"Oh yes, of course. He has been after me for years. What you experienced last night? I have been dealing with the same sort of violation for ages. At first, when I was a child, he did not bother much with me. Brief but vivid nightmares every few months were the worst of it. It was not until I began to mature into a young woman that the true torture began. I resisted for fifteen years; all the while, I took steps to thwart him. Forgive me for not mentioning all of this before; it is difficult for me to speak of it, but I see now that I must. I could at least have warned you, but I never supposed Rownar would go after you. Make a try for me, yes, but I never imagined…"

"No one could have. I understand, and I am all right." Which was not a total lie but was not complete truth either. She was not terrified down to her bones anymore, but she was shaky. In any case, her words to Morgan were true enough for the present.

"I don't mind sharing the techniques I have used to cope if it will help you. It's the least I can do after what you went through last night."

Numerous misgivings, tinged with a small portion of optimism, swirled inside Trista. Both vied for supremacy, and after a short intense battle, optimism won. "What techniques?"

"I learned to meditate, to clear my mind. It wasn't easy, particularly not at first, but with time, I was able to block him out, at least to some extent."

"That is encouraging. I must admit, I have never had the focus required for meditation. I do not have the aptitude for it."

"You focus well enough where magic is concerned. Meditation isn't so very different. I will teach you; then you can practice it each day."

Trista nodded. "Thank you. I will try anything you think might prevent a repeat of yestereve."

"One other thing helped."

"Yes?"

"Sharing Connor's bed." Although her cheeks reddened, Morgan continued, "Once I lost my virginity, Rownar could not have such a firm hold over me. I am sure you know that is the way of it when one is bound to a dragon."

A wry grin curved Trista's mouth. "I'm hardly a virgin, Morgan."

"As you say, but having a man in your bed is both pleasure and protection," Morgan said. "I am not saying you should sleep with Sebastian for that reason alone, but I see the way you two look at each other. Why not let what's meant to happen, happen? In this case, I think it might not be a bad idea."

"Hmmm, it is something worth pondering," Trista admitted.

"Indeed." Morgan grinned. "I'm sure taking him to your bed would be no hardship."

"True. Believe me; I am already more than aware of that." Trista confessed with a smile of her own.

"Do consider it."

Although she wanted to reject the notion, Trista resolved to do so.

****

Once Morgan left her to her own devices, Trista enjoyed the respite the peaceful afternoon offered. After returning to her room, she had a tray sent up rather than joining the others for lunch, then read her favorite novel.

The centerpiece of her room was an enormous four-poster bed made of maple wood. A forest-green counterpane draped the bed and covered most of the ivory linen beneath. To the left of the bed was a stand with an ewer and basin in ivory. To the right was a dressing table with the bare essentials upon it. Navy-blue drapes hung at two large windows to the left of the bed and were open to the sun at present. The remaining furnishings were a dressing screen covered in a blue, white, and green plaid pattern and a beautiful painting, a seascape with a storm on the horizon, over the bed.

It was a pretty space but one with few personal touches, as many of her waking hours were not spent there. She was more often found in her tower room during the day. Still, when she wished for privacy and a distinct lack of useful occupation, her bedchamber was a cozy, comfortable spot. Just as she acknowledged it was time to rejoin the others and face whatever needed to be faced that day, she heard a knock. Without waiting for a response from her, Sebastian entered.

"How do you fare today?"

"Well enough. And you?"

"Well enough. I have prepared a protection charm for you along with ones for Connor, Morgan, and myself." He held out a beautiful emerald necklace.

With great care, Trista accepted it and held it to the light to watch the stones shimmer and sparkle. "It's lovely." She closed her hand over it for a moment. "I can feel the power coursing through it. You have done a wonderful job." She held the jewels up to her neck, brushed her hair to one side, then presented her back to him. "Will you help me put it on, please?"

He obliged, managing to turn the gesture into a caress. Trista suppressed a shiver. She crossed to the cheval glass to see the effect.

He put a hand on her shoulder, met her gaze in the mirror. "It becomes you," he murmured.

Trista muttered her thanks, then took a deep breath. Although the words were bitter on her tongue, she made herself say them for the first time, recognizing their absolute truth. "I am sorry. I was weak last night, and, in truth, I have been almost from the very beginning. It's long past time I admitted it."

"Perhaps."

When he said nothing more, she pretended to occupy herself with straightening the few items on the dressing table. Then stopped short at the sound of his voice.

"Regardless, I was a fool ever to let you go."

Trista did not reply but found she could not move. Not toward him or away. She discerned then she was on the cusp of some new revelation or perhaps at the crossroads of a path taking her in a whole new direction. One careless word or gesture, and she might choose wrongly. So she waited for him to speak instead.

"I should have fought harder for you, for us. But at

the time, I was dealing with my own weakness and temptation. I was not strong enough to save us both then. Forgive me."

All of a sudden, she found she could move after all. She swiveled back around to face him and grasped both of his hands in hers. "There is nothing to forgive. I was strong in dark magic. Who's to say you could've saved me? Besides, I had to make the choice to save myself."

"And you did. We both did and now, here we are, so much better than before."

Deeply affected, she nodded, then belatedly made to go.

"Oh, by the way, last night you were not weak. Not at all." He shot her one fierce look. She responded with a surprised but pleased one of her own and decided that, after all, she was in no hurry for him to leave. Instead, she allowed him to stay, and they whiled away the rest of the afternoon.

****

The potion shimmered pink for an instant, then turned a sickly green, and a putrid stink rose.

"Damn it!" Sebastian shouted, then slammed a fist onto the table.

Trista pushed her frizzy hair back from her sweaty forehead and made a sound somewhere between a scream and a groan.

"What by all the gods are we doing wrong?"

"If I knew, I would fix it, wouldn't I? And we would be done with this." The irritable response she threw back at him matched her mood.

"We've been at this for too long," Sebastian said, his voice firm. "We need to rest, to stop for a while."

"Stop?"

"Yes, Trista, we need to stop. Instead, we need a walk in the warm sunshine and, afterward, a meal, for example. Then we can start again tomorrow. Come at it with a fresh perspective."

She bit her lip and said nothing. Connor and Morgan were gone in search of a dragon terrorizing a nearby village and would not be returning until the morrow.

Somehow, he must have read her mind because he said, "Come now, a meal alone together couldn't hurt. Or are you afraid?"

"I am not afraid of anything, least of all you." It wasn't the first lie she had ever told him, but she hoped and prayed it would be the last. Face set, she followed him out into the golden afternoon.

At his direction, they took the time. Being in the fresh air helped clear her head, and she admitted, to herself at least, that Sebastian was right; she needed this. Staring at the same four walls, working with the same ingredients, trying the same techniques over and over with little variation, and getting nowhere was guaranteed to drive her insane. Perhaps if she let her brain focus on other things for a while, the answers would come to her in time.

They said little as they walked, but the silence was not at all awkward. Without effort or conscious choice, her mind cast her back to the many other times the two of them had done this. On one level, it seemed like a lifetime ago; on another, it was as if it was only yesterday he had taken a similar journey with her.

The afternoon wore on, and they stopped at her favorite spot along the lake to watch the sun set. As it did, the wind died down, the birdsong quieted, and the riot of color faded gradually into the dark blue of the night sky. It was a beautiful natural occurrence Trista never took for granted anymore. It also was pleasant to share this experience with a man who, against all odds, still meant so much to her.

Once the sun drifted below the horizon and the world was bathed in twilight, Sebastian rose then offered her a hand. "Dinner?"

The interlude had been so very pleasant, and the afternoon had been far too short in her opinion, but so were many other good things.

With a sigh and a smile, she took hold of his palm and let him raise her from the ground. "Absolutely."

****

Dinner proved as pleasant as the walk. Sebastian felt quite rejuvenated, and optimism filled him on every front. After their brief respite, they went at their work with renewed vigor the next morning. So it did not surprise him when, mere days later, the spell was finally properly cast, and the precise mix of ingredients was found to make the potion viable. The spell wound through the air, through them, until at last, with a deft swish and flick of wands, his and hers, it was ended. The last notes of the enchanted dragon song died away simultaneously. Yet, all of it ceased far too soon.

"We will need to strengthen this if it is to enchant anything larger than a fox."

Sebastian nodded. "We'll work on it." He caught Trista's gaze. "You are stronger. You have more than you did."

The admiration he felt must have been apparent in his voice because she turned a sharp green gaze on him. "More even than when I was steeped in dark magic?"

"When we were both steeped in dark magic," he corrected. "Yes, far more."

Emotions whirled inside him. Fascination was not the least of them. As he immersed himself in them all and savored each and every one, they became more and more intense until he forced himself to step back. It was either that or... Gods.

He cleared his throat. "Well, we are getting there. It isn't perfect yet, but we are making progress."

"Definitely."

He rolled his shoulders, squared his jaw, then lifted his wand. "Again."

****

The potion glowed red, its light filling the tower room, and a puff of smoke drifted up from the cauldron. Sebastian beamed at Trista, then saw her widened eyes transfixed with joy.

"We've done it," she murmured. Then in a stronger, more confident voice, she repeated, "We've done it!"

His grin spread. "We have indeed." With a whoop, he grabbed her, pulled her to him, and spun her around.

For the first time since he met her, she giggled. The pure joy of the moment had him laughing as well.

As he slowed, then lowered her back to firm ground, his world shifted when he looked into her eyes. All it took was one heartbeat of gazing into them, and he was lost. Not kissing her now was not an option. He kept his approach gradual, giving her plenty of time to pull away and sever the connection between them, but she stayed breathlessly still.

When their mouths met at last, it was as though no time at all had passed. The familiar heat, coupled with her lips firming in response, was expected and welcome. Yet the reality of it all was a jolt to his system. All of a sudden, he couldn't get enough, and he dove into her mouth without restraint. For one heady instant, she met and matched him. Her hands stroked through his hair, and she clung. Meanwhile, his own hands gripped her waist, blindly steered her forward until the wall was at her back. His hands left her midriff then he leaned against the smooth stone. The muscles of his arms locked tight to keep from touching her the way he longed to.

When he left her lips to kiss his way down her neck, Trista gasped. His whole body trembled in response.

Sometime later, she whispered, "We shouldn't be doing this."

"Let's do it anyway."

He took her mouth again, but a moment later, she pulled away.

"Sebastian, what are we doing?"

"I don't know, but it feels incredible." And he resumed nibbling on her lower lip.

Then he got another jolt, this one not so pleasant. Trista shoved him hard enough to have him stumbling back a pace.

Her eyes were hot with a mixture of unacknowledged passion and ripe fury. With her face and neck flushed from his ministrations, she looked altogether desirable. Since clearly it would not be wise to point this out, he waited for her to speak while he got his breath back.

Chest heaving, she said, "If anyone ought to know what we are doing, it's you. I agreed to help you take on a dragon. I didn't agree to this." She waved a hand between them. "And besides, you left me. What were you thinking, kissing me that way?"

"I wasn't thinking. I was feeling." A little shaken now to realize how close he'd come to the brink, he stepped back from her. "That's always been the trouble with us. When I'm with you, I don't think; I feel. Then I act."

Trista edged away from the wall. "Yes, well, if you think I will hop back into your bed the moment you crook your little finger, think again."

Temper spiking, he said, "You seemed quite willing to a moment ago."

When she turned away, he was sorely tempted to turn her right back. It required tremendous effort, but he got himself under control.

When he was reasonably sure he could speak without shouting, he continued, "You were right to stop me, I admit. There are so many things we need to consider before going any further. It's only prudent."

"Such as?"

"Such as whether you have changed, whether we have changed, enough. When we were together before, we were weak. Both of us. Weak and self-destructive, and we fed off each other. I will not let that happen again."

"And you think I would? I assure you I would not."

"Still, you think we should take a step back?"

He nodded but let his gaze linger on her. "For now. Don't worry, when I'm ready, when I'm sure, when I want you, I'll let you know."

Trista closed her eyes and took a shaky breath. It wasn't until he was out of the tower room and well away that he took a deep breath of his own.

****

When they were ready to use their spells and incantations to lure and trap a single dragon, Sebastian believed it was only right Morgan and Connor be told. Trista was of the opinion that they ought to try it on their own first and then show the princess, but she made no open objection.

So, in spite of Trista's lack of enthusiasm, Sebastian told Morgan and Connor of the plan. Upon hearing of it, Morgan insisted she and Connor join them.

After some discussion, they decided an abandoned barn on the edge of Trista's estate would be the best location to try. No risk of harm to innocent servants or villagers and no worries about prying eyes. The barn and the meadow nearby were much smaller spaces than they would eventually need to work with but were quite large enough for one young dragon.

As they entered the structure, Trista looked about, taking in everything from the disused tools lying around to the lingering scent of hay and horses. "I suppose this out-of-the-way place will suffice, but can we really do this? Do you think we're ready?"

Sebastian shrugged. "I don't know, but we have to start somewhere. All the appropriate elements are in place. We've done our best and are as ready as we can be. Now we just have to do this and hope it comes together."

"Tell me again this is going to work."

"It will. If not now, then at some point, because we won't stop until it does."

They started with the spell. Sebastian and Trista

said the proper incantation, calling the dragon they wanted by name, then poured the potion on the ground. At Sebastian's signal, Morgan began to sing.

Tension filled Sebastian's whole body, locking all of his muscles tight, and he could sense it in the others, coming from Trista in particular, as he was most attuned to her. Yet, it was also present in Connor and Morgan, and it fed his own.

Soon the dragon called Cax appeared on the horizon, speeding straight toward them. The closer he got, the faster he flew, as if he could not wait to enjoy the delights the spell promised. The song and the illusion lured the creature. But as soon as he was enclosed beneath the barrier, he started to fight. He breathed fire against the net. He smashed against it again and again with all of his great strength. The net cracked like glass, and the crack spread inch by inch. Then, with one final decisive blow of the dragon's tail, the net shattered.

He rose, then spurted fire. Connor flung his sword and pierced him straight through the heart.

They all stood stock-still until Princess Morgan finally asked, "By all the gods, what went wrong?"

"I wish I knew. Forgive me, Your Majesty. I swear to you I will find out," Sebastian promised.

Connor said nothing, but Sebastian could all but see the tension pouring out of the slayer. Well, he could hardly blame the man. Connor could never have expected to have to kill a dragon on a moment's notice.

"The barrier wasn't strong enough, obviously. Nor was the taming spell." Trista said. She pushed back her hair with a shaking hand and then turned to the princess. "Sebastian and I will fix whatever is wrong.

We haven't come this far to fail."

Morgan nodded. "I know. Yet, time is of the essence. Please remember that. If there is anything Connor or I can do, you have but to ask."

Sebastian bowed. "Thank you, Majesty. We will find the answer. There is a solution; we just have not found it yet."

Without a backward glance, he and Trista returned to the manor house.

Chapter Eleven

"Trista and I want to test what we have. We want to try again." Sebastian said as they sat around the table together a week later.

"You want to test the potion on something smaller and less menacing than a dragon, this time perhaps? Splendid." Connor toasted Sebastian and Trista with his tankard of ale. "I commend you both for all of your efforts. Let us hope they bear fruit."

Sebastian shook his head. "No, I want to test all we have created on nothing less fierce than a dragon."

Connor held up a hand. "Wait a moment. Have you forgotten what happened a week ago? By all the gods, don't you remember what transpired last time? Are you sure you want to take such a risk again?"

"Yes, and I want to do it tomorrow, the sooner the better." Sebastian was quite determined on that point, but by their expressions, he could see Connor and Morgan were uncertain.

"We learned a lot from that first debacle," Trista was quick to reassure them. "We believe part of the reason the plan didn't work was because each spell must work in concert. Also, as we mentioned before, we know the magical net we created was not strong enough. We have fashioned a more durable one. Last but not least, we underestimated the strength of a dragon, and while the song lured as intended, it did not tame. Now it will. And so…"

"You want to test all of it again. On a dragon we will call to us." Morgan's pretty face was pale but also set and determined. "Very well."

"Morgan—"

This time the princess held up a hand to stay Connor's words. "Sebastian and Trista say they have perfected the spells. I trust them. I trust them almost as much as I trust you, Connor. Do you remember what you told me right before we went after Meglos? 'After you have trained and done the best you can to prepare, then all you can do is put your fate in the hands of the gods.' It's time to take that sort of risk again." She stretched out a hand across the table and grasped his.

"Put that way… In my heart, I know you are right. Still, I will want us to take some basic precautions."

"Of course," Trista said.

They went over all of the details he wanted in place. Then Connor glanced over at Morgan. "Did I really say all that? About fate and the gods?"

"Yes, you did."

He could only shake his head.

"Then we are all agreed?" Morgan asked after a pause. She raised her glass, and the others followed suit and lifted theirs. "To victory and triumph over every dragon!"

And may the gods protect us, Sebastian silently prayed as he drained his wine.

****

The next morning, the four of them again assembled at the abandoned barn. Sebastian and Trista prepared the ground with the potions they had spent weeks perfecting and conjured the enchantments.

At last, Sebastian gave her the signal, and Morgan began to sing. She sang until her throat was raw, and still no dragon appeared. She thought for a time that nothing would happen and was ready to consider this another failed attempt.

"Dragon, on the eastern horizon!" Connor shouted.

A tiny, dark blotch in the distance grew with every breath she took. Her voice quivered; whether it was with fear or excitement, she could not have said. Either way, the music never faded.

As it grew closer, it shrieked, a sound unique to dragons, one she would never mistake for anything else. Trista stepped forward with Sebastian and chanted as the creature hurtled toward them. Every instinct urged her to pick up her sword. Instead, Morgan repeated the song.

As it approached, she observed that all was as Sebastian said it would be. As before, the dragon was young, smaller than one fully grown, which still meant a wingspan of twelve feet. It was black, striped with red, and female.

Soon, the air stirred with the beat of her wings, and Morgan could feel as well as see the beast being drawn in. She did not want to pick up her sword, instead, she wanted to be right where she was doing exactly what she was doing. Her gaze fixed upon her quarry; she sang at the top of her voice as the dragon plunged straight toward her. The creature dove from a height of five hundred feet or more and breathed fire as she did.

Sebastian and Trista roared the last words of the incantation, and a silver net blinked into existence, ensnaring the dragon within it. It formed a dome over the immediate vicinity, then disappeared. As the dragon neared Morgan, it collided with the invisible barrier between them, the contact bringing the net trapping it into sharp relief against the sky once more. Roaring, the beast shot fire straight at her, only foiled by the magical mesh. Gradually, however, her movements slowed, the bursts of fire became less frequent, and as her eyes lowered to half-mast, she sank to the ground as if too weak to do anything more.

Realizing for the first time she had her own sense of timing, Morgan sang the last bars of the song. As the final notes died away, the others cheered as she walked the few steps to the edge of the barrier. Satisfaction rolled through her, and she could not contain the small, fierce smile which curved on her lips.

"She is well and truly caught, isn't she?" Connor remarked as he came up beside her.

"She is. Soon they all will be. I can't tell you how happy that makes me."

Sebastian twirled Trista in a circle. Both were laughing, but when they noticed her attention on them, Sebastian slowed and lowered Trista's feet back to the ground.

"Thank you both. This would not have been possible without you. Your kingdom and I will be forever grateful. As your princess and as your friend, I say this with all of my heart."

Connor held out a hand to Sebastian, and they shook. Then he took Trista's hand and kissed it. "You have my everlasting gratitude also. I have fought these monsters for over a decade. To know that soon I won't have to fight anymore means everything."

Trista brushed a stray hair out of her eyes, glanced at each of them in turn, then let her gaze rest on

Sebastian. "It worked. It really worked."

Sebastian face split in a grin. "Of course it did. I told you, we are the best magicians ever born."

"Indeed we are."

"So we've got her. Now what?" Morgan said.

The four of them looked at each other, expressions blank; then Morgan started to chuckle. The others soon joined her, and they all laughed until they doubled over with mirth.

"Can we transport that thing to Castle Belmere? And can you cloak it until we arrive there?" Morgan asked Sebastian once their collective hilarity spent itself.

"Surely. No problem at all."

"Marvelous. Make it so, then."

"When do we leave, Morgan?" Trista demanded.

"At first light. The journey is not a short one. I want to return to my father and get things underway as soon as possible. For now, the gods are with us. Rownar is or was trapped, and since he has not appeared, his wounds must be severe. This will not be the case forever. We should make the best use we can of this temporary respite."

"I agree. Still, time enough for a good meal, then maybe even a good bedding," Connor said in a cheerful tone.

Morgan's face heated, but she did not respond.

"Men," Trista grumbled. When Connor and Sebastian looked at her as if to say, 'what did we do', she added, "That's a rather tasteless and insensitive remark, as it is rather doubtful I will end the day with a bedding, good or otherwise. Added to that, you men often think of nothing but your stomachs and your..."

She shot a meaningful glance below Connor's, then Sebastian's waistline.

"That we do, darling." Sebastian replied.

"I fear I must agree," Connor said.

"*Humph*, remember we'll be leaving early tomorrow." Trista shook her head at them as they all trekked back to the house.

****

After Connor and Morgan retired for the evening, Sebastian remained. When Trista showed no signs of leaving the comfortable drawing room either, he poured both of them another drink. "Are you sure you want to take on Rownar with us? We—I could manage without you, Trista."

She scoffed. "No, you couldn't."

He covered her hand with his. "Don't do this to prove something to me."

The snort she let out was derisive in the extreme. "Don't flatter yourself. I want to do something to balance the scales. After all the terrible things I have done, that is the least I can do, don't you think?"

"So you are doing this out of some misplaced desire to atone."

When she said nothing, he took her silence as confirmation and went on. "First of all, it doesn't work that way. Each life is precious and unique and, as such, irreplaceable. Second, you need to consider the danger."

"Why? Do you?"

He was silent.

"I didn't think so. As I told you when this began, I live for danger. You know that better than anyone."

"Trista—"

"Be careful, Sebastian, or I might start to think you still care about me." She walked toward the door, and when she was about to open it, he stretched one hand over her shoulder, laid his palm flat on the panel, and kept it shut.

"Damn it, woman, you know very well I still care. I never stopped."

The soft skin at the back of her neck was mere inches away, and he breathed in the vanilla scent of her hair. As was about to place his lips to her nape, she spun to face him in one fluid motion. Her eyes were as wide with wanting as he felt, so, with no further words, he took her mouth.

When he let her come up for air, she whispered, "At the risk of repeating myself, I thought we weren't going to do this."

He stroked his fingertips over her cheek. When she did not protest, he gathered her into his arms and lifted her. "Looks like we are, after all." He carried her through the hall and up the stairs in full view of anyone who might happen by. Once through the door into her bedroom, he shut it with one good strong kick.

****

It all felt so familiar, but this only heightened Trista's anticipation. Being touched by him after so long was like a flood after a protracted drought. For nearly two years, in her heart and soul, she had been dead. Her body had lived and healed, but a part of her soul had remained barren and untouched.

For the first time in a long time, her heart, soul, and body were in complete accord instead of in conflict. She reveled in the sensation and him. She had thought never to be this close to him again. She had believed she would go the rest of her days never feeling truly alive again. Yet, here she was in his arms, and every part of her quickened once more.

She could not fight him or herself any longer; she didn't want to. So, she put all of her ardor, repressed for what seemed like forever, into the kiss. She put everything she had into encouraging him, enticing him. The resulting encounter, this first time, would be heated, passionate, and quick, she suspected, but no matter the tenor of their joining, she would embrace the moment fully.

****

She beckoned and Sebastian went to her willingly. Stripped raw, he hid nothing from her, certainly not his desire. With efficient, rough tugs, he dealt with her bodice and put his hands on her naked breasts. Never breaking kiss or caress, he guided them both to her bed. When the backs of her legs met the mattress, he paused long enough to press his aching flesh to hers.

Her body bowed in a swift involuntary reaction. He groaned then, hands leaving her breasts to grip her bottom; he lifted her up and into him. Rocking her evocatively against him, he pleasured them both. His control, which until then he held onto by the thinnest thread, snapped. He had to be inside of her now. With one murmured spell, quick as the beat of her heart, his clothes disappeared. Her eyes widened, and her breath hitched, but she made no demur.

Yet, he still took a moment, found breath and wit enough to say, "If you don't want me, tell me now."

"I want you. If you stop now, I think I might die."

His response was purely physical, entirely visceral. Repeating the same words, he vanished the last of her clothes as well and they were skin to naked skin at last. In one long, smooth, sure motion, he entered her. Lowering her, he buried himself fully inside her warm, willing body.

****

Trista let out a gasping moan. Pleasure rolled through her, and she could feel every inch of him. Then he moved. His touch sent heat racing like fire underneath every inch of her skin. As he thrust, he guided her, allowed her to sink back down onto him. He was stronger than he looked; she had forgotten how strong. His muscles bunched and rippled, and she found herself completely under his sway, physically, emotionally, and in every sense.

In no mind to share the reins of the engagement, he dictated the pace, the depth, each aspect of their joining. She discovered she could move only fractionally of her own volition, so she clasped her inner muscles about him as she sank down onto him and was rewarded with a groan. The tension infusing him ratcheted up a notch. He caught her gaze then consciously increased the timing and force of his thrusts. Then deliberately, he let himself go. All that reined power released at last, for her, or to be more accurate, for their mutual pleasure.

Already on the precipice, on the edge, seeing this in his eyes, knowing it to her very bones, she careened over with him. A maelstrom of overwhelming emotion mixed with unadulterated physical sensation swept through her. When they climaxed, it was simultaneously, repeatedly, and more strongly than they ever had before.

When it was over, she went boneless, and if he hadn't been holding her, she would have slid right out of his arms to the floor. For uncounted minutes, she let her body go limp while her mind drifted. As she relived their shared moment of utmost pleasure, she shivered. The fact that they were still in sync in this sphere even after all their time apart rocked her. Muscles quivering in reaction, he took his time lowering them to a sitting position so he could perch with her on the edge of the bed. Her breathing slowed, as did his. Then he tightened his arms about her and kissed her. Dreamily she kissed him back and at first, was not aware of him hardening again until he began rocking them both with a gentle motion, and the exquisite friction made her moan.

"Again? Already? You are quite tireless."

"We've been apart for almost two years. I won't have my fill of you anytime soon." The sensual promise made her shiver. His body surged up to meet hers, and she curved into him.

"Good," she murmured and kissed him ravenously.

Strong arms came around her, held her close for an instant, then, in a burst of energetic motion, he rose, reversed their positions, and adjusted her limbs until she was lying beneath him.

In spite of the fact that moments earlier she had been well-sated, they were both ready again almost immediately. This time he set a slower, steadier, more confident rhythm which left her reeling.

And still, there was more. Throughout the night, they made love over and over until they both all but collapsed from exhaustion. Near dawn, wrapped in each other's arms, they slept.

****

When the door creaked open, heralding her arrival,

Connor was ready and waiting for Morgan. Since he lay quite naked in his bed, except for the sheet riding low over his hips, he hoped his eagerness was more than clear to her. Inordinately pleased but not altogether surprised to see her, he held out a hand in her direction in case she hadn't quite gotten the message.

"I'd hoped you would come to me tonight." Connor caught her offered hand and kissed it.

"How could I stay away? This is the last night we'll be truly alone."

"Until we return to the castle, yes, I suppose it is."

Morgan shook her head. "Then we will have to be much more circumspect and far more discreet. In the castle, there are eyes everywhere. One misstep and the whole world will know about us if they don't already."

Feeling suddenly vulnerable, he hesitated, then murmured, "Would that be such a bad thing?"

"Not at all. But I dread being under the watchful eye of the servants, the court, my father. Out here with you, I have been free. I don't want to give that up."

"You don't have to, not yet." With gentle pressure, he tugged her toward him and the bed.

****

Dawn was breaking, and soon they would have to rejoin the world. Trista was not sure how to do that or even whether she wanted to. What was more, how would things be between them? So many questions. Well, if she did not ask, she would never find the answers.

"What now?" she queried.

"Now? We fight. We think and consider what we want if we live. We decide what we can and, more importantly, what we should do."

"I am sure of one thing: I have missed you, Trista. I've missed this. I've missed us. Whether we can have it again, I don't know, but trying can't be any worse than what we have been doing this past year and more."

In his arms, she stiffened, and her voice sounded cold even to her own ears. "This year and more was your choice. I suppose I can admit now it was the right one, but it was your choice, never mine."

"Yes, it was, and it was a choice I had to make, then. But now I am choosing something entirely different. I am not perfect. And neither, by all the gods, are you."

"I never claimed to be." Taking a deep, slow breath, she rose. "We'd best get dressed. Morgan and Connor will be awake soon, and they will have news for us, I am sure."

Having no idea what he might have done with her clothes when he magiked them off, she started to go to the wardrobe, thinking to put on a dressing gown. But he grabbed her hand.

"Whatever happens, I don't regret this."

Unable to resist him, she cupped his cheek. "Nor do I."

Chapter Twelve

Unable to wait a moment longer, Morgan galloped the last miles with Connor at her side and did not rein in until she gained the forecourt of Belmere Castle.

James rushed out to greet her. He barely allowed her to dismount before sweeping her into his fierce embrace. "Thank the gods you are safe," he murmured into her hair.

She clung to him for one moment, then pulled away. "I am safe and well, and I have news. Did you not receive my letter?"

"I did but not until long after you engaged Rownar and—"

James broke off. He narrowed his eyes then caught sight of Connor. He advanced on the younger man who had dismounted. With firm and purposeful steps, he soon reached the dragon slayer who had sworn to keep his daughter safe. Without hesitation, he punched Connor squarely in the jaw.

His wicked right cross found its mark, and Connor stumbled back a step from the force of the blow but made no attempt to defend himself from the attack. Morgan squeaked in alarm and rushed to get between them as her father continued punching her lover.

"You went after Rownar alone! You imperiled the entire realm! You endangered my only daughter!" More blows landed on Connor.

"Tell me why I shouldn't execute you right now!"

"Father, stop!" Morgan roared.

James knocked Connor to the ground with a blow, then fell to his knees to continue the attack. Trying to drag her father bodily off Connor had no effect whatsoever, even with Sebastian's help. But the sound of her voice got through to him at last. He stopped striking her beloved, at any rate.

"There wasn't any other way," she informed her father in a calm, steady voice. "Rownar would have eluded us otherwise. It isn't Connor's fault."

There was a long silence, and it was far from a comfortable one. Eventually, Connor broke it.

"I would give my life for hers. If at any time I had been given a choice, I would have chosen her."

James got to his feet in one smooth motion. Since he looked as though he still might quite like to land another blow, Morgan stepped right in front of him and put a hand to his chest.

Connor looked quite the worse for wear, between the bruise already forming on his jaw, his broken nose, the blood dripping down his face to his shirt, and the dirt covering him. Yet his dignity was still intact. He stood.

Moving one cautious step away from her father and toward her lover, she wiped his face with her handkerchief; then she left Connor to finish cleaning himself up as best he could while she dealt with her father.

"*Enough*. I am more than fine, as you can plainly see. There is no harm done. Since that is the case, you, Father, will stop behaving like a savage," she ordered. "Perhaps you did not realize we have guests."

Belatedly, he noticed the two strangers accompanying Connor and his daughter. He tugged down his waistcoat, straightened his spine, and greeted his visitors as he put on his more-ceremonial face. "So I gather. Please make the introductions."

Morgan did. The formalities thus observed, though with some awkwardness, she said, "Father, we have had a long journey. Food, drink, and rest would not come amiss, as well as a surgeon for Connor. In short, I think all of us would like a bit of time to freshen up. After that, we have much to talk about, and I, for one, would love to do so over a meal."

"Of course, of course." The broad wave of his hand included them all. "Come, you shall have food and every other comfort you could wish for; then you can tell me all."

Sagging with relief, Morgan started up the flagstone steps, and the rest of her companions followed.

****

An hour later, settled by the fire in the main drawing room, a hot cup of tea in her hand, Morgan felt distinctly better. Her father had refrained from beating anyone else to a pulp, which was all to the good. In addition, she was exceedingly grateful to no longer be on the back of a horse, even one so sure-footed as her Maribelle. To sit at her ease on an unmoving surface was welcome. The room was reserved for entertaining guests of particular importance, such as close kin or personal friends of the royal family, and so was quite appropriate for their present interaction.

Her father sipped from his cup of tea, then glanced her way. "So, you said you have news," he prompted.

Morgan took a final swallow of the strong, sweet liquid, cleared her throat then began. "Yes, we have come up with a new plan, one that Sebastian and Trista will help us execute. The only dragon we will kill is Rownar. As for the rest, we will capture them."

"Capture them?"

Morgan nodded.

"Capture them how and put them where pray tell?"

Never had she seen such genuine astonishment cross her father's face. His eyes widened and his jaw slackened. He set his cup down with great care. He looked astounded, not to say flabbergasted. Morgan hid her smile and did her best to explain. "The how is where Sebastian and Trista come in."

After she had thoroughly enlightened him, her father rubbed his chin and glanced over at her. "I don't like the idea of relying so much on magic. Spells can be broken, enchantments can waver, and incantations can weaken. I am much more comfortable when I can face my enemy with a sword in my hand. To my mind, that is the one sort of fight worth having. It is why I hired Connor to train a dragon-slaying army for me."

Trista scoffed, but before she could speak, Sebastian squeezed her knee. Trista's face hardened, but she remained silent.

"And we will still have need of it. Dragons, especially in large numbers, will not be at all easy to subdue, even with magic. We are in total agreement there, Sire," Connor said. "Yet, I think this new plan is our best chance. I have been battling the creatures for almost half my life with little success. It is time for a new approach."

"What is more, if we kill them all, we would

destroy the balance, perhaps irrevocably."

James raised an eyebrow at his daughter. "Are you quite certain of that?"

Morgan nodded. "It's what I believe."

James addressed Sebastian and Trista. "I have heard tell of you both, but not in several years."

Even from where she sat across the room, Morgan could see the high color standing out on Sebastian's cheekbones. "I can only imagine what you have heard. Not all of it is true. At least, that is what I would like to think. I can tell you that over the last several years, we have both abjured all dark magic."

"But not before causing serious damage to many."

"That's correct."

"That being the case, why should I trust you, particularly when the stakes are so high?"

"You don't have much choice. You need us."

When James said nothing to contradict the statement, Trista's lips curved up slowly.

Sebastian's expression remained dead serious. "Trista and I are willing to swear as many vows as you like, pledge our allegiance to you as many times as you wish, but none of that matters if you don't trust us. The only way to build trust is with time and action. We intend to help capture every dragon in this realm at great personal risk. Already we have come up with a spell only the two of us alone are strong enough to cast. I think we have already begun to prove ourselves, don't you?"

Again, no response came from James.

"Let time and our actions speak for us; that is all I ask."

After another long pause, James replied, "All right.

As you say, I don't really have a choice. But know this, if one whisper of dark magic reaches my ears, your life is forfeit, and so is hers." With a tip of his head, he indicated Trista. "This I swear."

Sebastian exchanged a glance with Trista, and though her jaw set, she nodded almost imperceptibly. A moment later, the two of them were on their knees, pledging their fealty.

That done, James took a large swallow of the brandy the servants brought round, then continued, "There is one more aspect to this, and it is one I am absolutely against: using the maidens."

"None of this will work without them." Trista's voice brooked no argument, not even from her king.

"That has been made quite plain. I don't have to like it." He exhaled and set his glass aside. "To put so many innocents in such grave peril does not sit at all well with me. A king protects his subjects; he does not endanger them, nor yet jeopardize their welfare. These young ladies are bait, and there is no way around it. Even so, I will agree, under one condition."

Trista opened her mouth to protest, then at Sebastian's sharp look, shut it.

"They will offer themselves of their own free will or not at all. No one will be forced. I will speak to my subjects from the balcony off the great hall, then send this proclamation throughout the land. Any young woman over the age of fifteen may volunteer."

They each murmured their approval of the idea, even Trista.

Morgan considered a moment. "It occurs to me, Father, what if a young woman wishes to volunteer, but her family does not agree? What then?"

James rubbed his chin a moment. "If her parents are dead set against it, and if the young girl in question is likewise determined and they cannot reach an accord, they shall come to us, and we shall resolve each issue on a case-by-case basis."

Morgan inclined her head, satisfied with the notion.

James rose to his feet. "Well, since that is decided, I am sure you are all still quite tired from your journey. Rest tonight, and tomorrow we will flesh out this plan."

Saying nothing more, he left them.

****

At the king's suggestion, Connor, Morgan, Sebastian, and Trista travelled, along with James, on horseback to Ashbridge moor the next morning.

"We will be there soon. I hope the journey has not been a tedious one, but it was necessary, I assure you. I felt it imperative you all see this place for yourselves. That way we can develop the best approach," James said.

As they travelled down the sloping track, Connor noted the strategic elements of the area.

"So, what do you think? In my humble opinion, tactically, it is most suitable. Nevertheless, you alone among us have fought dragons before and won. Will it do?" James asked.

Connor said nothing as he assimilated the details. Low hills surrounded the place to the south. The summit of one would be an excellent spot for Sebastian and Trista to cast their spells. It was deserted, free of inhabitants, and the north side was eminently defensible due to the mountains, which were too high for even the dragons to fly over with ease. There was a river to the east close enough to provide water for the troops and to quench any dragon fire. The terrain they stood upon stretched to the west and was rocky, a distinct disadvantage. Still, he had fought in far worse places.

"It will take work and planning to set the trap here, but what doesn't? All in all, we could not have asked for a more advantageous battle ground," Connor said.

James clapped Connor on the back. "I am most pleased to hear it."

"Sebastian and Trista will cast the spell and create their magical net over this entire valley, using the mountains for a border." Connor gestured to the snowy peaks. "Then the singing will start. The dragons will enter right enough, but once they have, they can never leave."

"But when they realize they have fallen into a trap, they will try to break away. It won't be pretty."

"No, you are quite right, it will not be pretty, but they will not escape. I will not let that happen. Once they realize what is going on and dragon fire fills the air, you will deploy the army. That is your part, Sire."

"I am aware." The king's tone grew a bit acerbic. "I have led armies before. In fact, I led them long before you were born, boy. The plan is sound. Each of us will do the job he or she is most suited for. That is as much as we can do, I suppose. May the gods protect and shield us and perhaps even favor us."

****

As arranged, the fastest messengers available were sent throughout the entire realm. A day was also set for the king to address his people directly. At the appointed time, the square before the castle filled to bursting, as they had hoped.

"My people," James began, "I come before you

today to ask something very important of you. It is something I cannot accomplish alone. Your willingness to make this sacrifice is vital to this kingdom, to the very world."

James was happy to note his audience was already riveted. "All of you know and have probably personally experienced the scourge of dragons upon our land. They are the bane of an otherwise idyllic existence. But for the first time, there is hope."

Silence fell. With his audience utterly captivated now by the power of that one word, hope, he explained the plan to capture the creatures. Silence reigned.

At last, a middle-aged man near the front of the crowd spoke up. "You want us to give you our children."

It was a statement, not a question, and the man sounded appalled. A rumble of discontent rose from the crowd.

Morgan jumped in. "We need their help, yes. Everything that can be done to protect them will be done."

"They are bait for the most monstrous living things in the world, and you think you can protect them?"

Disbelief permeated the man's words, and doubt soon settled like a miasma over the crowd.

"I know we can." Trista claimed with a toss of her red head.

James held up a hand to forestall further comments. "Nothing in this world is absolutely certain, but as the princess said, everything that can be done will be done. I would never ask any of you to take such a risk if I did not believe that risk is vital to our very survival."

Morgan spoke a word in her father's ear then, at his

gesture, stepped forward. "I was once as young and innocent as your daughters. My youth, which ought to have been blessed and joyful, was overshadowed by Rownar. I spent my early life first in fear of him, then learning to fight him. I would not wish the same on any other young woman in my kingdom. To make the world safe for every child now living and for all those children who will, by the grace of the gods, come after us, we need your help. It is not a thing which can be forced but must be willingly given. So, I beg of you, mothers and fathers, if you have a daughter who wishes to aid us in this, send her to me. Do not gainsay her. In return, I promise to fight alongside her, and I pledge never to give up, not while I draw breath."

A girl, whose pretty face was marred by a terrible burn on her left cheek, stepped forward. "I will help."

James only heard her because she was mere feet away, but even then, he could not be altogether certain of her words. "What was that, young miss?"

She repeated in a stronger, firmer tone, "I will help. I have a good enough singing voice, or so I'm told. Rownar did this to me when I was little more than a child." She gestured to her damaged face.

"What of your parents, girl?" James asked, his tone gentle. "What have they to say about this?"

"I ain't got none, Your Majesty. Rownar murdered them the same day he scarred me. I lived with my aunt, me mum's sister, until she died a year ago. My life has been hard; maybe it won't be quite so hard if we capture those demons."

"Your name and age?"

"Justine Lawson, Sire. I be just turned sixteen."

"Very well, Justine. You shall be our first."

She dropped into a clumsy curtsey. "I am honored, Your Majesty."

****

A gesture from King James signaled to Connor that he was up next. He found himself focusing on his new troops and ready to begin. He was happy to see how their numbers had grown during his absence. When he first arrived, only a few lieutenants had been selected for the dragon-slaying army; now, there were a thousand troops, give or take. He hoped those chosen for this special force would be open to his unorthodox training methods More, he hoped to give the common people some method of defense.

A colonel stepped forward and gave him a short introduction. That done, the man stepped back to allow Connor to address the soldiers specifically.

He paused a moment, partly for effect and partly to gather his thoughts. As he did, he looked around and studied those who would shortly be under his command. The mixture of the battle-hardened and the green suited him.

"Some of you are veterans of many wars. Others, though you are soldiers, have yet to prove yourselves in battle. Still others never thought to have to fight at all. No matter what category you fall under, from today, you are all on equal footing."

None of the soldiers were so inexperienced as to let their reactions to such a statement show, but Connor sensed an expectant tension throughout the group nonetheless.

"While the common people stand here wondering whether we can do what we claim and actually capture dragons, many of you standing here at attention are wondering why whatever experience you might have is now considered negligible. The answer is that none of you has ever gone up against a dragon. I have."

He paced from one end of the formation to the other. "Those of you in this regiment were chosen for a reason, however—for your skills, for your willingness to learn, for your ability to improvise. Any or all of these might have earned you a place here. You are the first line of defense. In the coming days, I will do my best to train you, to teach you all the basics you will need to survive, protect and defend. Some of you will not make it. But the odds of coming out of this conflict alive increase if you have training in addition to natural skill. Natural skill cannot be taught, of course, but technique can and will be.

"Some of you may think that since you have fought in so many battles, there is nothing new to be learned. You are wrong."

It did not surprise him that many of them, the older men in particular, were skeptical, even patently unconvinced. They muttered to each other and sent him narrowed gazes. Not in the least concerned, he proceeded to the next, far more exciting, part of his presentation. He signaled to Sebastian, who stood at his back.

One flash of magic, strong, beautiful, and bright as the sun, then a dragon appeared in their midst. If the situation had not been so serious, the reaction of his prospective troops would have been comical. Connor found little to amuse him in the panicked response. Many yelled and backed away. Some even ran. The reaction of the people was even worse, screams and a swiftly burgeoning chaos took over. Revived somewhat by the stimulus of the crowd, the creature, captured mere days ago, shrieked and charged the invisible wall of Sebastian and Trista's magical force field.

"Don't be alarmed; you are all quite safe. All of you know our plan. Here is proof we have already succeeded on a smaller scale. As you can see, the creature is contained."

"Forgive me if I need more than your reassurance to believe that."

Connor saw a stocky fellow of forty-odd in simple farm clothing with a scar across his left cheek.

"You doubt me? You doubt the word of your princess? If so, observe."

Silence fell as all those present, civilian and soldier alike, followed Connor's order. The dragon called Sil continued to thrash against her prison. It soon became apparent that the creature was well and truly caught. Soon enough, the quality of the silence changed, and it became tinged with awe as this realization sunk in.

"Even contained, this dragon is formidable, as you see. When the final battle occurs, there will be more of them to face than any of you, or even I, have ever seen before. They will be cornered. Then, if the gods are with us, they will be trapped, as this one is. There is nothing more dangerous than trying to accomplish this feat. This regiment will do its utmost to succeed, and they have my every confidence, but these soldiers cannot be everywhere at once. While they are the first line of defense, all of us must be prepared. So, if you want to live, you will listen and you will learn."

Quite certain now that everyone's full and undivided attention was his, Connor was ready to teach them the rudiments of dragon defense.

****

To Morgan's great elation, many more young women volunteered to sing, and many young men offered to fight with the regular troops, or if they were good enough, as part of the dragon-slaying army.

Soon the group of singers numbered two dozen and more. Morgan separated them by soprano and alto to begin with and told the girls to report to their new quarters after taking leave of their families. She had organized the quarters herself and hoped the girls would be comfortable there. She hoped also that more would arrive. The more powerful they were, the better. The gods knew, they would have need of all their strength if they were to defeat their sworn enemy.

Sure enough, her prayers were granted, and by the end of the day, another three dozen maidens arrived. Not only that, she believed down to her soul that the call, which went out to all the land, would be answered by many more.

****

The next several weeks passed in a state of tension which became more and more unbearable until it was all but untenable. There were no sightings of Rownar, not alive, wounded, or dead. No one believed him to be deceased, of course, and so they all lived in a heightened state of awareness, ready to fend off an attack at a moment's notice.

For the time being, Connor spent his days training the army. Sebastian and Trista worked on perfecting and expanding the spells both for attack and defense. Morgan supervised, organized, and educated the young volunteer maidens in music as well as basic self-defense.

Despite that all of their efforts might still come to nothing, Connor's pride grew day by day. It was no small thing to produce the first dragon-fighting army in centuries and the first organized one in the history of the world.

There was also Morgan. Each day she became more essential to him and, at least to his mind, they became more and more of a unit. The nights with her were his solace.

Every shared moment brought them closer. He often wondered what he would do without her if the worst happened and Rownar destroyed her. How would he ever let her go? Though they never spoke of it, he assumed she knew as he did that this could well be a stolen season, and that did not mean they would both still be alive at the end of it all. Would he survive a life without her in it? Why should he have to? She was his, and he was hers. In his more reckless, honest, braver moments, he would decide that was that and he would ask for her hand. Then his more prudent side would rear its head, and all the rational reasons for not offering for her would present themselves. In the end, he told himself he would wait, at least until the damn dragon hunting her was dead. Then, if the gods were good and they both survived, perhaps he would speak his heart.

Until that happy day, he would spend as much time as possible showing how much he loved her and bask in the warmth of her affection. He would take advantage of every moment the gods granted them and not waste even one.

With this thought uppermost in his mind, he went to her.

****

The tenor of their joining that night was what Morgan could only describe as fervent. Connor's gaze was avid, his whole demeanor keen, and his eagerness unmistakable. His touch was more ardent than ever, and he took her with passion and zeal as if he could not get enough of her and did not ever want to let her go. After they each relished a lengthy, heated climax, he simply held her.

When she turned her head to see his face, the look of utter longing in his expression all but stopped her heart. It seemed he was yearning for something eminently desirable just out of reach. How could she remain silent?

"What is it? What's wrong? Please tell me."

"I want to marry you. It's what I have wanted from the first. I know that now. In a perfect world, I would. And this is not something I intended to speak of tonight."

Morgan's heart felt as though it was going to burst right out of her chest, but she chose her words with care. "Why can't you?"

"For so many reasons. This battle, first and foremost, as you know. Do I even have the right to bind my life to yours when I might die at any moment? Then there is my lack of royal blood. Your father would be a fool to allow it. Even though he, in his mercy, decided not to execute me for treason, you must have dozens of far more eligible suitors. Added to all of that, I wasn't sure if, given the life I have led, whether… whether you would have me."

Her bursting heart soared, and she framed his face with her hands. "You are the strongest man I know. In spite of the hard life you have led, you are decent. I love you more with every breath I take. You are the one man I want to spend the rest of my life with."

A light dawned in those beautiful eyes she cherished so well, yet his expression remained wary. "But what about your father?"

She waved this away. "Oh, pish, when push comes to shove, my father wants my happiness. Nothing is more important to him."

"And the coming battle?"

"I will only be stronger knowing I'm to be your wife."

For a moment, Connor did not speak, and when he did, it was in a voice gone hoarse. "Morgan, I would do anything to make you my wife, anything except hurt you. Leaving you alone in the world? How could that do anything else?"

"At least I will have been yours, even if it is for a short while. And perhaps I won't be alone; perhaps there will be a baby."

His entire body trembled. "Is there?"

"Not yet. But I long to have your child."

"I want us to have a family. I won't deny it." He sighed. "You seem to have an answer for everything."

She beamed at him. "So I do."

He regarded her, his expression solemn, until her smile faded. "Be very certain, Morgan. If I ask and you say yes, I will hold you to it. Once we are betrothed, I won't let you go, even if it is the right thing to do. I am an honorable man, but I am not that honorable."

She merely raised her eyebrows.

"Let it be on your head then, as much as mine." He inhaled a deep breath and grasped her hand in his. "Morgan Elizabeth Talbot, will you do me the honor of becoming my wife? Will you make me the happiest of men?"

"Yes! Yes! Yes!"

Drawing her into a fierce embrace, he kissed her, sealing their betrothal. Then he opened the drawer of the bedside table and drew out a small object. It was a simple gold band with a tiny pearl in an old-fashioned setting in the center.

"This belonged to my mother. It is all I have left of her. Will you wear it?"

"But if it is the one thing you have left of her, I couldn't possibly—"

"She would want you to have it."

"If you are sure, then I would be honored." He slipped the ring onto her shaking hand, then kissed her knuckles.

When he released her fingers, she held them out to admire the exquisite jewel and let it catch the light.

"Now, the one final thing left to resolve is what in the name of all the gods to say to your father."

She snuggled back against him. "You'll think of something. You always do."

He snorted at that, but soon enough, he was asleep in her arms

.

Chapter Thirteen

Connor could not remember ever being so nervous. As he awaited the king's arrival in the audience chamber the next afternoon, he rehearsed what he would say. Or he tried to. Every time he settled on what he thought were the right words, other words, better words, would come to his mind. So he would rethink and rephrase over and over again until his head spun. In the end, he decided to go with the unvarnished truth.

"Good day, Connor. What can I do for you? The training of our army is progressing well, I trust?"

"Exceedingly well, Majesty. But I am here to speak to you on a matter which concerns the princess."

"Oh? Do please go ahead."

"Last evening, I proposed to your daughter, Sire."

James's jaw tightened. "I see. You have taken my advice and made a decision, it seems. And did she accept?"

"She did." Connor beamed. He could not help it. "She loves me and wishes to marry me. With your blessing, I would very much like to marry her."

"Ever since you encountered each other in my audience chamber, I have suspected this was coming. When you began bedding my daughter with some regularity, we spoke of it, although the conversation was brief. I could have put a stop to it any number of ways, yet I chose not to. So now I must ask you formally and in all seriousness, why do you want to wed my daughter?"

"Many would want her fortune, her power or both. I do not. I have no problem being her consort. I want to rule beside her, not over her. How many can say that? I do not want to change her. I desire the woman who was prepared to take on Rownar single-handedly, the woman who took her fate into her own hands. It is my great good fortune that her destiny is inextricably linked with mine. For this and so many other reasons, I am willingly bound to her, whether married or no. Most importantly, I love her with all my heart, and every piece I have left of my broken, damaged soul belongs to her."

James said nothing, so Connor soldiered on.

"I am painfully aware I have little to offer. I am more than cognizant there are other matches which would be far more politically expedient, but I promise you, I can make her happy."

James held up a hand. "You have done more for my kingdom, for my child, and for me personally than anyone. By training her, you may well have saved my daughter's life. That is a debt I can never repay. In addition, I happen to like you. I will speak to Morgan and learn of her feelings on the matter myself. Once I have, I will inform you both of my decision. For now, you may go."

Connor resigned himself to a wait, bowed, and departed.

****

The very same afternoon, James called his daughter to his private apartments. When she arrived, he bade her make herself comfortable in his sitting room. He sat in a red brocade wingback chair while Morgan settled herself on the settee covered in golden silk.

"Connor has asked for your hand, as you knew he would."

"He spoke to me first, and I accepted; I am sorry about that, Father, but I—"

"Such a breach of protocol does not concern me. The one thing that does is what you want. Are you certain it is him you want? You are still young enough, after all, and there are other men, men of power and influence, attractive men, intelligent men. You have seen next to nothing of the world, daughter; perhaps there is another man out there for you that you have yet to meet."

Morgan shook her head. "There is no other man, not for me."

"Still, there is no rush."

"Father, I love him, and I do not want to waste any more time. I am not some heedless girl who has no notion of her own heart. If it were not for needing to finish this and defeat Rownar at last, I would marry him tomorrow."

His jaw went slack with the shock. "You are seldom so impulsive. He must be a very rare sort of man."

"He is. He loves me. I have never been loved so well before. And it isn't in just his words. It's in his actions. It's in the very fabric of who he is. He has treated me as an equal in this fight when few could or would have. He is honest, even when it isn't easy. He is loyal to a fault, and he is the bravest man I have ever met."

"I understand." James laughed a little and held up a hand. "No need to enumerate the rest of his many virtues. I have encountered more than a few of them myself." He cleared his throat and ran a hand through his hair in an awkward sort of way. "Forgive the intrusion on your privacy, but I must ask. The bedding, all is well there?"

A hot blush rose in Morgan's cheeks. "It is."

"This is what you truly want?" he asked once more. Even though his heart broke a little at the idea of letting his only child go, her happiness was important to him above all.

"It is. I cannot imagine my life without him. I cannot, I will not give myself to any other."

"Then, I will consider it, of course."

Morgan put her hands to her lips to stifle her involuntary gasp. Her smile blinded, and her eyes sparkled with joy.

James looked at her with an indulgent smile. "Now calm down and give me a night to sleep on it. I will breakfast with you and your prospective suitor in the morning, and I will have an answer then."

After she hugged him within an inch of his life and kissed him on both cheeks, Morgan dashed happily off, presumably to inform Connor.

****

When Morgan entered the dining room, she was not exactly nervous, but neither could she claim she was calm. Until her father formally approved and she heard the words with her own ears, she would remain edgy. His blessing meant a great deal to her, and while nothing would ever keep her from marrying Connor, she would far prefer to do so with her father's consent than without it.

The smaller, more-private dining room her father preferred was furnished with a table and chairs of maple wood and was large enough to seat ten. Morgan also favored it; it was so much cozier and far more comfortable than the grander public dining room, which was primarily used for more formal occasions involving heads of state and could seat as many as seventy-five people. Today, of all days, Morgan was grateful her father found it far too impersonal for everyday use.

She forced her steps to slow as she entered. Proper greetings were exchanged, and they sat.

As soon as they did, Morgan demanded, "Well?"

James shook his head. "Impatient as always, eh, daughter?"

When she said nothing in reply but instead glared at him, he shook his head again. "I agree to your marriage with two stipulations. First, you take care of my daughter, Connor. Love her and honor her. Second, allow me to throw you the grandest engagement ball ever seen, only to be surpassed by the most magnificent wedding."

"I swear upon my life; I will love and care for your precious child all my days."

James leveled his steely stare at his prospective son-in-law. "See that you do." He directed his attention back to Morgan.

Happy tears filled her eyes and spilled over. "Truly?"

"Truly."

She rose from the table and wrapped her arms around his neck.

"Be happy, daughter," he whispered as he kissed

her cheek.

Connor rose then executed a deep bow. "I am forever in your debt, Sire."

"Not as long as you honor your vows. Or, if you must, consider it recompense for the shots I took at you. The damage I did to your pretty face when you returned here was perhaps unwarranted."

Connor inclined his head then he kissed Morgan's hand. Before he released her, he held her gaze a moment. As he brushed his lips against hers, she wondered, was fate repaying her for all the years of loneliness, isolation, and struggle? If so, she hoped it would continue because, for once, all was right with her world.

He broke the contact and steered her back to her chair. Once she resettled into the comfortable seat, her father demanded, "So this engagement ball, how soon can we have it?"

Morgan beamed.

****

The rose garden at Belmere was celebrated far and wide. It contained more roses per square foot than any other garden in the known world and of every conceivable hue.

Each of the four pathways had a different shade of rose along it and were named accordingly—the white drive, the pink avenue, the red way, and the yellow lane. Each color pertained to the four directions of the compass: to the east was white drive, west was yellow lane, go north to follow the red way, and head south to the pink avenue. A clearing in the center included those four colors and countless more besides. It was a riotous rainbow of every shade when the flowers were in bloom.

Since the rose was by far her favorite flower, Morgan was exceedingly fond of the place. As a child, she had played there with her mother, and some of her happiest memories occurred in the rose garden. She still went there often to breathe in the sweet scent and drink in the beauty. So it was the most natural thing in the world to have Trista meet her there, where the roses were beginning to bloom.

As they entered the garden to enjoy the fine spring morning, she held out both hands to her new but very dear friend. "I have wonderful news. I am to be married. Connor asked for my hand, I accepted, and my father has given his blessing to the match."

"Congratulations! I wish you joy." Trista caught the princess in a tight embrace.

Once Trista released her, Morgan tucked Trista's arm about hers, and they strolled. "Now, all we have to do is get that handsome magician of yours to propose."

"Oh, Morgan, I am not sure he ever will or even if he should. When we were together before, we were not good for each other, and that's understating the matter."

"But what about now? I assumed things were going well between you. You told me things were very different."

"So they are, but I suppose a small part of me is waiting for it all to go to hell the way it did before. Things are better between us now than they have ever been, and I love him more than I ever have, but still..."

"Trista, you must stop dwelling on the past. Focus instead on the present and the future. To that end, will you be my bridesmaid?"

A smile broke over Trista's face. "I would be

honored."

Morgan all but clapped her hands in excitement. "Wonderful! There is so much to do. You must help me with all the details, not just for the wedding but for the engagement ball as well, which will be held before we know it."

So they made a start as they ambled along in air filled with the fragrance of roses.

****

As promised, the ball was unlike anything the country had ever seen. Nobles travelled from miles around to dance attendance on the princess and her chosen consort in a very literal sense.

Years had passed since Trista attended such an event. She had forgotten she had liked them well enough in her first youth. Unfortunately, those occasions grew stale and empty after a while, perhaps due to their frequency or, more likely, because the people were all the same. Such events had been her mother's lifeblood, however, and her father renovated the old manor house with this in mind. The ballroom there was a touch less grand than the one she found herself in tonight.

Numerous candles in their wall sconces cast soft light upon perfumed ladies in gowns of such elegance and richness that to look upon them was an unmitigated pleasure to the eye. Even the men were resplendent in their formal attire. Rich velvets of navy, brown, deep forest green, and black set up a favorable contrast with the pastels of yellow, pink, and sky blue most of the women wore. The chandelier, which hung from the ceiling in the middle of the room, was lit, and the crystals sparkled like diamonds. Already, couples whirled around the flagstone floor in time to a waltz played by the musicians in the far corner.

Since the spring night was fine, the terrace doors all along one wall were open, so the guests might have access to that area if they wished to take the air. More likely they wished to court, she suspected, but as she was happy enough with her own courtship at the present, she was not disposed to mind.

As soon as he entered, she knew it. Sebastian drew her attention like a magnet. It was all she could do to keep her body from following suit. Thank the gods she did not have to struggle for long. His eyes were for her alone as he crossed the room as if he were as drawn to her as she was to him.

He bowed. "Might I have this dance, my lady?"

Trista looked first to her princess for permission, which was soon granted via a slight inclination of the head. Then her gaze clapped right back on Sebastian. "The pleasure would be all mine, sir."

Trista had not had any notion Sebastian was such a wonderful dancer. She had taken lessons in her previous life as a noble woman of good family, before admitting who she was and accepting the magic in her blood. Inevitably, she danced far better than all the poor partners she often had. Tonight, with him, for once there was no need for her to lead. He was so very skilled and, sure at last she had found the right partner, she relaxed. It felt as though she were flying yet held safe in his arms.

"How is it we never danced before when you do it so well?"

He smiled. "We were, if you recall, far too busy doing other things."

Remembering magic, spells, and the greatest enchantment of all, him, she smiled back. "I suppose you are right. Still, we should do this more often. We should make a point of it, because you are wonderful."

To prove it, he whirled her into a tight turn and twirled her over the floor.

When Sebastian waltzed her right out of the ballroom and onto the terrace, it seemed quite natural and right. She did not question it. Her one coherent thought was that there were all sorts of magic and that this evening was full of the best kind.

When the music ended, instead of bowing, he held her gaze. "What are we doing?" Sebastian asked. Then he laughed a little. "You would think by now we would know the answer to that, yet it seems one or the other of us is always asking that question. Still, I can't keep myself from asking it again now."

Trista tried to coax her pleasure-addled mind to work. But all she managed was, "We are enjoying each other, as we have been these past weeks."

"But what if I want more? More than just having you in my bed? What would you say?"

"You said there were things you had to decide first. Like if this is what we should do. Are you saying you have decided?"

"I'm saying I don't know if it is what we should do, but I know I need you and love you. I think, no, I know, I could not do any of this without you. I am saying the more that I want is you with me, always, for the rest of my life, however long that might be. I want you to marry mc."

Trista could hardly bear to hope, but she couldn't help it. "Are you sure? You are so certain I have changed, that we both have?"

"We are better, stronger than before. Can't you feel it?"

Tears filled her eyes. "Yes, I can. I wasn't sure if you did. Even more, I wasn't sure if I ought to trust it."

"You should. Say you will be my wife once we get through this."

She shook her head. Sebastian started to protest, but she placed a finger to his lips. "I don't want to wait. We have wasted enough time already. Too much. Let's marry now before we risk our lives going up against the strongest dragon in the world.

He beamed. "Oh, I think that can be arranged."

A few glorious minutes later, when Sebastian returned her to the ballroom, she could not contain her joy. It must have showed in spite of her efforts to mask it because Morgan noticed.

"You are glowing," Morgan commented from behind her fan. "What's happened?"

"Something wonderful which I will not share right now. Tonight is yours and yours alone. My news can wait. I promise to tell you very soon, but for now, your betrothed is headed this way."

"Oh, come Trista, you must tell me."

But Connor bowed before them and asked Morgan to dance, saving Trista from a reply.

****

The wedding ceremony held a month later was simple and beautiful, as Trista wished. The single indulgence she allowed herself was her dress. Morgan's seamstresses worked day and night on a silk-and-lace creation of the palest sky blue, which went well with the pink roses and baby's breath in her hair. Connor and

Morgan stood as witnesses for them. The archbishop officiated, and James was the only other person in attendance.

The tiny chapel, decorated with violets and white roses, resembled a bower. Candlelight shimmered down on the evening ceremony as they spoke their vows. With eyes for no one but each other, Sebastian and Trista promised to love and cherish one another for the rest of their lives.

In spite of the unvoiced but still evident disapproval of the archbishop, they also celebrated a tradition far older and more pagan. After exchanging the customary vows, Sebastian took a dagger, blessed and prepared for the purpose, and sliced a small cut into his palm.

"My heart is laid at thy feet. With my body, I thee worship. All I have and all I am is yours. Let our blood bind us, each to the other. Let our flesh and bone knit. Let us be as one from this day forth."

Trista cut her own palm, then repeated the words. With braided silver cord, the bishop bound their hands together.

"I now pronounce you husband and wife," the bishop intoned. "You may kiss the bride."

More than happy to obey, Trista's lips met Sebastian's in a kiss, both passionate and pure. Joy filled her heart and soul, as she joined her life to his.

After the ceremony, they adjourned to James's private apartments to consume a light supper of white wine, chicken, and fresh fruit to celebrate with those who mattered most.

As the evening wore on, the bridal couple longed to be alone. At last, James declared it was time for the bride and bridegroom to take their leave.

As Sebastian and Trista prepared to go, Morgan grasped Trista's hands then kissed her cheek. "Be happy, my dear friend."

****

Alone with Sebastian in his chambers, Trista strolled about, feeling a trifle dazed. She took in very little of the room but retained a brief impression of heavy oak furniture, fabrics in a wine red and gray, and little else. The masculine effect created suited him very well.

Coming to her side, her new husband offered her a glass of wine. "Are you all right? You seem a little flummoxed."

She focused her wayward wits and smiled. "I am fine. I'm more than fine. I am, however, finding it a bit hard to believe that we did it, that I am your wife. From almost the moment I saw you, I hoped and dreamed, of course, but I never ever believed it would actually happen. Now, here we are."

"Yes, here we are indeed." He poured a glass of sherry for himself.

"I won't ask you if you have any regrets because it is far too late for them."

"Regrets? About marrying you? I have none. No, we've found each other again, and that is all that matters." He lifted his glass in a toast, and they both drank.

"I am glad." She hesitated, then said, "I have so many regrets. Not about tonight, about before."

"Tonight is a new beginning. We can't forget or discount the past, nor should we, but this is a time to put it aside." Gently, he took her glass, set it on the table, then placed his own beside it. "Nothing, not dark magic or dragons or the coming battle are part of our world right now. Tonight, the past and the future do not exist. The one thing that does is you and I, together. Nothing else matters right now."

With a wave of a hand and the glow of magic, the roof above them grew transparent, leaving only the sky full of stars. Trista gasped; she simply couldn't help it. He rarely used his power so, but when he did, it was always a treat. A delightful indulgence, an extravagant luxury she reveled in.

He could not make time stop. Even a sorcerer does not have that privilege, but he could make it slow. This he did for them both on this one night.

She was his now, and he, thank the gods, was hers, and they would both relish it. The realization that they would never be apart again, that nothing less than death could separate them, made Trista feel curiously free. Even though she was more than aware death might come, her heart was light as air. Nothing could dim her joy. Unable to contain it, she used her magic to brighten the very stars he had revealed until they shown like the sun. His eyes widened, then, with a besotted smile on his lips, he kissed her.

If they had been in sync before, that was nothing compared to now. He knew exactly how to touch her, just when to deepen the kiss. She, in her turn, knew the precise moment to move them forward, closer physically and emotionally to each other. She knew when to offer herself up to him, body and soul, and did without hesitation.

Clothes disappeared, and his hands were everywhere while his mouth caught her breast. Liquid fire raced down her veins as his tongue laved one nipple in slow, wet passes, and his finger and thumb lightly tweaked the other in counterbalance. Without conscious thought, her body made this perfect rhythm her own. She became a willing servant to it and him.

****

When Sebastian lifted his head, Trista moaned in protest. He bent for one last long, slow lick, then focused his attention elsewhere, like the apex of her thighs. Skimming the tips of his fingers over her silken skin from waist to knee, he shuddered. Gripping her hips, he led her to his bed, and they toppled onto it in a heap. As his palm seized her knee, it seemed the most natural thing in the world that she would part her legs. He brushed his fingers over her, then into her, and found she was ready for him.

One deep shuddering breath later, their bodies joined. In and out, over and over, each time, spikes of pleasure prickled over his skin as he slid into her. Even better was their steadily increasing strength and duration. The realization that this sort of body-and-soul intimacy would be theirs for the taking for the rest of their life together rolled through him. There was nowhere else he wanted to be and nothing else he wanted to be doing.

Overcome with emotion and overwhelmed by sensation, the raw power of his culmination stunned him. He had no choice but to surrender to it and her. She was still right there, with him every step of the way, even in the heart of the maelstrom. As her climax began, the stars brightened and pulsed. His completion triggered hers, and she followed him a heartbeat later into utter ecstasy.

As they returned to earth, the little points of light dimmed. Sometime later, he was not sure quite when the roof reappeared over them. For the longest time, he held her, savoring their connection, one of both body and soul. To feel so much a part of another human being, to know the connection was strong and perhaps even, given the magic in their blood, eternal, was amazing. To love and be loved was the sole thing that mattered in this mad world. He knew then he would do anything to protect it, to keep it strong. Anything.

"I love you, wife."

"And I love you, husband."

Wholly at peace for perhaps the first time in his long life, he wrapped his arms around her and slept.

****

Later that evening, as Morgan and Connor took their ease in her bed, she posed a question.

"There is something I have wanted to ask you for some time. One day, I will be queen. Does it bother you?"

"That I am to be your consort rather than king, you mean?" Connor shrugged. "Not in the least."

"And thank the gods for it. I am not complaining, but are you certain your feelings on this issue won't change?"

He held her gaze. "Morgan, I have never wanted to be king. I wouldn't know where to start, anyway. You, on the other hand, were born to it. Born and bred to rule with the skill and compassion I see in you every day."

"Thank you for the compliment, but what of you? What do you want? How do you see our life together? Tell me, and as your future queen, I will do my best to make it happen."

A myriad of emotions swept through him, gratitude at her consideration being but one. He was moved that she would value his happiness so highly. Admiration and anticipation also played a part. For the first time, it sunk in that his life would soon be his own, and he could make of it whatever he willed.

He refocused on the question at hand. Such a serious, far-from-idle query deserved due consideration, and so he pondered for some minutes before answering. "I think, for a time, I want to enjoy a bit of peace. No dragons to battle, no travel to the next village. Nights spent in the same bed, your bed, and mornings waking in your arms. All day spent in whatever pleasurable pursuit takes our fancy. Time to just…be."

Her smile grew tender and a touch wistful. "That sounds lovely. But I know you, such a life might satisfy you for a good long while, but not forever."

"Not forever," he agreed. "There are a thousand things I could do. I can and will continue the training of the army, subject to your approval, of course. Otherwise, I want time to discover who I might become. I have been a dragon slayer all my adult life. I don't know how to be anything else. I am not even sure whether I can become something different or will even want to in the end, but I think it's high time I try. I love horses, training them, breeding them, racing them. Perhaps I'll explore that. I wouldn't mind seeing something more of the world without a battle at the end of the journey. Hell, I would like a bit of time to read something other than books on dragon fighting or strategy."

"You won't miss it? The adventure, the visceral excitement of hunting down a dragon? I confess I worry

I might, and I have only been a slayer for a few weeks."

One decisive shake of his head put paid to that idea. "I very much doubt it. That life, well, it lost its appeal for me long ago. I have lost my taste for it entirely, and I am ready to embark on the brand-new adventure of being your husband. It is not any less dangerous or unpredictable a proposition, and well, I know it." He grinned, and she humphed.

After a moment, however, he sobered. "I also want to be here to advise you when called on and to support you when necessary. I want to be a true partner." He tilted up her chin then placed a gentle kiss on her lips.

After a moment's contemplation, Connor asked the same question of her. "And what of you? What do you want? What do you wish for out of life? Soon, you will be free of Rownar. Have you thought about what comes next?"

She pursed her lips. "I want much the same as you, I suppose. I want to be free and to know my people are likewise. When I think in more detail about it, I realize for years, this kingdom has been devastated, all but shattered, by the dragon scourge. I want to repair my realm. I want to heal the very heart of it while healing my own."

"That is a most noble ambition, and I would be honored to work along with you to reach it. If you wish it, I will rule beside you, never over you, as your second in command, if you like. I can and will carry out any and all of your wishes."

"And this is, in truth, what you want to do?"

"It is. In all ways, I am your majesty's most willing and devoted servant."

To prove it, he rose and walked to the door of her

chamber, turned the large metal key in the lock with a distinct click, then rejoined her in her bed.

****

The morrow would bring battle. They all knew it. Weeks after their return to Belmere castle, Rownar had at last been sighted on the eastern plain. Having a better idea of his approximate location would help when casting the spell, and being assured he would be well within range of the song was a boon. The time was now.

Restless, Morgan slipped out of bed and left Connor sleeping. She found herself wandering the library, always a place of comfort and refuge for her. Caged as she had been from her childhood onward, she soon discovered the best way to be free was to lose herself in a good book. Fortunately, being royalty, she had access to thousands of volumes in a library filled with histories, plays, mathematics, geographical studies, and even novels. Fairy tales of knights and ladies, chivalry, and dragons fired her imagination and broadened her narrow world. The two-story room was lined with bookcases made of wood polished to a gleam. It was well-lit by windows during the day and by sconces holding scented candles during the night. Leather couches to curl up on completed the picture. It was the most extensive library in the kingdom, arguably the world, and it was her playground of choice.

Choosing a book was easy, focusing her attention and remaining engaged was far more difficult. Even though the novel was a favorite, on her third attempt to read the first page without having taken in a word, she gave it up as a bad job and put it back on the shelf. She was about to return to bed when the sound of the door opening stopped her.

Her father entered. "Can't you sleep, daughter?"

She shook her head. "I am far too edgy. Everything hinges on tomorrow's battle, and I cannot stop going over and over it in my head. Is there anything we have missed? Anything else we might do to prepare?"

"If there is anything we've left undone, I can't see it. There is little to do now but wait. And pray we all come through this alive."

"I suppose you are right. Good evening, Father."

She got several paces. Then James stopped her.

"Morgan, no matter what happens, I am proud of you. If your mother were here, she would say the same."

"Thank you. That means so much to me. I sometimes wonder what she would think of all this, and I question whether she would agree with some of the decisions I've made. It helps hearing from the one who knew her best and esteemed her so highly that she would be proud."

"You should know also that she loved you more than anything, and so do I."

Morgan hurried over and embraced him. "I love you, too."

They held tight to one another for one more moment. Then, her father withdrew. He sniffled a bit but tried to conceal the fact by wiping surreptitiously at his nose and turning away.

"You ought to try to sleep now. So should I. We all need to be at our best when we go up against Rownar and his kin."

"Yes. Good night then, Father."

He kissed her forehead, and she headed back to her

rooms.

****

"What's troubling you?"

Leaning back into the pillows, hands crossed beneath his head, Sebastian looked over at Trista. Only she would ask such a question because she alone would realize there was indeed something troubling him. Sebastian was not sure if he was grateful or annoyed.

"Aside from the fact that we will be going up against the strongest dragon in the world tomorrow? What if it doesn't work? So much depends on our part in this succeeding. If it fails…" Horrifying images of that eventuality raced through Sebastian's mind, and there was nothing he could do to stop them.

"There are other factors involved."

"Yes, but…"

"It all hinges on us, on the effectiveness of our spells and the strength of our magic. Sebastian, we have done everything we can. We have done all it is within our power to do. We have tried our best to make certain all goes as planned, that our incantations work, that the potion is indeed potent. For once, I have used my powers for good, and no matter the outcome, I am glad of it. The rest is in the hands of the gods."

"The fate of our kingdom, perhaps even of the whole bloody world, rests on this. And while I agree with all you just said, I can't help being a little tense."

She raised her eyebrows at him. "A little tense?"

His lips curved up a bit. "Hmmm, maybe a bit more than a little," he admitted. As he felt some of the very tension they spoke of ease, he decided he was, after all, grateful she knew him so well.

"I should say so." She settled herself in a more-comfortable position on the bed. "Try to relax and get some sleep. We have to be awake long before dawn, and it is best we are both rested."

"I can think of one sure way to relax."

"Oh, can you, now?" She faced him. "All right then, husband, but you'd best be quick." She sighed, but her lips twitched and her eyes danced.

"Oh, I can be quick, but I think, in the end, you'll want me to take a very, very long time."

****

When Morgan returned to her chamber, she found, to her surprise, that Connor was no longer asleep.

"Morgan, there you are. I woke, and you weren't beside me. Is everything all right?"

"I was restless, that's all. I went to the library and tried to read but couldn't concentrate. My father joined me, and we spoke for a while. I did not mean to worry you. I'm so sorry."

"No, no, it's fine. You're sure you're all right?"

"I am still worried about tomorrow."

"So am I, but we have done all we can. You know that better than anyone."

"True, I have been planning this for years. It has been my entire life for the past few months. If we fail, I don't know what I'll do. That's assuming I live through it, which is not a foregone conclusion."

"We won't fail. You can't possibly believe that we will."

"No, I don't. I have not come this far and done all I have done to fail."

"Brilliant." He gathered her close and kissed the top of her head. "One way or another, it will all be over tomorrow."

She longed to speak again, to open her heart to him one last time, but before she could, he put a finger to her lips.

"Shh, no more talk, not tonight. Try to rest." He framed her face in his hands and kissed her with a gratifying thoroughness. Then, with a sigh, he settled her against him and shut his eyes.

In spite of the uncertainty of the morrow, Morgan felt safe and loved. Taking strength from that, she relaxed mind and body, and slept.

Chapter Fourteen

All was in place. Sunrise was chosen as the moment to begin after much debate and discussion. Dragons were at their weakest, and white magic at its strongest then. It was something to do with the light overcoming the darkness in nature as well as magic.

Shivering a tad in the pre-dawn chill, Trista and Sebastian spilled the potion onto the ground to form a protective circle, one which would shield the maidens from all harm while they sang. Once done, Sebastian nodded in satisfaction.

"Good. This will hold. Now it is time to prepare the ground on which we will capture them."

Thrice, they pronounced verses in the old language, then thrice more in their native tongue as they went round to form a perfect sphere, he in a clockwise direction, Trista, counter-clockwise. Both of them poured out the potion they had earlier had so much trouble concocting as they went. The ring they created, glowed.

Sebastian took the path leading up the hill to their designated vantage point, and Trista followed. From there, they would create the illusion which would draw the dragons even closer. Lastly, they would cast the final spell to create the net that would trap any dragon who flew within it. That spell, the final trap, they left dormant, ready to be brought to full life once the first of the dragons they lured arrived.

The illusion of deepest, darkest desire was a simple one, but only in comparison to the other magic they would use to create the net to hold the dragons captive and tamed. All things considered, that spell was a rather complicated one. Yet its complexity did not worry Sebastian. He recognized the scope of his own power just as he recognized Trista's. Both were an integral part of him, and he trusted that their combined strength would be sufficient, and so it was. Together, they conjured the illusion, the protective circle, and the trap as well, and though it required effort to maintain it, they succeeded.

As they waited in silence, he held Trista's hand. She was the one solid thing in a world about to go mad, and he hoped to be the same for her.

At last, the first rays of sunlight appeared, and on the princess's signal, she and the maidens started to sing. Even from their perch high above, Sebastian could hear the terrible beauty of the song.

Come to us, dragons; you have naught to fear.

All we are and all we have are yours.

Come drink of the wine of my soul; come taste the flesh of my heart.

Never to separate the whole, my sisters and I offer up every part.

Come to me, dragons, and tarry here.

All I am and all I have is yours.

Hear my song, listen to my voice, and let my spirit guide.

Come to me and set all else aside.

Sebastian detected their approach first. The dark magic burgeoning and rising in the air was, to him, unmistakable. He beckoned to Trista.

"The dragons are coming. We need to cast the final spell now!"

She lifted a hand at the same moment he lifted his. "Are you ready?"

Trista nodded. Gazes locked, powers melding and merging, they conjured the magical net as they chanted in unison. Blue light from their fingertips combined, pulsed up and outward, then rained down to form the solid infrastructure of the net. As one, they spoke the words of the spell.

Let dragon's evil be forever enclosed within this space

Captured and bound to this place.

So our people no longer live in fear

Let this net we cast set all dragons apart

And protect all we hold dear.

Keep them safe by our art.

This wish is precious to mine and me,

As we will, so mote it be.

The wind rose. What they had not expected was the sheer number of dragons, first ten, then twenty, then more. At that point, Sebastian stopped counting.

Each and all hurtled toward them at speed. When they first saw the illusion created to tempt them, the creatures slowed. Incapable of fighting the song and the illusion, the dragons circled toward the ground like moths to a flame, unable to resist.

****

Waves of heat from dragon flame, gusts of wind made by dragon wings, and the force of magic buffeted them on the hilltop. Never had Trista used so much of her power before. The effort of spinning the enchantment, casting the protective spell and weaving the net, plus the energy necessary to keep it all going, was monumental. Not even at the height of her dark magical power had she ever expended so much energy. She flagged, then slipped.

"There are too many of them. I had no idea there were such a great number of bloody dragons in the whole world, much less in our country. I am not strong enough. I can't hold it!" She gritted her teeth.

"You can. You are the most stubborn person I know," Sebastian insisted.

Frantic, she shook her head. "No, I can't!"

His beautiful mouth curled in a snarl. "Damn it, woman! You can, and you will hold! Because if you do not, you will die, and then I shall. Those people down there are depending on us. King James, the princess, and Connor are all expecting us to come through, and that is just for a start. Countless lives will be lost if we do not succeed. You may not be capable of doing this alone, but we can do it together. Don't you dare give up!"

Bearing down and digging deep for strength, she followed her instincts and did as he ordered. She searched her mental and physical reserves and found, to her surprise, there were still some to be had. Or perhaps she was tapping into his strength, the strength which was always there so she could call on it whenever she needed it most. Either way, she held. She even started to feel energized by the experience. Much as she had been when practicing dark magic, she was aware of a severe depletion of her reserves, but didn't actually feel it, nor could she bring herself to care, not in that moment. All that mattered was that he was with her, and she could go on doing this magic forever.

What was more, it was working, and that was beyond encouraging. Dragons called by the song were then captivated by it, as well as by the illusion of all their desires, as planned. Once close enough, the net, precisely as predicted, caught them. So long as they could manage to cope with them all, the whole strategy might, in fact, work.

****

Deep in his new, hidden cave, the song pulled Rownar out of the depths of sleep. In the dark of his lair, he rose, compelled to do so, like all of his kind. With a roar and an amazing spurt of flame, he headed for the surface. Flying as fast as the wind, healed at last and at full strength once more, he shot out of the dark mouth of the cavern into the open air.

One thought dominated his dark, primitive mind: revenge. He would have his vengeance against Morgan and her new protector. Somehow, he was certain she was part of the song which pervaded his mind. He would claim all the song promised then end her.

With that, he took flight in the vanishing dark.

****

Even through the chaos, the smoke, and flame of dragons, Morgan could see that things were going as planned. Too many dragons to count filled the sky while more arrived with every moment. Perhaps half of these were trapped in the net all but immediately. The other half were captured after only the slightest twinge of resistance.

As she sang the dragon song, Morgan concentrated her entire being on calling Rownar to her. Still, he had yet to appear. She wondered whether an injury might be keeping him away. Then her link with him roared back into life.

Close, he had to be close. Singing all the while, she searched the sky. Finally, a dark spot appeared on the horizon, and she knew it was Rownar.

Swifter than any other creature on the planet, he closed the distance between them in no time at all. As he executed a wide, banking turn, she unsheathed her sword,

****

Rownar travelled far but swiftly, until at last he found the place. Before his eyes, gold shimmered, and jewels sparkled. Atop great piles of it, maidens were perched, ready and utterly in his thrall.

But there was something wrong. Even in his clouded brain, he could discern that much. If there was anything he knew to be true of humans, it was that they never went down without a fight. They never just surrendered, not in all the centuries he had dominated them. Yet all this was here for the taking? But the song made any kind of rational thought difficult, if not impossible. It was far easier to float along and enjoy the beauty of the music. Curious, he noted the other maidens who stood by. These were the source of the song filling his ears, his mind, and every fiber of his being.

Although a mist which he now suspected to be an illusion, somewhat obscured his vision, Rownar could still make out his fellow creatures. One by one, they landed, as tame as kittens, at the feet of the singers as soon as they got within range. Shaking his head to clear it, he fought the lure of both the song and the illusion. That music would be their downfall. It was a trap. The knowledge penetrated his brain in one blinding flash of instinct and intuition.

Straightaway, he spoke mind-to-mind with the other dragons, in particular with those still in flight. *"Crush them. Silence the song."*

For many of his brethren, it was too late; dozens were already captured. However, such was the strength of Rownar's will that the most resilient were able to draw on it and break free of the spell. Once they did, the dragons joined him in making his, Rownar's, command a reality. The dragons shot fire toward the singers. A magical shield rose around them. One purple dragon slammed straight into the force field. The impact sent the creature flying backward right into the net. Seeing this woke up still more of Rownar's companions and alerted them to the danger they were in. The other dragons also attempted to rush the singers. When they, too, found themselves caught within the silvery magical net, their unmitigated fury broke loose, but in vain.

Rownar fought with all the more ferociousness for that, and many of the other dragons not already confined followed suit. Fully breaking the hold of the song at last and not yet within the net, he lurched up, avoiding the magical trap, and, with an almighty roar, dove straight for Morgan.

****

Once Rownar appeared, and the dragons started to resist, James knew the moment had come.

Mounted on his stallion in full armor, he held a hand up high so all his soldiers might see it. "Attack!"

He and his troops thundered into a barrage of dragon fire.

****

Below, the whole chaotic scene was laid out before them like some diorama with smoke billowing through it. Although the bulk of his attention was on maintaining his magic, Sebastian watched closely all the happenings in the valley. So when Rownar arrived, he knew right away.

"Trista, do you think you have a bit of magic to spare?"

She threw a quick glance at him. "Not really. Why?"

"Look, in the east."

Rownar dove straight at the soldiers in formation as though for some specific target Sebastian could not see.

She must have known his thoughts right away because she shook her head before he could even speak. "Oh no, you can't be serious. You want to take him down? There's no way we can do it. Not with all of the other spells we have to worry about. It's not part of the plan, and with so many things in play right now, it's not a good idea. We cannot concentrate on a specific target, even if it is Rownar."

"We won't be able to take him out altogether, but we might damage him. I am talking about one short, swift burst of power from both of us. We might turn the tide of this entire battle. I have enough left for that. Do you?"

"I suppose it's worth a try."

Sebastian flashed her a grin. "On three, then. One. Two. Three!"

Two simultaneous bursts of bright blue magic hit Rownar squarely in the chest. As expected, it did not knock him out of the sky, not even close, but it did jostle him enough to spoil his aim, foiling his first flaming salvo at the army.

Sebastian whooped; he could not help it. "Good work! We stopped him, at least for now."

"We did, but let's not lose focus," Trista chided, her tone gentle yet reproving.

Sebastian sobered in an instant. "Right." He threw all of his power back into sustaining the spells, bolstered by their victory.

****

Connor used his shield to protect himself from the burst of flame Rownar shot at him, which, thank the gods, was somehow thrown off target. Employing his every skill, he exploited each and every technique he knew in order to survive. Beyond that, keeping Morgan safe by distracting Rownar was his first priority. Making sure the dragon did not go after her was paramount.

For a while, the plan worked. Rownar wanted Connor's blood almost as much as he craved Morgan's. A sweep of the dragon's tail, wide and unexpected, hit him. The backlash sent him careening.

An instant later, the world went black.

****

With Connor down in his daughter's defense, James's instincts took over. It was clear to him the creature was doing his best to get to Morgan and finish her. The fiendish brute took his wife years ago. He would be damned if he would allow it to take his daughter too. There had to be an end, and if he had his way, it would be now.

With a thunderous yell, he rushed Rownar. As he

hoped, he was a diversion. Rownar gave the king his full attention. The dragon shot fire in his direction.

Rownar swiped out at him with a front claw. The sheer force of the blow bore James to the ground. It was then he understood. The bastard meant to play with him before killing him. Forcing himself to his feet, he faced the beast. When he reared, James dashed forward with sword raised, striking a blow to Rownar's underbelly. Seconds later, Rownar retaliated and took a sizeable chunk out of his shoulder, bit again, then would not let go. James screamed. His body writhed in pain, and, desperate, he smashed his shield into the beast's snout.

Rownar shook him as though he were the rabbit to the dragon's hound. He lost hold of his shield. The ground rose before him with a speed he never could have imagined, and he hit with a bone-jarring thud.

The pain engulfed him as Rownar tore off a leg, then an arm, and cast him aside to turn his attention back to Morgan. He had very little time to think, only enough to offer a prayer to the gods for the safety of his daughter.

****

Connor came to with a face full of dirt and the roar of dragons ringing in his ears loud enough to deafen him. The shadow of one circled overhead. It was Rownar. With a groan and a curse, he hauled himself to his feet, drew his sword, and hurried to engage. As he raced forward, he caught a glimpse of gorgeous, thick brown hair flying, and his heart stopped. Morgan was face to face with the demon spawn who had been the bane of her whole existence and his. And, he realized, he would never make it to her in time to be of any help, not with his sword arm, in any case.

In one smooth, rapid move, he sheathed his sword. Then, with hands as steady as if he were shooting at a paper target, he caught up his crossbow, then nocked an arrow. Rownar hovered some twenty feet above the ground; wings splayed wide. Connor loosed the arrow. It tore through the delicate material of the wing. Rownar shrieked in fury and pain. His massive jaws snapped at Morgan as he went down but clamped shut on air.

****

Time slowed and seemed endless, but at last Connor reached her side. "Let's finish this," he said. "Together."

Bleeding profusely from various wounds and grounded now, Rownar writhed and spewed fire as far as he could. "You cannot escape me."

"No, it's you who cannot escape us," Morgan replied.

Together, they pierced his dark heart.

For a heartbeat, the connection between them flared and was even stronger than it had been before her first night with Connor. Through the link, Morgan experienced all of his fury, his refusal to accept his own downfall, and it flowed like acid in her veins. Then at the last, the realization of his final defeat and inevitable death crashed in upon him. As Rownar drew his last breath, the connection between them faded, then severed.

For one instant, she savored her victory. But it was not over yet, not anywhere close to being over yet. There were plenty of other dragons who still needed to be dealt with.

Needing energy, physical as well as magical, for

the battle, the other dragons feasted on Rownar's remains. The creatures ripped him to shreds, and Morgan knew they would not stop until every bit of dragon flesh was picked clean from his bones. Sickened, she turned her face away from the hideous sight.

She battled them while she suppressed both grief and triumph and did what Connor trained her to do. She fought, and, for a time, at least, that became her world.

Chapter Fifteen

The number of dragons arriving slowed. With no new dragons making an appearance, Sebastian began to hope, but it wasn't until long after Morgan and Connor destroyed Rownar and the rest were caught that he was sure the illusion could be shattered.

"We can let the illusion go now, Trista."

"You're certain?"

He studied her for a long moment. Her every muscle was locked tight, and sweat beaded on her forehead. Although her body was nearing the limits of its endurance, her mind was still fixed, determined and unwavering. It was clear she had taken his earlier advice to heart and would never give up. Not while she still had breath in her body. He stepped into her line of vision. When she did not react, didn't even blink, he touched her outstretched forearm, the channel of her power.

"It's all right. You can stop now, my love. It's over. We did it."

Her gaze shot to his. "We've won?"

"Yes. Rownar is dead. The rest are captured. No other dragons have arrived for over an hour."

"It's been that long? That's the last of them? Truly?"

He nodded. "The maidens will continue to sing for a time, and the spell of protection about them will remain until reconnaissance can be done so that there can be no question. As for the net entrapping the creatures, it can be closed. It will not fade, not for centuries. We have done what we set out to do. You can relax now. You've done so well. You can let go."

With gentle pressure, he encouraged her to lower her arm. By infinitesimal increments, the tension in her eased until, all at once, the last of it left her, and she sagged, her legs no longer able to support even her slight weight.

Sebastian sucked in a breath as he caught her by the upper arms to steady her. "I've got you," he murmured.

She drew in air. "It's done, and we are victorious. Thank the gods."

"Yes, praise be."

All at once, her expression stiffened, and she shifted back to look at him. "Are you hurt?"

"No, I am fine. Tired to the bone, but fine. You?"

She exhaled in relief, then assured him, "I am more exhausted than I have ever been in my whole life, but otherwise I'll do."

He smiled. "Splendid. We should join the others." Arms around her, supporting her weight, he led them slowly down the path back to the moor.

****

The battle lasted a day and a night. It took that long to get all the dragons captured, contained, and subdued. When it was finished, the sun rose over great devastation. Scorched earth, piles of ashes, burned corpses of men and two dragons, as well as singed grass, could be seen for miles around. The dragons seized remained still, as though both paralyzed and hypnotized.

The devastated landscape before her was shattering. The desolation profoundly saddened, and greatly distressed Morgan, and the grief she felt at the loss of her father was even deeper yet. Though she felt hollowed out, for the first time since her eighth birthday, she also felt free.

She had no idea how long she had been standing there when Connor joined her. Saying nothing, he put his arms around her and held her close.

After one long moment, however, he let her go. Once he released her, he knelt. "The king is dead. Long live the queen."

Shaken at seeing him thus, the knowledge that queen was exactly what she was now began to sink in. She held out a hand to him. Lowering his head, he kissed her blackened-and-bloody knuckles.

"I pledge you my fealty, from now until my death."

Morgan cleared her burning throat. "Rise, Sir Connor O'Malley, and know I am your liege lady, and I honor your devotion."

He got to his feet as his queen commanded, and after a moment, he offered her his arm as they walked through the carnage.

"Where are my father's remains?" she asked after they had gone some distance.

"His body has been brought to the castle. It is already being cleansed and prepared for burial, Majesty."

"And its condition now? Don't lie to me, Connor; I saw Rownar all but tear him apart."

He grimaced. "The physicians were able to put him back together, for the most part. They reattached his limbs and cleaned up superficial wounds. His face was, by the grace of the gods, unmarred. He is certainly not what he once was, but he is fit to be seen."

The vise-like grip pain and terror had on her heart eased at least a little, and Morgan managed a nod. "Thank you for seeing to all of this. I am constantly in your debt, it seems."

He touched a gentle hand to her cheek, then shook his head. "Not for such a thing as this, never. It was my honor and privilege to be of service to you and His Majesty. Is there anything more you would have me do? I stand ready to do anything Your Grace requires."

There was nothing more she wanted than to go home, clean off the filth, and rest, but she was queen now. There was much still to be done. "The wounded, are they being tended?"

"Yes, and most have been brought to the hospital tent as instructed, though there are some still in the field. Those are being carried in as we speak."

"Losses?"

"Few, Your Grace."

"Did any of the maidens die?"

"No, none. Only fifty of our soldiers died in battle. Some may yet die from their wounds, but we will do our utmost to prevent it."

Morgan sighed. Fifty lives lost. Less than she had feared and fewer than she had expected. "Praise be," she murmured. "May the gods watch over them and their families."

As they walked again, she said, "I want to see Sebastian and Trista as soon as possible. Where are they?"

"As to that, I cannot answer, but I can find out."

He turned to go, but she stopped him with a hand on his forearm. "No, send someone. I would have you near me a while."

"Of course." Connor signaled and a young soldier stepped forward. After he gave the man some murmured directives, the fighter set off.

Connor gave his full attention back to Morgan. "Daniel, there, will find them and bring them to the hospital tent. I thought you might wish to go there to meet them; that way you could be briefed on the condition of the wounded while we wait."

Morgan let out a breath and nodded. "An excellent notion. Lead on." They headed in the direction Connor indicated.

****

Sebastian and Trista arrived at the hospital tent, looking the worse for wear.

"Thank the gods you are both whole and unharmed," Morgan said as she embraced them.

"Report."

The order from their new queen was so brisk and succinct that Connor, Sebastian, and Trista were all taken aback.

After exchanging one swift look with Trista, Sebastian began. "The spell is holding, Your Majesty. Every dragon enticed here is now contained, unable to harm anyone or anything anymore, not even others of their kind."

This time Morgan's heart eased more than a fraction. "Excellent. What can you tell me about the strength of the spell over the long term? Will it wane?"

"In the normal course of things, such a spell would dissipate, but bearing in mind the long lives of dragons,

Sebastian and I accounted for that when we prepared it. In fact, that is part of what took us so long to create it and make it effective."

A slow grin curved her lips. "How long?"

"Ten centuries, give or take a decade." An answering smile played on Sebastian's lips.

"Aside from Rownar, were any other dragons killed?"

"One other, Majesty. A dragon called Pern died of his wounds about an hour ago. The rest are confined and tamed, quite unable to harm one another or anyone else," Connor said.

"Good. First, we must gather all our wounded from the field and bring them here. I understand that operation is already underway. Once it is done, those well enough to be transported should be prepared for travel. Then we can move out and go home. After that, burn the dead dragon."

Relief combined with fatigue had her swaying on her feet, but Connor was right beside her to steady her. "You must rest."

"No, I'm fine."

"Majesty, you haven't slept for over twenty-four hours."

"Neither has anyone else. I will be all right."

When she voiced another feeble protest while still feeling altogether unfocused, he gathered her up, gathered her in. "I insist."

When she struggled against his hold, the edges of her vision went black. Blood from the slice in her thigh pooled on the floor, and all she could hear was Connor's sharp voice informing the rest of the company of what she already knew, she had been wounded.

Then she knew nothing more.

****

After he carried her to the hospital tent, Connor refused to stir from her side even while the surgeons worked on her. The wound in her thigh, once cleaned and stitched, was not quite as serious as it had at first appeared. "The wound is not deep, and when it is fully healed, it should not affect her movement. The loss of blood is a concern, but she is as robustly healthy as she is resilient. Given a bit of time and rest, she will soon recover, thank the gods, and long live the queen."

"When will she wake?" He could not pry his gaze from her face; it was so white and still, so unlike her usual lively, mobile expression.

"I cannot say, but often when the body is injured, it will take the rest it needs. If she does not wake within a day, then there may be cause for alarm. Once she is strong enough, we will move her to own rooms in Belmere castle, but for now, she ought to remain where she is."

"Very well, I will stay with her until she comes around."

"As you say, my lord. Under normal circumstances, as the queen's personal physician, I would remain at her side, but with this battle, there are many wounded and in need of my immediate care. In fact, it was her express wish that I should offer whatever assistance I could."

"The queen would not have it any other way. She would want her people tended to."

"Even so, the queen remains my top priority. Never doubt it. If you need anything, anything at all, send a nurse to find me. I will come check on her progress in one hour."

"Thank you." Connor managed the two words, and they were sincere and heartfelt, but already his entire focus was on Morgan as he searched her face for any signs of returning awareness. Finding none, he settled to wait.

****

"How is she?" Sebastian demanded later.

"She's worse." Connor could not temper his curt response; he had no attention to spare for good manners right at the moment. Not when the woman he loved thrashed with pain and delirium.

"Has the doctor been by? What did he say? Is there not some remedy?"

Connor shook his head. "He tried a fresh ointment consisting mainly of honey to stop the spread of the putrescence but said it's up to her now. It all depends on whether her body is strong enough to fight it. He wanted to cut off her leg, but I refused even to consider it. Not yet. There's time for that if the situation becomes dire. Her temperature is spiking, and that's also a real problem, but the only thing that can be done to remedy that is to keep her cool by bathing her in ice water every two hours."

"I will make certain there is an unlimited supply available," Sebastian promised.

Connor looked up at him from his chair beside Morgan's bed. "Do you know of any white magic which might help?"

Before Sebastian even opened his mouth, Connor knew the answer. "No. I am sorry. There is some dark magic that might but—"

"She would never want that," Connor said.

Sebastian agreed. "I did look at the ointment, and it appears more than sound. Healing is not one of my gifts, and I know of nothing more effective than what is already being done. I'm sorry, Connor."

"No, no, it's all right. It isn't your fault."

"What happens if she dies?

"Is there a plan in place, you mean?" When Sebastian nodded, Connor said, "If she dies now without an heir, the crown goes to her nearest male relative, a young cousin from Farrow. The man has never set foot here, yet the kingdom would be his."

"That will not go unchallenged. I am sure there are others who have a claim and would put themselves forward. Not to mention, the council would never sit still for it. It would mean civil war."

"It would. I cannot think about that now. To be honest, I do not care. The whole world can burn for all the difference it will make to me. All I can think about is her. If she dies…"

Sebastian gripped his shoulder, and small, cold comfort though it was, it was a relief to realize he wasn't alone.

"I am so sorry. If I knew of any white magic that would heal her, it would already be done, but I don't. I wish there were." He tightened his grip. "Do not give up. She is strong, and I know she will fight to get back to you." He patted Connor on the shoulder. "If there is anything else I can do, anything at all, let me know."

Connor did not look up as Sebastian left. Instead, he straightened the covers over Morgan and smoothed back her sweaty hair.

****

Trista bolted upright, straight out of a fitful sleep.

Disoriented, with no idea where she was, it took a moment for her to recognize that she was in her room at Belmere.

Seeing Sebastian approach, she demanded, "Is she any better?"

He shook his head. "Not at all. She is very ill. She might even be dying."

Trista struggled to sit up and untangle her legs from the twisted blankets, though exhaustion dragged at her. "Damn it, I should never have left her."

Sebastian guided her back down. "You needed rest. You hadn't slept in days, and besides, Connor is with her. It is a terrible feeling, knowing there is nothing you or I can do."

Numb, Trista nodded. "Rarely have I ever felt so helpless."

"Our magic doesn't work that way; you know that."

"I know."

"But even so, I wish there was something, anything. She is our queen, and I am honored to be her friend, and I would give my life to help her."

"I am close to so few. The last thing in this world I want is to lose her."

He wrapped his arms around her. "I understand, love. Let us hope it won't come to that."

"But what if it does? There is other magic that does work that way. You know it as well as I do."

His face paled with fear, and his eyes grew angry and cold. "Don't even think it. The queen would rather die than be saved by dark magic."

"Perhaps, but I can't bear to watch while the life drains out of her."

"Trista, no. It comes with too high a price for you both. Put it out of your mind."

"It's a price I would be willing to pay. It would be for her."

"But it wouldn't stop there, and you know it. As quick as that," he snapped his fingers, "you would be back to where you were when—"

"Where I was when you left me. Maybe. Or maybe this time, I could resist."

"I'm not willing to take that kind of risk with your life. It is so tempting, believe me, I realize, but you can't. We can't. No matter the inducement. Otherwise, we're both back where we started, and what has this all been for?"

"What if she dies?"

The whispered question hung between them for a long moment, then Sebastian fixed his unblinking stare on her. "We aren't gods. Who lives and who dies isn't up to us, not most of the time anyway. Please promise me you won't do it. Promise me you won't use black magic to save Morgan's life." When she hesitated, he demanded in a harsh voice, "Swear it!"

Again, Trista was on a knife's edge, at a crossroads between two difficult, if not impossible, choices. Go one way, and there was a vortex of blood, and pain and dark magic, but she knew from experience the descent would feel amazing. At first. Sooner or later, however, she would hit the ground, and there would be nothing left of her when she did.

On the other side lay a shadowy, painful and seemingly endless road, one she would perhaps have to travel without one of the few people who mattered to her. The single difference was that she had no idea what would be left of her when said journey was over. Would it be worse? Whether it would be worse for her, she wasn't sure. For others, it would be. Losing Morgan, their queen, would definitely be worse. Of that, she had no doubt.

Besides, she had worked long and hard to pull herself out. She'd be damned if she would be so weak as to back away now. But, gods, the sacrifice. Well, no one said it would be easy. In a moment of clarity, it struck her that it was all about what she was willing to live with. Was she prepared to lose her soul? And even if she was, was she likewise ready to lose Sebastian, along with everything and everyone she had ever cared about? All for a theoretical eventuality that might not even manifest itself but instead remain hypothetical? Perhaps the queen could live without magical intervention after all. Put like that, the answer was easy. Hell no.

"I swear it on my life and by the magic in my blood."

Sebastian took a huge breath and his features relaxed. Relief all but oozed out of his every pore, and as he closed his eyes, he paused as if savoring it. "That's all right, then," he murmured. In one quick motion, he pulled her to him and held her in a tight embrace.

"Shall we go see her? It would mean a lot to her to hear your voice."

Trista nodded, and they made their way to Morgan's chamber.

****

There had been pain, pain greater than any she ever experienced, but it was gone now, thank the gods. In its place was the feel of the warm sun on her face. Since she wanted to see it as well as feel it, she opened her eyes. When she did, she found herself flat on her back on a beach of pure-white sand with the sea mere feet away. Sitting up, she drew her knees to her chest and stared out at the blue water. The place, wherever it was and however she had gotten here, was so beautiful, so serene. She wanted to stay forever.

"Morgan."

Somehow, she was not surprised to hear her father's voice. When she turned her head, there he was, tall and strong as ever. "Father." She rushed into his arms, and they were warm and solid as always. After a pause, she asked, "Am I dead? I'm dead, aren't I? I must be if you are here."

He smiled down at her, and his tone was as tender as she recalled. "No, my darling. You aren't dead."

"But you are. So, forgive me, but I don't understand."

He hesitated as if searching for the right words. "You are hovering in between, and for a short while, you are not one or the other. Even better, you are one of the few allowed to choose which way you will go. Live or die; take your pick. But before you do, there is someone else who wants to see you."

A strong, ocean-scented breeze wafted over her face, and in the distance, a figure shimmered into being. For a moment, Morgan could not believe what her senses were telling her. Even from so far away, the identity of the newcomer was unmistakable. It was in her build, her movements, the color of her hair and complexion, and a thousand other small details. It was her mother.

Without conscious thought, her feet flew across the sand. Her mother raced toward her, and a heartbeat after that, they embraced. After a time, Delphine drew back a bit and framed Morgan's face.

"My girl, so beautiful. So tall and grown up. I cannot find the words to express my joy at seeing you after so long," she murmured. Then she pulled her daughter close again.

Morgan's tongue tripped over itself as she struggled to speak to her dearest mother after so many years. She had so much to say to her. "We captured them, Mother, every last dragon in Esterhaven. And I killed Rownar—the one who took your life—with Connor's help. I hope you aren't too disappointed in me. In truth, even his miserable life was not mine to take, and I should perhaps have left it in the hands of the gods, but I could not."

"I know, Morgan. I saw, and I could never be disappointed in you." Delphine shook her head. "I am so very proud of you. Watching over you from afar for most of your life has been my greatest joy and privilege. I am so sorry I could not be there in the flesh to comfort and guide you. That has been my most profound sorrow. Let me guide you now."

With a tilt of her head, Morgan assented.

"Connor O'Malley is a man worthy of you. I approve. I have no right to suppose my approval matters, but I want to make my support plain."

Morgan beamed. "Oh, I am so glad. You are my mother; of course I want your blessing."

"Thank you, dearest, that means so much to me. The two of you are well-matched, and it does my heart good to see it."

Whether time worked the same way back on earth, she had no idea, but they talked of everything and nothing for what seemed like hours to Morgan until, finally, she had to ask again. "Are you sure I'm not dead?"

Delphine laughed, and Morgan experienced a flash of poignant memory at the sound. "No, no. It's as your father told you, you are in-between, and soon you must choose."

"That's simple, then. I want to stay here with both of you."

"It is anything but simple, daughter. You cannot make this decision solely based on a desire to remain with us. You must think of what you leave behind, a kingdom with no one to rule it, a betrothed who loves you and whom you love, friends who care a great deal for you. A life," James said.

"But how can I leave the two of you?" She twisted in a slow circle. "And this place is paradise. It's so beautiful. I don't ever want to leave."

"It is wonderful, isn't it?" her mother said. "There's nothing I want more than for you to stay so we can be the family we were always meant to be, but you have more, so much more to do."

"No, I—"

With no warning, a voice echoed through the world, coming from nowhere and everywhere at once. It was Connor, begging her to come back. A moment later, he professed his love in such simple, eloquent terms that tears filled her eyes. She had supposed in a place like this, she would be beyond tears, but not so.

In the end, it all came down to a few very simple words. *"Please, Morgan, my love. Come back to me."*

"Go, my sweet girl. Your father and I will wait for you. We will see each other again. Now hurry!"

Laughing and crying at the same time, she hugged her father, kissed her mother's cheek, and raced toward Connor's voice.

****

For three days, the fever raged, and Connor never left her side. He ate little and slept even less. It all became a blur of cold cloths, ice baths and calming words said during Morgan's fevered hallucinations. Until, in the small hours of the night, he collapsed from fatigue.

Hours later, Connor woke with a jerk and a gasp, unsure of his surroundings. Glancing about, his mind caught up, and he recognized Morgan's bedchamber at the castle.

When he pressed a hand to her forehead, he found it blessedly cool. Tears prickled in his eyes as he murmured a grateful, heartfelt prayer to the gods, then rushed to fetch the physician.

When he arrived, the doctor took her pulse, examined her wound then put a hand to her forehead as Connor had done. The man's relief was palpable. "She does appear to be on the mend. As you noted, her fever has broken. Her pulse is strong. Her wound seems to be healing. There is far less pus, and I see no signs of rot. She isn't quite out of danger yet, but she is much improved. We will continue with the current regimen. The queen is young and strong, and her nature is overcoming even the greatest of obstacles."

"Is there anything else that ought to be done?"

"Not until she wakes. When she does, give her water, no wine or mead. Then let her consume broth and nothing else for the first two days, so that she may slowly regain her strength. Otherwise, we'll see."

"All right." Connor rose. "Thank you."

The physician bowed deeply. "It was my pleasure, Lord O'Malley."

****

Her return to consciousness came in waves. First, she was aware the mattress beneath her was her own. Next, she was cognizant of a sound that was part and parcel of those waves. A deep, regular, soothing sound that was somehow familiar filled her ears.

For a time, Morgan puzzled idly over what it might be, then smiled, heartened. It was Connor's breathing, and, judging by the regular rise and fall of the noise, he was asleep nearby. How close, she could not at first determine since her eyes refused to obey her brain and open.

With supreme effort, she managed to force her lids to flutter up, and the first thing she saw was her beloved's dark hair, his head resting on the bed beside her. Although she longed to run her fingers through his thick mane, she hadn't the strength. Drained from such great exertion, she let her lids fall shut.

When she next woke, Connor's bright gaze was the first thing she perceived. A silent prayer of thankfulness ran through her head.

"Come on, come back now, darling. Come all the way around. That's it."

With no idea how much time had passed, she did as he instructed, anxious to rejoin the world. "What happened?" She was shocked to discover her voice was a croak from disuse.

"Hmm, you collapsed from your wounds, coupled

with dehydration. Then putrescence filled the gash and you developed a fever. You have been unconscious for four days now. Why on earth didn't you tell someone how seriously you'd been hurt?"

His voice held censure but so much concern and tenderness too, that she smiled. "Because I had no idea the cut was that bad. I let some dragon claw me. Stupid. It wasn't even Rownar, and at first, I didn't even feel it. I thought I stopped the bleeding, but I was wrong. Besides, I had other things, things quite as important, to tend to."

"And your own life, that's not important? God's blood, Morgan!"

He scraped back the stool he sat on with such force he almost upset it, then rose to pace. He swore under his breath but with great vehemence. At long last, he stilled and faced her. "I was sure I was going to lose you this time. You defeated Rownar, yet here I was, terrified victory would come at the cost of your life. After everything we have been through, I was positive you were dying. Damn you."

He swept her hand into his, then held it to his lips. An instant later, the moisture of a single tear slid down her palm, and shock filled her. "It's all right, Connor. I am here, and I am very much alive. Please do not distress yourself; I can't bear it."

"I could not bear it if I lost you." The words were harsh, but he passed a hand over his face, wiping at the added moisture he found there.

She tilted her head, the better to look him straight in the eye. "I am not going anywhere. That gods-forsaken dragon is dead at last, and I have my life back. I'll be damned if I'll die now."

He barked out a laugh. "I have never been so happy that you are such a stubborn woman."

She managed a weak chuckle, but then her head flopped back onto the pillow. She was disturbed to discover even this short exchange left her exhausted.

"Rest now. All is well. I won't leave you."

Too tired to do anything else, she did as he bid her.

****

After that, Morgan's recovery was, thank the gods, rapid. Although, in her opinion, not nearly fast enough. Each day brought greater strength until, after two long weeks, the physician pronounced her strong enough to leave her bed.

"For only a short turn about the room at first. Then you may increase the distance over the next seven days. But you must not overtax yourself," he said. "If you continue to improve, after seven days, you may resume normal activities."

"That is all to the good, but there are many things I must see to personally, matters requiring my physical presence, ones which will not wait any longer."

"You are the queen. There is no one on this earth more important, and you must take care of your health above all. Everything else must be postponed."

"No. Further delay is not acceptable." She ticked off points on her fingers. "There are many other wounded to tend. My father must be buried and mourned. Trustworthy people must be sent to seek out any remaining dragons. We believe we captured them all, but how can we be sure? We cannot be, not until we search this whole country. On a happier note, I have my coronation to organize, but even so, it is a royal event and must be planned. As much as grief overwhelms me, and as much as I would have it otherwise, I still must be crowned as soon as the traditional period of mourning is over. My rule must be solidified. The one thing I cannot do is remain an invalid any longer."

"I understand, but, Your Majesty, I cannot in good conscience recommend any other course than the one I have laid out.

"The physician is right, Your Grace," Connor said. "No arguments."

Morgan started to protest, but Connor held up a hand. "Your kingdom needs you hale and whole, as do I. You must do as the doctor instructs and make a full recovery."

"Perhaps a compromise? What if people come to you? You could grant audiences here. If necessary, you could even hold a council meeting right in this room. I mean, why not? It is large enough, barely, and it would be less taxing for you. Your people would get the benefit of seeing their queen is alive and, if not in perfect health, at least on the mend. Would that suffice?"

Morgan thought it over. She weighed the risk of seeming weak against not appearing at all. In addition, she calculated what damage could be done in a land with no one at the helm, even temporarily. She then weighed this against the damage done to her health by curtailing her recuperation. If she were incapacitated or even if, the gods forbid, she died, it opened the possibility of leaving her kingdom permanently rudderless. "Indeed, it would."

"Splendid. I will make the required arrangements." He kissed her forehead. "You rest. That's an order, Your Majesty."

She scowled but did not object further.

****

The next morning Morgan prepared to receive the council as best she could. She donned a dressing gown and had her hair washed, brushed, and braided. Deeming herself as presentable as it was possible for her to be at this point, she signaled her maid to open the door to her room. Connor stood beside her as she bid them all enter.

The whole group of thirty filed in, and it made for a tight fit. As their gazes fell on her, she noted that most appeared relieved to see her health was improving, some even to the point of tears. She nodded to each in turn and murmured words of greeting and thanks.

Soon enough they settled, and she called the meeting to order.

"The primary reason I have summoned you here today is to assure you I am indeed alive and well. Not fully recovered yet, perhaps, but on the mend. I appreciate all of your hard work and sacrifice during my convalescence. It will not be forgotten. Secondly, I am aware numerous pressing issues must also be decided. So, let's make a start. On what is to be done with the gold and the jewels of the dragon hoards, the overall value of each dragon hoard is even now being determined by our accountants. The gold and gems are being transported here and put into the treasury. Once the grand total is calculated, it will be divided thus: each and every person in Esterhaven shall receive a certain portion over and above anything taken from them, with a larger amount given to the maidens who sang the song and the soldiers who fought.

All the injured and families of the dead will receive

more, likewise, for their sacrifice. Some ten percent of the total shall be used to heal the wounds of this land. To wit, the barns destroyed, shops burned, forests scorched, livestock killed, and crops decimated shall be rebuilt using this portion of the gold. Another five percent shall remain in the treasury against difficult times which may come in the future. All this will be done after Lord Sebastian Hale and Lady Trista Norris cleanse every piece of any and all dark magic."

This plan met with the approval of the entire council and was adopted forthwith. Pleased it was considered so exceedingly suitable, she beamed upon them all. The most important business done, she pressed on and presented another matter.

"Now is as good a time as any to make an announcement which coincides with this issue. We hereby appoint Sebastian Hale and Trista Norris as our royal sorcerers. Together they will safeguard us and our realm using the great gift of their magic. We would honor them by trusting them with this duty." She turned to her two dear friends, whose expressions were mirror images of shock. "Do you accept?"

After a swift, speaking glance at one another, Sebastian bowed and Trista curtseyed. "We are honored by such a trust and accept wholeheartedly."

Morgan beamed. "Excellent. We are pleased and are quite certain you will both meet your obligations."

She raised her voice and addressed the entire governing body. "Unless there are any further issues?" When no one spoke, she continued, "Then we are adjourned until a month from today. In the meantime, enjoy the profound and glorious absence of dragons."

As the council filed out, she drew in a deep breath.

In spite of the fact that she felt better every day, she still tired easily. Yet, there was more to tend to, and so she could not rest yet.

"Members of the privy council stay." When only her few most trusted advisors remained, she began. "As you are all no doubt aware, the time for my coronation draws near. I would hear your thoughts on the matter."

****

The day the physician pronounced Morgan recovered was the first Connor could breathe easy again.

"You are certain she is entirely healed?" he asked for at least the tenth time.

"Quite certain, my lord. Our queen is young and exceedingly strong."

"Thank the gods for that."

"Indeed, my lord."

"I am right here, you know," the subject of their discussion complained.

The physician cleared his throat. "Yes, so you are. Apologies, Your Majesty."

"So, then I can resume all normal activity? I can take up my life again?"

"Yes, I am happy to say. May the gods shield you forevermore."

"And you. I will not forget how you saved my life. Go take some much-needed rest."

He bowed. "Call on me if you have a need." He bowed low once more and left them alone.

As his knees turned to jelly without warning, Connor dropped into the nearest chair, which happened to be the one he sat in while watching over her. "Thank the gods."

She stroked a hand through his hair and over his cheek. He lifted his face to look at her.

"It's all right. The danger is over now. I have regained my customary rude health. There's no need to worry anymore."

He swallowed so loudly that he knew she must have heard it even from where she stood. "I can't just turn it off. I will be worrying about you for some time to come. I can't help it."

"I know." She tilted her head. "I, on the other hand, feel alive. I feel strong and vital. I've cheated death, at least for now, and I want to celebrate."

His gaze shot up from his contemplation of their joined hands and locked with hers. It was like a match to flame. "Are you sure? The doctor's only just left."

"Oh, I'm sure. I almost died, but I did not. What better way to feel it and know it than this?" She pressed her lips to his, and the kiss was heated, passionate, and uncontrolled.

Connor couldn't touch her enough, couldn't get close enough. He had been scared down to his very core that he would never be able to do either again. He needed every inch of her naked skin against his, and he needed it now. He took a deep shaky breath and tried to get himself under control. Even though the physician proclaimed her recovered, that didn't mean the vigorous activity his body demanded was advisable.

Morgan urged him closer and began doing away with his clothes, all but tearing them from him. His inner self roared with triumph, and he could not stop himself from responding in kind. Clothes, his and hers, ripped, and he didn't care as long as they were gone and out of the way. Mere moments later, he was inside of her in the depths of her huge bed.

Alive. She was alive, and his was all he could think as they touched the pinnacle of sensation.

In the aftermath, he ordered, "Don't ever scare me like that again."

She laughed, the sound soft, sultry, and everything feminine. "I'll try, but I make no promises. Fortune is fickle, and who knows what we may face in the future. Besides, if I have something like the last few minutes to look forward to, I might want to scare you quite a lot."

Connor rolled on top of her as she giggled. "Not funny." But his lips twitched in spite of himself.

"It's a little funny."

He shook his head as she laughed uproariously and kissed him everywhere she could reach.

****

Over the days of her illness, her father's body had been preserved, Sebastian and Trista had seen to that, and now came the time to bury him. A cold drizzle fell, and the smell of damp leaves filled Morgan's nostrils as she stood at her father's grave. She felt numb. All throughout her convalescence, her father's death had not seemed real, and part of her refused to accept it. At any given moment, she had expected him to enter her room with his usual flourish and order her to get well.

Now, however, reality was all too tangible. Half the kingdom was in attendance to observe the funeral rites. His once-vital body was soon to be lowered into the ground, and she was uncertain how to go on or even if she could manage to. Yet, as she gazed at the stricken faces of her people, she knew she must. She had to find a way to move forward. It was what her father would want, and it was what her people needed.

Connor squeezed her hand gently, offering his wordless support. She returned the pressure and thought of how lucky she was. He was always at her side, she realized, and in a very short time, she had come to rely on him. He was her rock, and, despite her loss, she was not alone. That notion gave her strength.

She signaled to the archbishop, and the service began.

****

Morgan wore black to symbolize her mourning even on the day of her coronation one month later. The dress was of heavy, shimmering satin—as fine a fabric as could be had—made in the style she favored, with a bit of silver embroidery edging the neckline and the sleeves. Her jewels alone relieved the severity of her appearance. Large, finely crafted, professionally cut diamonds in a silver setting hung about her neck and dangled from her earlobes. The entire effect was quite austere. Thank the gods black became her because, despite efforts to convince her to do otherwise, she would not put off her mourning gowns, not even for such a momentous occasion. In fact, it was only to stabilize her kingdom and solidify her rule that she agreed to be crowned so very soon after her father's death.

On one other point, she refused to budge. Connor would be recognized as her consort and crowned the prince of the Corillium Isles, a part of Esterhaven located off the west coast. He had been offered and had refused the crown matrimonial, but her betrothed would be a crowned prince; she had insisted on at least that much. This would all occur during one ceremony, not a separate one, as her new ministers recommended. In all other ways, she allowed her advisors to guide her in the tradition and protocol of her coronation.

The grand music swelled, and she walked down the cathedral aisle toward the throne. On the raised dais, Connor awaited her, along with the archbishop and several of her closest advisors.

First, a golden crown set with rubies was brought forth. Connor, resplendent in black breeches, white shirt, dove-grey tunic, and black cloak, knelt.

The archbishop intoned, "I crown thee, Connor O'Malley, Prince of the Corillium Isles."

Everyone present, save the queen herself, bowed. Connor stepped back and returned to the new queen's side, taking his place at her right hand. Then, a far-richer crown, on a cushion specifically designed for the purpose, covered in red velvet and edged in gold, appeared. Made of silver and set with sapphires, the crown was the most exquisite, well-wrought piece of its kind anywhere in the world.

Now the archbishop faced her and stated with great reverence and ceremony, "Morgan Elizabeth Talbot, I crown thee queen of all Esterhaven."

When she faced her subjects, they all bent a knee. Then, as one, they rose, and shouts of, "Long live the queen!" echoed through the cathedral.

Chapter Sixteen

Months passed as she adjusted to her new role as queen. During this time, she called on the training in government given to her by her father, and she discovered she needed every bit of it.

Overseeing the peaceful, smooth transfer of power from her father to herself and putting her plans for the dragon hoard into action kept her busy. Matters such as choosing her own advisors to serve on her privy council as well as drafting new legislation filled her days.

Next, the parceling out of the dragon gold was organized and accomplished. In addition, tremendous time and effort was spent revitalizing the kingdom as a whole. New infrastructure was built; roads and homes were constructed as promised.

She had few free moments, but the work was more than fulfilling. It all came together as she had hoped and prayed it would.

A quiet contentment and a deep sense of accomplishment filled her even after all she had lost. She began to believe her parents might possibly be proud of her.

One fine morning, a brisk rap on the door echoed through her bedchamber. "Come," she called.

Instead of one of her maids, as she expected, a footman entered. "Forgive the intrusion, Majesty, but King Ferdinand of Linford is here begging an audience.

He says it's urgent, and he must see you at once."

She raised her eyebrows but rose from her dressing table. "Very well. I will receive him in the main audience chamber presently."

Connor strolled in from his adjoining dressing room, put his arms around her, then kissed the back of her neck. As the crown prince and consort of the queen, he was ensconced in the chambers next to hers although they had yet to wed. "Did I hear you say you would receive someone? It's early for even an informal audience, is it not?"

"It is, but King Ferdinand requests it. He was a dear friend of my father, and it's urgent, apparently. Will you join me?"

"Of course." He kissed her hand, and they made their way out.

****

Once seated on the throne in the main audience chamber, she signaled to her guards, and King Ferdinand was allowed to enter. When he remained steps away from the entrance, she beckoned him forward. "King Ferdinand, this visit is most welcome. I was told the matter was rather pressing. I hope there is no problem?"

The man came ahead, but his stride was hesitant, and his posture stilted. Ferdinand acknowledged Connor with a brief nod, then bowed very low to the new queen. A contemporary of her father and still rather attractive, whatever troubled him had taken its toll.

"Indeed, I fear there is a problem, one which has been plaguing my country for decades, but one it's rumored you now have a solution to."

Morgan widened her eyes. "Indeed. While I cannot speak to the accuracy of these rumors, I would be honored if we could be of any assistance whatever. Tell me, what can I do?"

"Word of your capture of every dragon in your kingdom has spread, Your Grace. When I heard of it, I set out without delay. The kingdom of Linford has long been hard hit by the pestilence of dragons."

When, overcome by emotion, he could not go on, she prompted, "This is well-known. So, what would you have of me?"

The king took a deep, steadying breath. "We wondered, how did you do it? Could you advise us? Could you help? The devastation is most acute, and the situation is grave. We would do much to rid ourselves of the creatures. If you could... We throw ourselves on your mercy, great queen."

He dropped to his knees and said nothing more as if he could no longer bear to speak of it. Morgan studied his face. Pale, drawn, and desperate as he was, compassion swamped her. She was all too familiar with what it was to be a ruler with no way to help her subjects.

Stepping forward, she held out both hands to him, then lifted him to his feet. "Of course, I will help, Ferdinand. Our kingdoms have always been allies, and you and my father the best of friends. I have thought of your kingdom and your situation often and always intended to help, but there has been much to see to here in my own land. Forgive me for not acting with greater dispatch. Let me offer you my sincerest apologies for not contacting you sooner."

Relief suffused him. His shoulders relaxed as if a

great weight had been removed from them. Morgan was gratified to see it. "No, there is nothing to forgive, Morgan. I have known you since you were a child, and I know your heart. You have had your own problems to deal with. Dragon battles, the death of your father, and you, yourself, were wounded, I hear. But now that all that is passed, I would be forever grateful for any aid you could grant us."

"Of course, of course. There are others we should speak to and matters to arrange, but I assure you, all that can be done will be done."

She turned to Connor. "My prince, could you send for Lord Hale and Lady Norris?"

He bowed. "I can and will."

"We will arrange quarters for you." She clapped her hands, and a maidservant appeared. When the girl curtseyed, she ordered, "Prepare rooms for King Ferdinand in the east wing."

"Thank you. I can't tell you how much I appreciate this."

"No, no, it's nothing. Go, take some refreshment, wash off the dust of travel, and rest while I set things in motion. In an hour or two, rejoin me here."

With much thanks and many more expressions of gratitude, Ferdinand took his leave.

Alone, Morgan put her mind to the problem and directed her entire focus toward finding a solution.

****

As arranged, Ferdinand met Morgan in the audience chamber two hours later, only this time, Connor, Sebastian, and Trista joined them.

"I believe we may have a plan. Or the beginnings of one, at least."

"Thank the gods and Your Majesty's mercy for it. Please, do tell me."

The queen gestured her chief magician forward. "Sebastian."

"We'll start by offering instruction to any magician who wishes to aid the cause. Send him or her here, and we will share our spells, our potions, and our technique. None are as powerful as Trista and myself, but we now believe there are ways to get around this problem."

"Depending on how many wish to serve in this way, if certain countries have no one willing, then we can send someone to them who has been trained."

"How long will such instruction take?"

This time Trista answered. "It depends on the skill of the magician, how powerful he or she is, and how well he or she takes instruction. Weeks at least, perhaps even months."

Ferdinand's face fell. "But what are we to do in the meantime? Every hour wasted means more lives lost."

Alarmed at his death-like pallor, Morgan hastened to answer. "No, no, do not distress yourself, and do not despair. We will not waste even another hour. Lord Hale and Lady Norris have agreed to go with you and begin the process." She rose and held out both hands to him. "King Ferdinand, we care for your people as we do our own. You and yours shall be first to benefit from a plan we should have put into action long ago."

Ferdinand brought her joined hands to his lips. "Your kindness shall not soon be forgotten, Majesty."

"I thank you, King Ferdinand. I would repay kindness with kindness. It has always been so between our countries. Soon I hope to extend the same courtesy to others. In the meanwhile, let us discuss details."

****

Some weeks later, Morgan invited all of the court to a grand summit at the castle. This one week of consultation and discussion was an acknowledgement that the dragon scourge was not confined to any one country but was a challenge for the world at large. Many dignitaries from neighboring countries attended. Already word had spread to every part of the world of the defeat of the dragons in Esterhaven, and all the other nations wanted the same for their own people.

In celebration of the newfound freedom throughout the land and for the amusement of their visitors, the summit would conclude with a grand ball. It was intended as a concrete expression of their newfound unity and commitment to a better world, one free of dragons for all time. At least such was the hope, but right now that seemed to be a long time away. For the moment, they were in the council chamber, which was full to bursting. With members of her own council, plus similar representatives from twenty other countries present, the room could barely accommodate them all.

"But will it hold?" Balthasar, king of Aldston demanded.

"It will hold. My oath on it. If there is anything in this world I know, it is magic, and this spell will hold." Sebastian assured the group at large.

"As you say. Then, I must ask, will you help us?"

He directed the question to Morgan, and several long moments passed before she ventured a response. "We are prepared to offer all of you the specifics of the spell, the potions, everything required. We will even offer the services of magicians trained by our own Lord Sebastian Hale and Lady Trista Norris, if you have none of your own of sufficient skill. In addition, we also recommend the more magicians who perform the spell, the better, especially if they lack adequate ability to cast the spell alone. We offer all this and in return require one thing only."

"What is that?" Balthazar's tone was wary and reluctant.

"That you will ever think kindly of Esterhaven, and that we will live in peace."

Salvatore, another monarch from yet another distant land, snorted. When Morgan shot a sharp look at him, he did his best to paint on a sober expression, but she remained unconvinced. She raised an eyebrow at him, then gestured for him to speak whatever was on his mind.

"Forgive me, Your Grace, but you want us to live in peace? All of us? Impossible."

"I realize that." Tone dry as dust, she continued, "Fight amongst yourselves if you must, but none of you will commit any act of aggression toward my realm. At least, not without just cause. I trust my country will never give you grounds."

Connor stood. "I realize what Her Grace is asking is a tall order. It will require a great deal of trust on all sides. But, gentlemen, ladies, think of it… a world without dragons. Think of what she is offering you. Isn't it worth any price to have such a world? I want such a world for us all."

"As do I," Morgan said. "The only way this will happen is if we work together."

"What if we cannot make this promise or if, later, we break it? What then?"

"In such a case, Balthazar, I ought to, and indeed

have been advised to, refuse to help any such country. This I will not do. I will not deny innocent people aid whether they are my subjects or no. No matter that they might even one day become my enemy. However, such a thing will not be forgotten. I would beg of you to consider my offer. Let us unite in peace."

The royals and dignitaries exchanged glances. "Respectfully, we would like time to consider, Your Majesty."

"Of course. As I said, no matter your decision, mine will remain the same."

They all rose, but before any could take their leave, Morgan added, "I would ask for your answer by noon tomorrow. Now we know how to conquer them, we should not waste a moment. Time is of the essence."

"As we know all too well, Your Grace. You will have your answer by midday."

All bowed and went out.

"I still am not at all sure that was wise." Trista murmured once the last person left.

"Perhaps not, but it was right. Doing so must engender goodwill and improve our world," Morgan replied.

"Still—"

"What would you have me do, Trista? Allow the blameless to suffer as I did all my life? Let innocent babes lose their mothers and fathers? Permit children to live scarred? Ask young maidens to sacrifice themselves body and soul to a dragon? These are things I will never allow, not if it is within my power to prevent them. Now, I will say no more on the matter."

Trista curtseyed low. "Of course, Majesty. I beg your pardon."

"Granted, but I mean this. I will not discuss it further, Trista."

"I understand."

"Good." She faced her betrothed. "Connor, what do you think? How many will agree?"

"I am not sure. I am no judge of such things, but a fair number, I would say."

"Sebastian?"

"I agree with Connor. Most will decide in your favor, I think. There are some few who may not, of course, but… with no real incentive to do as you ask, we can only hope most see sense."

"May the gods hear us." Morgan said the familiar words, but never had she meant them more.

****

Before noon the next day, they gathered once again in the council chamber. As soon as Morgan was settled at the table along with all the others, she asked, "So, can I assume each of you have come to a decision?"

Balthazar rose and cleared his throat. "We have. In fact, we have reached a consensus. We will accept whatever help you are willing to offer to remove the blight of dragons from our world. Other matters remain to be settled."

"What other matters?"

"Disagreements will arise. Dissension is a normal result of our very different cultures. It is the very nature of the world. When such problems occur, I propose that we, all of us, should meet to discuss them just as we are doing now before any aggressive action is taken."

Morgan blinked, then her lips curved. "That is an excellent, not to say inspired, suggestion. All of you have agreed to this?"

"We have."

"Let me add my voice. I also approve of this action with all of my heart."

"And so we are all in accord?"

Connor searched all the faces. Servants handed glasses round and poured wine.

"Then let us toast. To a brave new world with no dragons in it."

Chapter Seventeen

"When will we marry?" Connor asked the question of the beautiful woman in his arms and his bed, whose hand rested over his heart.

With a lazy finger, Morgan traced a path over his chest. "Soon. My father would not want me to be in mourning forever. I thought, on the first day of spring? It is just a few short weeks away. That is the soonest a royal wedding could be arranged. What do you think?" She raised her head to peer at him.

"That sounds perfect." He framed her face with his hands. "I want you to be my wife, and I don't want to wait anymore. We both know this existence is damned unpredictable. Either or both of us might have died in battle, and even though Rownar is gone, that does not mean there aren't other threats, ones we can't even see. This world is not only fragile and our place in it precarious; it is finite. I want to make the most of whatever time we are given."

"You're right. Life is too short to waste any more time. So, it's decided, on the first day of spring, we'll marry."

His lips brushed hers in gentle affirmation, and he held her close in his arms.

****

Morgan felt like a bride, pure, beautiful, and full of only joy. Dazzling in gleaming white satin with a veil of shimmering silk tulle, she waited in the vestibule of the church, ready to join her betrothed.

He was resplendent in his wedding clothes of white-silk shirt, dove-grey satin waistcoat, trousers of black brocade topped by a wool jacket in a dark grey, and black boots polished to a glossy shine. It was the love and devotion shining in his eyes that captured her, however. Her own love for Connor filled her heart and made her soul sparkle as bright as the spring sun when she held out her hand to him, and they said their vows.

She remembered the words well enough from Trista's wedding and had, of course, known them all of her life.

Connor began, "My heart is laid at thy feet. With my body, I thee worship. All I have and all I am is yours. Let our blood bind us, each to the other. Let our flesh and bone knit. Let us be as one from this day forth."

As she repeated the words, she knew she had never meant anything more.

****

As soon as they gained her chambers, Morgan took Connor's mouth. There had been so many people to greet, so many who wanted to wish them well, and that was kind and heartwarming. However, in all honesty, the one thing she wanted, after several hours, was to be alone with her new husband. After what had been an interminably long wedding reception, enjoyable in its way but seemingly unending, she wanted nothing more than to bask in the feel of his mouth on hers, and now she was, but he had something else in mind.

Pulling back from the kiss, he dropped to his knees before her. Locking gazes, he wrapped his hand about her ankle then caressed upward in slow motion. As he did, her cheeks grew heated, and the muscle of her calf quivered. On a trembling breath, she stroked a hand in his hair and biting her lip, she moved her free ankle to widen her stance.

****

Feeling absurdly triumphant, Connor lifted her skirts, brushed them up then aside and put his mouth to her lower belly. Kissing his way down… Just before he claimed her warm, wet center, he lifted his gaze to her, waiting, wanting, needing to see her eyes, to have her assent. When his lips brushed, feather-light, across her most-sensitive flesh, she gasped. When he pressed his mouth to the spot more firmly, her hand gripped in his hair, locking him to her. It was all the answer he needed. As he licked, her lids lowered on a moan, and he let himself go, the act of giving her pleasure heightening his own.

He took his time and savored, her taste and scent imprinting on his brain, and as he did, he brought her to the brink more than once. He could have stayed that way forever, but Morgan's reactions became increasingly edgy, then grew to bordering on frantic, and he knew it was time. With one deep thrust of his tongue at her core and one firm press of his lips, he sent her flying. Gripping the backs of her legs to keep her steady, he held her through it. As the contractions started and grew stronger, he did all he could to draw it out, let her ride it out, and when her climax was over, he kept her legs from going out from under her.

Finally, he lifted his head and murmured, "I wanted to do that all day, wife."

"I know, husband."

His eyebrows lifted as her pretty face flushed.

"I mean, I didn't know what you wanted, not in precise detail, but it was clear you wanted me. I could see it in your eyes. There were times when I had to stop looking at you. It was too much. We were not alone, and I was terrified everyone would see right through me. I was petrified they would know all I wanted was you."

In one fluid motion he rose, then smoothed her skirts back into place. Remembering what he had said to her the first night they met, he asked, "Do you want more?"

"Gods, yes. I want your clothes off and you inside of me. Now."

When she trailed hot open-mouthed kisses down his neck, he growled deep in his throat, then shook his head. "Or maybe the clothes can stay put for now. Getting them off would take far too much time. I do not want to be apart from you for even that long."

On a breathless laugh, she said, "Me either. Still, we could…" She tugged at his shirt.

At her urging, he lifted his arms and it came off. After she let it fall where it would, he did the same for her, making short work of the bodice of her gown, as well as doing away with her chemise. Both naked to the waist now, she brushed her breasts against his chest.

Every muscle in his body shook with the pent-up desire postponed for far too long. It had been building all day, had increased exponentially in the past half hour, and was now reaching flashpoint. Groaning, he took her mouth and unbuttoned the placket of his trousers, unable to wait. Panting, he pushed her skirts out of the way once again, more roughly this time, and lifted her up and into him. An instant later, he wrapped her legs around his waist. With one thrust, he entered her.

His vision blurred, then went dark, and he didn't give a damn. He simply couldn't bring himself to care. Who needed sight when he could feel? The silken skin of her breasts under his hands and the clasp of her inner muscles about his rigid length were more than enough to carry him right to the edge. Then, when his vision returned mere moments later, he was grateful after all, because he could see her face. Her flushed cheeks, her soft lips, and her eyes, heavy lidded with need, were all a man could desire in this world.

He was also grateful for his hearing. Every gentle sigh, every moan, every gasp which filled his ears fed a craving for her that would never be fully satisfied. Not until they both found the peak and tumbled over, and perhaps not even then. Then she arched and undulated beneath him, and he was there. Transported, he let himself go, and his beautiful wife followed him into blissful, sensual oblivion.

When he returned, his head pillowed on her breast, he murmured their vows to her once more. "My heart is laid at thy feet. With my body, I thee worship. All I have and all I am is yours. Let our blood bind us, each to the other. Let our flesh and bone knit. Let us be as one from this day forth. In truth, I vow all this to you."

She cupped his cheek. "And I to you."

****

The summer evening fell outside the window as Connor joined Morgan in the library, as he often did. He approached his wife with trepidation. He knew quite well she would not like what he was about to propose, not at all. Yet, he was also certain that this was something that must be done. So, he squared his shoulders and prepared to broach the subject.

"Another nest of dragon eggs has been found, in Hammersmith this time."

She lifted her gaze from the book she was reading to peer at him. "If you are about suggest what I think you will suggest, the answer is no. You are my consort, and I need you by me, as you have been these last months. I do not need or want you pursuing the latest rumors of baby-dragon nests. With Sebastian and Trista both gone to help other countries be rid of the things, this is the worst possible time for you to be away as well."

"Morgan, it is critical we find and destroy or capture all of the dragon eggs and young dragons out there. Most eggs will die without a dragon mother's care, of course, but do you want to take the risk of even one surviving? I will tell you plainly I do not. Because I won't have everything, all we have done, be for nothing."

"Nor would I, but—"

"But nothing, this is how it must be."

"And it has to be you, of course. No one else."

"I am the very best at what I do. I know what signs to look for better than anyone else does. If I go, there is less danger to others and to your kingdom as a whole. In addition, it will take far less time if I am there."

"If I consent to this, how long would you be gone?"

"I would have to be away for six months at the very least, a year at most." His heart ached at the mere thought. What a romantic fool he had become. He lived well enough without her for the first twenty-eight years of his life, so, of course, he could withstand a year sans her company. Yet, he had not known then what he was missing.

Her chin firmed. "All right, if this must be done, then I will go with you."

"Morgan, you can't. Your rule is too new, too fresh, yet."

"In actuality, a royal progress to commemorate the coronation of a new monarch is a time-honored tradition. The people could see me and perhaps even grow to love me. We could be certain all dragon eggs are gone from our land at the same time. Best of all, you and I would not have to be apart. An excellent plan on all counts, I don't know why I didn't think of it before."

A tiny glimmer of hope sparked in him, one he ruthlessly put out. "But shouldn't you solidify things here before traveling about the countryside?"

"Politically, things are as solidified as they can be at this juncture. A royal progress could do nothing but strengthen them."

"And if you got with child? For all we know, you might already be pregnant."

"I am not yet, but I yearn to be."

Her expression softened, and his own heart filled with equal parts utter, poignant longing and abject fear at the prospect. Women died in childbed every day, and children were often stillborn. He could scarcely bear to think of it.

"Be that as it may, if I were to get with child, I would remain wherever I happen to be until the birth. You could stay with me or continue on for a brief time, then rejoin me before our child is born."

"I would, also, of course, travel with the best physician and midwife to be had. Really, there would be no more risk than if I stayed here. And, in a way, much less, because I would not be worrying about you quite so much or be bereft of your company."

He considered all she said. "All right."

"All right? Truly? You'll allow me to come with you?" With a laugh, she shook her head. "What am I saying, I am the queen. In the end, it is for me to decide. Still, I want your blessing and approval if at all possible."

"So I should hope," he muttered. He crossed to her and framed her face with his hands. "I don't want us to be apart any more than you do. I want us to be together, partners in everything."

She beamed. "Excellent. I will make all the necessary preparations. When do we leave?"

He couldn't help but smile back as nostalgia surged through him. "As soon as possible of course."

It seemed they would begin their married life with another adventure. Most fitting.

Epilogue

Twelve years later

The young prince and the diminutive fairy-like duchess played well together on the bank of the river near the castle. They splashed in the water, then raced off into the meadow and sped right past their indulgent parents, laughing all the while.

Trista, Sebastian, Connor and Morgan sat together on a large blanket, taking their ease while finishing the last of a fabulous luncheon and sipping champagne. Eleven-year-old Michael, the heir apparent, rushed after little Diana, aged ten, and threatened to douse her to within an inch of her life once he got his hands on her. All appearances and threats to the contrary, the prince was, in fact, very gentle with her. Much of their childhood had been spent in each other's company, and they were close companions.

"They look well together, do they not?" Morgan asked the group at large.

"Indeed they do." To Sebastian and Trista, Connor said, "Does she show any signs?"

Sebastian shook his head. "Not so far, but it's early days yet. Evidence of magic in the blood can manifest itself up to the age of thirteen."

Morgan shot a look at her husband and, after getting raised eyebrows and a shrug, she cleared her throat. "There is something we would like to discuss with you both."

Sebastian looked up from contemplating his daughter to turn his languid attention Connor and Morgan's way. Trista, her gaze suddenly sharp, fixed on Morgan's face.

"We realize they are still quite young, but we would like to know how the two of you would feel if our children were to marry."

"An arranged marriage? I am surprised you would suggest such a thing, Morgan. Don't you wish for your son to have a love match as you did?" Sebastian glanced over at her in surprise.

"Indeed I do. What I propose is this: we suggest the idea in perhaps another ten or even fifteen years. I would never pressure or coerce them, but we would merely put it to them as a possibility worth exploring. Always supposing neither has their heart set on another, and always supposing it is what they, too, wish. It is the dearest wish of my own heart that our children should one day marry. What do you think?"

Trista gave the idea some consideration. "Do you think he will accept the magic in her? That would be my first concern. My second would be that this would be, as you say, what they both wish."

Connor tilted his head and eyed the two children, now chasing each other and shouting like little hooligans. "Already he accepts magic in his life. He embraces that the two of you have power and that Diana may have it as well. None of this seems to bother him. I think he would value whatever talents she comes to possess"

"So long as that is the case, I have no objection.

Indeed, I would welcome the match." Trista smiled, reached over and gripped her friend's hand, then glanced over at her husband. "Sebastian?"

"I approve of the notion."

"I also agree," said Connor.

"It is settled then." Morgan raised her glass of champagne. "To the happiness and joy of our respective children. Perhaps they might even one day find joy together."

They toasted as the children ran in the warm, bright sunshine of a cloudless afternoon, entirely free of dragons.

A word about the author…

Shirley grew up in Baton Rouge, LA, and started writing at an early age. Always talkative, when she was eleven, she began to put her thoughts on paper, writing stories inspired by two of her favorite writers, Laura Ingalls Wilder and Madeline L'Engle. As she grew older, she developed a love of romance and decided to try her hand at paranormal romance. In addition, she has written several unpublished screenplays. In 2016, her novel, *If the Shoe Fits* was published by The Wild Rose Press and was featured in the 2017 Louisiana Book Festival. Shirley is also a narrator, and her novel, *The Crystal Flame*, is narrated by her.

Shirley graduated from Nicholls State University where she majored in History and minored in English. Since graduating (she doesn't like to think about how long ago that was) she has worked at some of the best libraries in the Baton Rouge area. She makes her home there and enjoys spending time with family members. She also loves seeing movies, reading, and shopping with her niece.

Currently, Shirley is hard at work on her newest venture, a series about a vampire trying to develop a treatment for his condition.

****

http://www.shirleypmccoy.com

****

If you enjoyed this story, leaving a review at your favorite book retailer or reader website would be much appreciated. Thank you!